CHRISTMAS COMEBACK
(to me)

Caroline Akervik

ISBN: 978-1-68046-961-5

Published by Satin Romance
An Imprint of Melange Books, LLC
White Bear Lake, MN 55110
www.satinromance.com

Published in the United States of America.

Cover Design by Caroline Andrus

To Tommy
I miss you. I wrote this story because I needed a little Christmas
after you passed.

To my Lakeshore peeps, you all are a part of the creation of this
story. I am so blessed to have worked with such a fantastic group of
people for ten magical years. You are the best and you are always in
my heart.

CHAPTER 1

R ear ending a reindeer, even a faux one, is a bad beginning to any morning, especially to a December morning during the holiday season. Erik, or *Erik the Wall*, Engen, formerly one of the most feared and admired goalies in the International Hockey League, glared through the snow-obscured windshield of his black Dodge Challenger Hellcat at the brown, antlered figure approaching his car. As it was after seven in the morning in December in Noelle, Wisconsin, it remained dark and overcast.

The two-legged reindeer with the soft curves of a female and a flashing red nose made her way over to the driver's side of his car. Shaking his head against the absurdity of the image, Erik rubbed at the bridge of his nose. Of course, only in Noelle would he literally bump into a reindeer on his way to his sister's home. He'd driven through the night after working a full day, and he was exhausted. This development was the pièce de résistance.

The reindeer apparition appeared at his window and

knocked assertively on his window with an undeniably human, leather-gloved hand. He lowered his window, and snow and cold air immediately swirled into the warm cab of his car. The reindeer costume-clad woman whose lime green Prius he had just rear ended had her glasses off and was trying to wipe them off on the furry sleeve of her reindeer outfit.

"Give me a minute. I can't see a thing right now. My glasses are photochromatic, and they're fogging up."

Stella Larson. His heart lurched. Of all the reindeer to hit, why did it have to be *her*? She hadn't recognized him yet, but she would. Despite the reindeer apparel, she appeared much the same as the last time he'd seen her. Beautiful. Was this a cruel cosmic joke? He could have rear ended anyone else's car in the town of Noelle, Wisconsin, but it had to be one belonging to the girl, now the woman, he'd jilted more than a decade before. It seemed to be more than a coincidence, more a cruel twist of fate.

He watched her as she further smeared her glasses. Back in high school, Stella Larson hadn't worn glasses, but otherwise, she hadn't changed at all. She remained tall and lean with long lines and a graceful posture. Her complexion was as fresh now at twenty-eight or twenty-nine as it had been when she was seventeen. If possible, her cheekbones were even more elegant. There was a dusting of freckles across her nose, and he knew that behind those smoked-up lenses were green eyes with ridiculously long lashes. Her thick, curly blond and brunette mane lay in a loose braid that had escaped the reindeer hood and draped over her shoulder. She'd always been the kind of woman that men and women stopped to stare at, she was just that beautiful, and, he had to admit, Stella made a very cute reindeer.

"Are you all right?" he asked. His voice came out like gravel. He cleared his throat.

"I'm fine. Fortunately, you were barely moving, but I need to get a better look at my car. I can't really see out here."

"I didn't see your car. I am sorry."

"My car is tiny," she acknowledged, "and the windows are so darkly tinted on your sports car. Is that dark even legal?"

Erik gritted his teeth. "She's a Hellcat," he replied, patting his black dashboard.

"Excuse me?"

"My car is a Hellcat, a Dodge Challenger."

"Whatever," she shrugged. "Let's exchange insurance information to be on the safe side. I'll take a good look at my car once I have it in the garage." Her voice was warm and husky, exactly as he remembered it. She was also being surprisingly good natured about the whole incident, but that was likely because she hadn't recognized him yet.

"Why are you dressed like a reindeer?" The words burst out before he could stop them.

She smiled, perching the now hopelessly smeared glasses on her nose. "Oh, for work."

"But you're dressed as a reindeer, Stella. What sort of work do you do that involves being dressed as a reindeer?"

It was at that exact moment when he said her name that the green eyes narrowed in recognition. "You!"

"Guilty as charged," Erik smiled the charming, half smile that had once made him a candidate for *People* magazine's Sexiest Men of 2016 before his life had taken a one-eighty degree turn, and all of his dreams and hopes for the future had ended or at least changed course.

Ominously, her hands went immediately to her hips. "Erik Engen, what are you doing back in Noelle?" Those memorable eyes narrowed at him. He'd dreamed of them more times than he liked to remember or admit in the years since he'd last seen this woman. Stella pronounced the name of the town, Noelle, the way all the natives did, in one syllable, with a long o.

"I'm here for the Nutcracker Festival. I'm amazed that it took you that long to recognize me."

"My one contact was bothering me, so I went with glasses today. It's an old prescription. You're here for the Nutcracker Festival? Is your father all right? He generally comes back to be the Grand Marshal each year."

"Not this year. This year, I'm serving as Grand Marshal. Dad took my mom on a surprise anniversary cruise."

"Your sister could have been Grand Marshal. Freya lives right in town." Stella pointed out suspiciously. Erik imagined that many of the native Noellians would be suspicious of him.

"Freya's nine months pregnant and due any day. I was the only family member who was available and guaranteed to be physically able. Are you that unhappy to see me?"

She snorted softly. "What you do or where you are, Erik Engen, no longer has any impact on me. You made sure of that a decade ago. I moved on."

He repressed the feeling of disappointment that rose in him. Stella Larsen still hadn't forgiven him for how he'd treated her when they'd both left Noelle so long ago. She hated him, that much was clear, but he found himself wanting to continue this interaction. It had a spice to it that he found engaging. Like the love-struck seventeen-year-old boy he'd once been, he couldn't get enough of Stella.

"I know where to find you if I find any damage to my car, Erik. You're staying at the Lingonberry Lodge, right?"

He nodded. "Yes, and I'll be there through the holidays."

"You realize that this Devil beast is completely inappropriate for Noelle in December. I'll bet it's rear wheel drive."

"It's a Hellcat. Are you suggesting your Prius is the right car for these conditions?" Erik scoffed.

"It's fuel efficient and cute," Stella defended. "I think we're done here. I'll be in touch if I need to be. Otherwise, I'm sure we'll both be quite content never speaking to each other again."

As she turned to go back to her car, Erik began to roll up his window. He paused, watching her. "Stella," he called out, "you never answered my question. Why are you dressed as a reindeer?" His gaze swept up and down her willowy, reindeer pajama-clad figure.

"I'm the art teacher at Leif Erickson Elementary School," she explained. "We're having our family holiday sing-along today, so the entire specialist team dressed as Santa's reindeer. Unfortunately, it's my luck that I'm dressed like this when I ran into the boy who once broke my heart," she muttered, holding her hands wide. Again, she spun away from him.

The boy who once broke my heart—that sounded promising to Erik. "Technically, I did run into you. Why is that your luck?" He called after her, wanting to extend the conversation. A decade since he'd broken up with her, Stella remained vivid and electric with energy in a way that most of the other women he'd encountered were not. Why was she teaching art in Noelle? Last he'd heard of Stella, she was working as a professional muralist all over the globe. What had brought her back to the town they'd both grown up in and then been in a rush to leave?

She pivoted in the snow to glare back at him. "I don't consider it good luck," she explained, "to have you literally run into me in your devil car on the day that I'm ridiculously dressed up as Rudolph the red-nosed reindeer."

Despite his fatigue and his anxiety about what he was facing in the upcoming days, Erik laughed out loud. Stella had always challenged him. If he could see her again, maybe being back in Noelle wouldn't be as bad as he'd anticipated.

Stella got back into her lime-colored car under the streetlight that was garland wrapped and topped with an enormous candy cane. Erik gripped the soft, heated leather of his steering wheel tightly. He hadn't wanted to return to Noelle this holiday season. Of course, he fully intended to take care of the business that had brought him back, the Nutcracker Factory that was the base of Engen Ornaments, the Engen family's multinational corporation. He'd even make an appearance at the Lingonberry Lodge with the rest of the family on Christmas Eve, but then he'd be on his way. Still, a few weeks would be the longest he'd been back in Noelle for years.

Back when he'd been playing professional hockey, he'd even missed a couple of holidays. In the years since he'd retired from hockey and had been working for Engen Ornaments, he'd spent no more than a day or two in town on any given holiday. Erik's role at the company had always involved a great deal of worldwide travel, and this was just as he liked it. To be honest, he preferred to stay away from Noelle and the Nutcracker Factory that had been his grandfather's creation and was the bedrock of the family business. It's not that his memories of Noelle were bad, but they were tender. First, his grandfather had died, and then he'd broken up with the girl of his dreams, Stella Larson, to pursue his dream of playing professional hockey.

Erik repressed a slight feeling of unease. He'd returned to Noelle for less than pure reasons. Oliver and Meg Engen were on an anniversary cruise. That was the truth, but the board of Engen Ornaments had sent Erik to evaluate the future of the fifty-year-old nutcracker factory that Ole Engen had founded in Noelle and that still employed a good number of the residents of the town. The Engen Nutcracker Factory was the main business in town and deeply connected to the town's identity. Every year, the Nutcracker Festival attracted many tourists in the final days leading up to Christmas that culminated in the Nutcracker Ball on December twenty-third. During the Festival, the citizens of Noelle participated in all sorts of winter activities including snowmobile races, pond hockey, ski jumping, Christmas craft fairs, and ice sculpture carving contests. Fittingly, the sign on the highway coming into town bore the legend, "Noelle, Wisconsin, home of Engen Nutcrackers."

Would that remain the case after his work here was done? Erik pondered. With a heavy sigh and a sick feeling in the pit of his stomach, he eased his car back into the flow of traffic which was predictably slow but steady for a morning commute in the driving snow. As he cruised along, he noted Hans Christian Anderson Street was decked out with the usual Christmas paraphernalia. Noelle was one of those typical Wisconsin small towns with brick storefronts at a variety of heights lining the two-lane main thoroughfare. Black, antique looking streetlamps glowed softly on both sides of the street. The entire town was decorated with an overwhelming abundance of holiday cheer. "Like Christmas exploded," Erik muttered under his breath, shaking his head.

He proceeded down the street, resisting the automatic urge to take the right turn onto Linnaeus Street. That turn led to the hockey rink and was one that he had made countless times throughout his childhood and teenaged years. Still, his eyes went to the white aluminum building, the Noelle Municipal Hockey Rink, where the high school hockey team, the Noelle Chill, practiced and played their games. Glimpsing a large, new addition on one side of the rink, Erik craned his neck to peer at it. He recalled Freya had mentioned there was now a girl's hockey team in town too, the Force, that practiced at the rink. So, it made sense that they'd added a second rink to the facility. During his brief visits to Noelle in the past few years, he had thought that the northern Wisconsin city seemed relatively unchanged. Now, observing his hometown with a more critical eye, he could see real changes. Most downtown storefronts were filled. There were two new hotels right where you turned off the highway, and he'd seen several new restaurants as well. Apparently, Noelle was growing.

Erik made a gradual right turn and pulled up the pine tree lined driveway to the craftsman-style home his grandfather had built and lived in named Lingonberry Lodge. Ole Engen had wanted his dream home in the heart of Noelle, right by Muir Park, the several acre park in the middle of the town with its abundant nature and cross-country ski trails. He'd bought up a big chunk of land and built his dream house there, overlooking Noelle Creek. Erik had spent a lot of his childhood in the enormous but whimsical house.

The wood carvings that Ole had loved and excelled at creating filled Lingonberry Lodge. He had immigrated from Norway as a young man, and the Lodge reflected his old-world tastes but with modern amenities. At more than four thousand square feet and with eight bedrooms, it was too much house for any one family. Erik's sister Freya had converted it into a high-end cross-country ski lodge. She and Benji, her husband, had built their own home directly behind it.

CHAPTER 2

Upon entering Leif Erickson Elementary School, Stella took an immediate left and headed for the gymnasium and her dear friend, Jayda Watkins, the Phy Ed teacher. She made a beeline through the cluttered equipment room to the tiny Phy Ed office which was located behind it.

"Jayda? Jayda?" she called out. "Where are you?"

"I'm out here," came the disembodied answer from out in the still darkened gym.

Stella pushed the door wide and paused for a moment, taking in the Christmas-lit extravaganza. *Wow. Jayda always goes all out for the holidays. What a sweetheart.* While the main, overhead lights were off, one side of the gymnasium as well as the dividing wall between that side of the gym and the cafeteria side were covered with multicolored Christmas lights. In the center of the gym side, lights decorated an elaborate string crawl-through maze as well. Jayda was busy setting up holiday themed stations for her students, all of which were modeled around a winter sports concept. Stella recognized a couple of the stations, including bobsledding with scooters, a snowball toss using white bean bags, and penguin bowling. There were several other new stations, as well, that she didn't immediately recognize.

Jayda, a bit shorter than her lifelong friend Stella, was muscular and fit with a curvy figure. She wore her corn rowed hair pulled back in a high ponytail, and had a cafe au lait complexion, an incredibly warm heart, and a tendency to always up the ante at Christmas time. Jayda and Stella had been in the same kindergarten class decades before and had been inseparable ever since. When Stella had come back to Noelle after her brother Elias's death, working with Jayda had been a major selling point for her to finally put her art teaching license to use at the local elementary school.

"Jayda," Stella called to her friend who was setting up the penguin bowling pins. "This place looks amazing." She held her hands wide to encompass the Christmas-ready gymnasium. "The kids are going to love this."

"Thanks, Stella," Jayda beamed. "I think it looks nice, too. I tried to go with more of a polar bear, penguin, North Pole emphasis this year."

"What was last year?"

"That was holidays around the world. Don't you remember?"

"Your gym at Christmas time is always amazing. This is nothing like Phy Ed when we were kids." Stella reflected, whistling low. "All we did was run the mile and play *Fishy, Fishy, Cross My Ocean* with Mr. Chipley."

"Mr. Chipley," Jayda chuckled, "wasn't interested in having to take any equipment out. He was old school. A jump rope and a basketball were all that he wanted to take out of his equipment room."

"He was terrifying. Since he retired, I think he's been

teaching Driver's Ed for Safe Driving Academy. Can you imagine being a beginner driver with Mr. Chipley in the car?"

Jayda snickered. "No, I'll pass on that one. I try to make the holidays joyful in here. You know, not all our students look forward to Christmas, Stella, so I try to make it a special for them while they're here at least. And you're one to talk. You're sure to win the classroom door decorating contest. How can any of us compete with a three-dimensional display of Rudolph's Bumble putting the star on the Christmas tree with Santa's elves? That is totally over the top. You put us all to shame."

Pleased, Stella beamed. "I do think this year's door decoration turned out well. I loved those Rankin Bass holiday movies growing up. I try to go with one of them as my Christmas door decoration theme each year."

"The fact that you are a professional artist makes the whole thing unfair," Jayda snorted. "My door decoration of the Minions in Santa hats can't begin to compete. You've got this contest in the bag, especially since you had the kids create all the elves. Did you really have to continue the elves all the way down the hall?"

"Remember, you get extra points for student involvement in the door decorating contest," Stella crowed. "My Gifted and Talented students did a really nice job on the elves. They were too cute not to share. Jayda, I have to tell you something. You're never going to believe who I just saw, I mean, who ran into me...literally."

"Give me a minute," Jayda replied as she lined up the last two penguin bowling pins. "All set," she spun around, her braids, fanning out behind her. She set her hands on her hips. "Okay, so lay it on me. Who did you see? Is he cute?" Her eyes were bright with excitement, sensing her friend had something juicy to share.

"Erik Engen, former star athlete now corporate executive, estranged son of Noelle, literally ran into my Prius."

The amusement drained instantly from Jayda's pretty features. She knew better than just about anyone else how much Erik Engen had hurt and embarrassed Stella when he'd broken up with her right after their high school graduation. "Erik Engen. Geez, Stella. He's here? In Noelle? Already? He usually comes to see his family on Christmas Eve, and then he's gone the next day. You actually saw him?"

"We spoke. Err, I ran into him. No, he ran into me with his monster black sports car on Anderson Street, right in front of Jan's Bakeshop. He bumped into my car on the way here this morning."

"And?" Jayda prompted, her eyes, big. "You're okay, right?"

Stella nodded.

"Your car."

"Not a scratch."

"What happened?"

"Well, his car collided with mine. I didn't recognize him at first, my glasses steamed up when I got out of the car. You know I usually wear contacts, but the right one was bothering me this morning, so I had these old glasses on. Once I could see, I recognized who it was."

"No damage to your car?"

"No, not a scratch on my Prius," Stella gestured with her hands. "We're both fine really, but it was a complete shock seeing him. I wasn't expecting it at all, and I had to be dressed like this, as a reindeer." She rolled her eyes expressively. "The first time I see my very first boyfriend in almost a decade, and

I'm dressed in furry pajamas." She shook her head in bemusement.

She had Jayda's complete attention now. "How could you be? Expecting to see him, I mean. He's only been back in Noelle a handful of times since high school and then only for a day or two. I wonder why he's here so early this year." Jayda nibbled on her full lips. "Darius," she mumbled, referring to her husband. "He'll know something about it."

"That's right. Darius works at the Engen Nutcracker factory," Stella replied, snapping her fingers. "If there's something afoot at the factory, Darius will definitely know what's up. Will you ask him, please, Jayda, for me?"

"Darius was just promoted to a manager at the Nutcracker Factory," Jayda replied, her pride in her husband evident in her voice. "I'll text him. He's home with Lyrique today," she said referring to their eighteen-month-old daughter. "She's sick, nothing serious, a low-grade fever, and she's tired. I stayed home with her yesterday, so Darius is home today. They should be on their second or third cartoon by now."

"How's Lyrique doing?"

"She's happy to be home all day drinking ginger ale and watching Puppy Dog Pals with her dad. She much prefers it to daycare."

"There has to be a reason for Erik to be back. He hates Noelle."

"You seem awfully interested in what Erik is doing back in town." Jayda's eyes narrowed suspiciously. "Do you still have feelings for that man?"

Stella blushed. "Of course not. I…ah… just don't want him to cause any problems at the factory," she stammered.

"I hope it's not something to do with the factory. Darius

and I just finished building our house last summer. We want to stay in Noelle. This is our home. We love it here."

"Don't jump to conclusions." Stella patted Jayda on the shoulder. "I hope it's not something to do with the factory," she muttered. "That would be awful. It's so important to the town."

"We'll see," Jayda stated. "I'll get the scoop from Darius tonight. Maybe Erik's back in town to see his family. I know he travels a lot for the company. Maybe he really is here to spend time with his sister, Freya, and her family."

"Maybe," Stella agreed doubtfully.

"Hey, ladies," Addie, a second-grade teacher and Jayda's and Stella's good friend, strode into the gym. Addie was tall, brunette, taught boot camp classes at a local gym several nights a week, and possessed an irreverent sense of humor. "What's going on in here?" She glanced between Jayda and Stella. "It's too early in the day for a serious conversation. What's up?"

"Erik Engen, Stella's first flame who dumped her years ago, is back in town. He ran into her car this morning, and we're wondering why he's back," Jayda succinctly summarized the situation. "Of course, this all happened while she was dressed in reindeer pajamas."

Addie took all this information in as she leaned up against the gymnasium wall. "How did he look? Terrible, I hope, being that he dumped you."

"No, good," Stella admitted. "Really good. He's totally hot."

"And he's in Noelle because?" Addie prompted.

"He's an Engen," Jayda explained. "We suspect he may be here for something to do with the Nutcracker Factory."

"Slow down, Jayda. You must remember I'm not a local. I

don't know the life history of everyone in town. I need some background."

"Addie, the Engens own the Nutcracker Factory as well as a big, multinational corporation called Engen Ornaments. The company started with the Nutcracker Factory. Now, Engen Imports sells all sorts of decorations and holiday supplies. The entire family used to live in Noelle. Freya Weber and her family still do, but the rest, Erik and his parents, moved to Chicago when they shifted the corporate headquarters there," Stella explained. "We were discussing what Erik's doing back in Noelle."

"He has family here," Addie shrugged. "I don't see any mystery. It's Christmas time. It makes sense." Addie was of a practical bent.

"True, and I don't remember Erik hating Noelle," Jayda reflected, considering. "He just wanted to get out of here to play professional hockey."

"Ooh, professional athlete," Addie commented.

Jayda continued, "Hockey was Erik's dream, and he went after it which meant leaving town. Stella, you went after your dream, too, of being a professional artist, right?"

"I did," Stella admitted. "I traveled all over the world creating art. It was fun, exciting, and exhausting. And then, I was ready to come home. Don't get me wrong. I still enjoy traveling for my art, just not year-round. Living out of a suitcase isn't fun. It's kind of nice having roots."

"You did your thing, and then you moved back here. So why are you jumping to conclusions about this Erik guy?" Addie pointed out.

"It's hard for me to be positive about Erik Engen," Stella replied. "He dumped me," she explained.

"Mm hmm," Jayda nodded with a wise smile. "And it still bothers you, doesn't it?"

Stella shook her head.

"I'm thinking the lady protests too much." Addie wiggled her eyebrows suggestively.

Jayda winked and nodded. "Erik's tall, dark, and completely built, and Stella is still hung up on him."

"You two are completely off base," Stella shook her finger at her two friends. "No one likes to be dumped. It hurts your pride. That's all there is to my feelings concerning Erik Engen, hurt pride. Whose friends are you anyway?" Stella teased.

"Well, if what you've told me is true, he's not a total villain. You both left town chasing your dreams. Everyone knows most high school romances don't stand the tests of time and distance," Addie noted. "I don't know the guy, but maybe he was being proactive by breaking up with you."

Jayda raised a finger to her lips, evaluating her gym set up, wondering if she was missing anything. "I need to get more pins for bowling," she decided, then headed back to the supply room with the other women trailing along behind her. "You know I'm loyal to you, Stella, always, but I remember Erik as a decent guy. I certainly hope he still is and that things are okay with the factory for Darius and all of the people in town who work there. You know what Erik does now, right?"

"No, not really," Stella answered. "No one discusses Erik with me. To be honest, there's no reason to. I knew he quit hockey because of hip injuries, and I heard he's worked for Engen Ornaments for the past few years."

"He's vice president there now. He's the one behind how the company has modernized. Engen Ornaments has gone international because Erik Engen has the golden touch, I guess. He goes into companies, straightens them out, and then either sells them or drives them along. Something big must be going down at the Nutcracker Factory if he's here." Jayda sounded anxious now as she gathered another armful of plastic bowling pins and handed them to Stella.

Addie glanced at the clock. "Shoot. Where does time go? I have to get going. I'm meeting a parent in three minutes. See you ladies later." She dashed out of the gym.

Stella and Jayda filed out of the supply room and wended their way through the maze of Christmas centers to the bowling area where they worked together to set up more pins.

"Is this right?" Stella asked Jayda as she finished setting up a set of penguin pins.

"Yes, just like in a bowling alley." Jayda approved of her friend's efforts.

"It's amazing that Erik's a corporate bigwig now," Stella muttered. "I can't imagine him sitting behind a desk. He was always this total jock and all about sports. I mean I know he did well in school, but Erik as a businessman, I don't see it. He was always in motion, couldn't sit still."

"Well, from the little that Darius has told me, Erik is a big shot and not simply because his family are the biggest shareholders in the company. I guess he's really good at what he does."

"Mr. Engen, Erik's father, isn't the CEO anymore?" Stella asked.

"Not for years. He was right after they went public. Now he's mostly retired but serves on the board."

"It's not that I'm surprised that Erik's successful," Stella explained, thinking out loud. "He went to Princeton after all. He has a degree in finance, and he always had his eye on the big prize. He was the kind of person who puts his nose to the grindstone, a hard worker. When hockey didn't pan out, I guess he used his second parachute, his degree."

Jayda laughed. "He always went after what he wanted. He went after you," she pointed out. "You wouldn't give him the time of day junior year, but he didn't give up. Then, senior year, you two were inseparable."

Stella wrinkled her nose. "That's ancient history."

Jayda set her hands on her hips. "When was the last time you saw him?"

"Other than this morning? The night we broke up," she admitted. "We were at a graduation party. I can't remember for whom. I remember it was one of those combination affairs for a couple of kids. Baseball players, I think." She shook her head. "It was at a big house right outside of town. They had taco stations set up in the garage and all sorts of games laid out on the yard. Erik came up to me looking all serious, said we had to talk. We both knew that we were going to colleges that were far away from each other. He'd committed to Princeton his junior year. I had done early admission to my college. Looking back at those final weeks of senior year, I guess we avoided the subject of what would happen after graduation. A bunch of our friends were there, at the graduation party, I mean, mostly playing volleyball. Erik asked me to play kubb, that Viking lawn game, with him. We walked over to where the kubb blocks and sticks were laid out, and he said that he thought it would be better if we broke up before we went to college. Just like that, with no explanation or discussion. He totally blind sided me." She crossed her arms over her stomach. "To this day, kubb and tacos make me feel sick to my stomach," she admitted.

"Ouch," Jayda acknowledged. "But he wasn't entirely

wrong, you know. Addie's right. Most high school romances break up in the first semester of college."

Stella nodded, giving a dismissive wave of her hand. "I don't disagree now, with hindsight and maturity. Erik was focused and practical. I'm not saying he was wrong, but he did break my tender, little, teenaged heart."

"That was the very last time you saw him?" Jayda questioned.

"Mm hmm," Stella agreed.

"No way," Jayda muttered. "Then he crashed into you."

"Well, I've seen him on TV, in magazines. Maybe I've even looked him up on Facebook a few times," Stella elaborated. "But I haven't talked to him since that night."

The bell indicating it was time for students to enter the building rang. "Dang, let's discuss this later, Stella. This is too juicy. Tell me the truth, is Erik Engen as handsome as he was back in high school, all tall, brooding, and hot?"

Stella considered, reflecting on the man who'd once been the first boy she'd ever kissed. "If you go for that sort of thing," she shrugged.

"You do," Jayda grinned. "At least, you did, and I'm guessing you still do."

"I'm older and wiser now, but yes, he did look amazing," Stella admitted with a wink. "He's older, has some scars on his face from hockey, but they just make him look dangerous. He still has that muscular, Thor-appeal going on. I'm sure he probably has a supermodel girlfriend tucked away somewhere."

"Ooh, you're wondering if he has a girlfriend. Interesting, but who wouldn't want a piece of the Nutcracker Prince? Honey, you could give any super model a run for her money, even when you're wearing a reindeer costume," Jayda responded as third grade students began to file into the gym. She put on her microphone headset. The volume of the students' chit chat rose as they headed to their respective warm-up stations.

Stella lingered for a moment. "You know the old saying, once burned, twice shy," she muttered to her friend.

"I'm still not entirely sure who did the burning and who got burned," Jayda remarked, eyeing her friend sagely. "But I do have some questions for Darius tonight, and I plan on getting some answers. I'll let you know what I find out."

Erik parked his black Hellcat in the parking lot, then hesitated before getting out of the car. Momentarily lost in reflections, he stared up at the rambling brown and crème building that had once been his grandfather's home and where Erik himself had spent so much time as a child. The lodge blended a Scandinavian emphasis on wood and other natural materials with big windows and hints of prairie craftsman style, including horizontal lines and a gabled roof that extended out over the welcoming front porch. Ole Engen has designed his home to blend in with the natural environment around it. Towering hundred-year-old white pine trees surrounding the house and snow on the ground created a very picturesque setting. Erik exhaled slowly, rolling his shoulders. No matter where he traveled or how much of the world he saw, arriving at Lingonberry Lodge always felt like coming home.

He would be staying at the lodge for the next ten days leading up to Christmas and then over the holiday itself. Erik, his parents and extended family made it their custom to stay in the lodge when visiting, to give his sister and her family their space. Freya and her husband, Benji, lived in their thoroughly modern bungalow out back.

In the past few years, his older sister Freya had converted their grandfather's home into a popular cross-country ski lodge. At first, Erik and his father had had mixed feelings about her plan to share the family home with paying guests. But, in the end, both had agreed with her observation that the house was simply too enormous for one family. By making it into a lodge, Freya had ensured that it was maintained in a manner that Ole Engen would have approved and that it was financially sustainable.

Lingonberry Lodge, the house, and its ten acres of land were located at the head of some world-famous cross-country ski trails. Deeper in the woods and beyond the park were snowmobile trails connecting popular supper clubs and Northwoods watering holes. In northern Wisconsin towns like Noelle, snowmobiles were almost more popular than cars as a means of transportation during the long winter months. Erik itched to get out on those trails, flying along on a snowmobile through the familiar winter wonderland. He hoped there would be time for his favorite winter activities including snowmobiling and playing shinny hockey during this holiday season in Noelle.

Predictably, Freya had lavishly decorated the exterior of the building with pine boughs and immense quantities of crimson ribbon in honor of the holiday season. From previous Christmases, Erik knew that white lights covered the pine trees ringing the house. But, as it was morning, these were currently turned off. He could also make out some new additions to the yard display including wire frames of illuminated deer, a sleigh, and snowmen. Even in the morning light, he could envision the full night spectacle of Lingonberry Lodge decorated for the holidays. Freya loved everything about the holiday season, and her passion for this time of year was displayed throughout the grounds and inside the lodge.

Grabbing his briefcase and suitcase from the trunk of the car, he headed up to the mahogany double doors. He took a deep breath and was reaching for the handle when it flew open. His tow headed and very pregnant sister Freya leaped into his arms, pushing him back. She was nearly his height. "Erik, I'm so glad to see you!" She hugged him exuberantly. As she drew back, she chattered away, "Of course, I'm sorry Mom and Dad couldn't make it, but I'm so glad you're here and actually staying for a little while this time. You're always so busy, and you don't come home nearly enough. The kids are super excited to see you. They're at school now." With her high cheekbones and chiseled features, Freya was unmistakably Erik's sister. But where Erik had darker skin and complexion, she was fair. She wore her hair chic and short in a white blond pixie. Always stylish, this morning, she sported a long red tunic over black tights. Her cheeks were rosy, her complexion fresh, and she was clearly in the last trimester of her pregnancy.

"Come in. Come in. We're so excited you're here. I didn't expect you until noon."

He set his bags down in the entrance foyer, stepped inside, and drew the door closed behind him. He squeezed Freya's hand. "It's great to see you, too, Sis. You look amazing. You are one of those pregnant women who glow. Wow, and would you look at this place." He turned slowly in a circle, taking in the virtual Christmas explosion.

The lobby of the Lingonberry Lodge which had once been

his grandfather's parlor, was impressive and a testament to Ole Engen's skill as a woodcarver. Much of the interior was decorated with an abundance of rich oak woodwork. Ole had had a passion for carving the trees, wildflowers, and grasses of the region, and these were incorporated into his woodwork. The pièce de résistance of the lodge was undoubtedly the staircase, featuring balusters connected with an extended scene of animals from the area. The oak trusses of the roof were exposed, and they gave the space an open and expansive feel. Of course, the entire space was richly decorated for the holiday season.

"Have you had breakfast yet?" Freya questioned.

"I've been drinking coffee to stay awake for the drive here," Erik admitted. "I worked until late last night, and then it was too late to get on the road. I tried to sleep until about three AM, but my mind was spinning, thinking about the Nutcracker Factory, and seeing you and Benji and the kids. So, I just got up and packed my things and hit the road. I think I'll sleep better now that I'm here."

His sister eyed him soberly. "Mom told me why you came. You know the factory is important to this town. It's practically Noelle's identity. You have to walk softly if you do anything. Remember, we live here."

Erik rubbed at his itching eyes. He yawned. "Freya, we can discuss this later. I'm not up for it right now."

"I'm sorry, Erik. Let's get your things into your room, and then you can come over and have breakfast with me."

"Freya, I'm going to take a rain check on breakfast. I'm too tired to be hungry."

Her expression was disappointed. "You'll come to dinner though?"

"Of course," he wrapped an arm around his sister, hugging

her close. "I can't wait to see the kids, but right now, I'm about to fall over."

Erik didn't wake up until nearly four that afternoon. He was disoriented when his eyes first opened. The pale fading light coming in his childhood window was familiar, but the decor was not. The bed was an immensely comfortable, midcentury walnut platform. Freya's clean somewhat stark aesthetic was apparent in every detail of the room. He appreciated the high thread count bedding, his down comforter, and even the gossamer curtains that hung in the windows. He found the smoky, gray-blue wall color soothing, and the green plants scattered about were a nice touch. But he missed his own childhood room, the dark blue privacy curtains he'd bought himself, the familiar dents and dings that he had made growing up in the space, his posters of Wayne Gretzky and Mario Lemieux, even the headboard on which he'd carved his own name and his hockey number, thirty-one. The room and the house had changed, but he'd known that from prior visits to Noelle.

Crossing his arms behind his head, he wondered what else had changed. Stella Larson's lovely face popped into his mind's eye. If anything, she was even more beautiful, more vital than she'd been as an eighteen-year-old girl, and she'd been a knockout back then. For a moment, he considered whether and how he could orchestrate another encounter with her. Fortunately, he had some time to try. The thought pleased him.

He heard children's voices from somewhere out in the hall and then Stella hushing them.

The children were home! Feeling more excited and optimistic than he had in a long time, he swung his legs out of the bed.

Once comfortably attired, Erik headed down to the den which was right off the lobby. Freya had gone with a Scandinavian Christmas theme in this room. That is, white lights and tomte—mischievous Swedish elves that were handmade in red and white wool—decorated the room. A massive field stone fireplace in which a well-stoked fire roared dominated a side of the room. The front desk was tucked into a recessed alcove in one corner. Behind this desk, a door led into Freya's office.

A large leather couch, a matching armchair, and a flat-topped log that functioned as a footrest were set before the fireplace. The arrangement invited guests to get comfortable, take a seat, put their feet up. An enormous but tastefully decorated Christmas tree occupied the opposite side of the room. The tree was also covered in white lights and decorated only with Swedish straw ornaments and more tomte. Erik thought wistfully of the large, colored Christmas tree bulbs and random assorted ornaments he remembered from his childhood tree. In her own home, Freya's tree was always colorful and decorated with kid-created ornaments, but everything at the lodge was tasteful and elegant. The guest reviews always praised the lodge's decor. The den was redolent with the smells of pine, clove, and citrus. No doubt his sister was diffusing some of her essential oils.

"Oh, you're up. I hope the kids didn't wake you." Erik heard Freya's throaty tones before she appeared from the corridor that led into the kitchen.

"It was time for me to get up. That's the best rest I've had in weeks. I've been traveling a lot, and then we've been swamped with the reorganization of Engen Ornaments." He shook his head, exhaling slowly. "It feels really good to be home."

Coming over to her brother, Freya gripped his hand. "We're so glad you're here. It was tough trying to keep the kids out of your room."

"Did I tell you, you look amazing, Sis?"

Freya chuckled. "Lies. I feel like a beached whale at this point in the pregnancy, but I appreciate the compliment. Still, I have no complaints. I feel good. I'm still skiing a few times a week. Two of my friends and I go, and Benji stays with the kids," Freya stopped speaking abruptly and eyed her brother with some concern. "Are you sure you want to stay here at the lodge? It's booked full of guests for the Nutcracker Festival. Please let me know if you would rather stay in the house with us. I can put Hayden in with the twins." She gripped his arm, "Sit down, Erik. Don't just loom over me. I want to put my feet up." Freya sat down on the armchair and set her Ugg-booted feet on the ottoman with groan of satisfaction.

Erik sat opposite her on the immensely comfortable couch. He relaxed back into the deep cushions. It suited a big man like himself.

"No, no. I like staying here. The paint and furniture may be different from when we grew up, but the light coming in the windows is the same. The way the wooden floor creaks when you walk on it is the same, and it feels like Grandpa is around. I really like staying here. Besides, you have a young family, and you need your own space."

"Or is it that you don't want to deal with the kids' noises and messes?" she arched a thin, elegant eyebrow at him.

"I plan on spending lots of time with you, Benji, and the kids. If I stay here, I can come and go as I please without disrupting anyone. Besides, my old bedroom is a quiet place to work, and I do need to work. It's the main reason I'm here."

Freya glared at her brother.

"And to spend time with my fabulous sister and her family. Really, the lodge is perfect. I don't want to put anyone out of their beds. I'll be fine here," Erik replied definitively.

"You'll plan on having all of your dinners over with us?" Freya prodded.

Erik nodded. "Of course. How's Benji? And the kids?"

"All of us are good and super excited to see you. Of course, everyone in town thinks that you're here to be the heavy and either fire people so you can mechanize the Nutcracker Factory or shut it down. Is that why you're here? Dad couldn't stomach it, so he sent you to be the axe man?"

Erik flinched. "Well, it's a little more complicated than that."

"Engen Ornaments is doing well, even with the increasing competition from Amazon. You know that Nutcracker Factory is the heart and soul of this town."

Erik held up his hands. "Freya, give me a break. Let me at least settle in and see everyone before we start this argument. As a member of the Board of Directors of Engen Ornaments, rest assured your voice will continue to be heard. We'll have plenty of time to talk about Engen Ornaments and the Nutcracker Factory, but we don't need to do it this very minute."

"You don't have a lot of time," Freya pointed out. "The Board Meeting is scheduled for the twenty-third, the day before the night before Christmas, the night of the Nutcracker Ball."

"The Nutcracker Ball," Erik echoed. In his mind's eye, he pictured the center atrium of the Engen Nutcracker Factory decorated for the annual dance filled with formally attired people. For a moment, he pictured a younger, less certain Stella Larson than the one whom he'd encountered that morning. Her face had been a little fuller then, the green eyes just as vibrant. He pictured her in a long gown, perhaps one she'd worn to a school formal with him. *Would Stella attend the Nutcracker Ball?* He found the thought intriguing.

"Erik," Freya interrupted his recollection.

"I know. I know. I have less than two weeks to finish fact finding and polish my proposal before I present to the Board."

Suddenly, two small children burst into the room and onto Erik. Both were flaxen blond and adorable and six, in the rug rat category. "Hazel, Felix!"

"Oncle Erik. Oncle Erik, I lost a tooth." Hazel pointed to the gap in the bottom row of her teeth.

"I pulled it out for hew," Felix announced, who was still working on the letter r sound. "I got blood on my fingews. It was awesome."

"I didn't even cry," Hazel added.

Erik knelt and drew both six-year-old children into his arms. As they giggled, he closed his eyes and inhaled them. They smelt of gingerbread, milk, and warm, active child.

"Hi, Uncle Erik."

He opened his eyes to see his sister's eldest standing by the door. Hayden Weber was nine, getting taller, and increasingly awkward. His longish, dark hair hung forward over one eye partially obscuring it.

"Is that how you greet your uncle?" Erik asked, setting the younger two down and holding his arms wide.

Hayden didn't move. He gave a small wave. "I'm good. Mom, can I go play video games?"

"Don't you want to spend time with your uncle? You haven't seen him in forever."

"I said hello. Can I go now? We're on a mission."

"You're being impolite, Hayden," Freya reprimanded her son. "Come on over here, and welcome your uncle properly."

Hayden did as he was told, but his arms were limp in the hug he gave Erik.

Erik noticed that he continued to glare at his mother. Clearly, a fight between the two had preceded his arrival.

"Now can I go, Mom?"

With pursed lips, Freya nodded.

Hayden turned and disappeared down the hall.

"Hayden," Erik called after him.

"Let him go," Freya rubbed an anxious hand over her forehead. "Hazel and Felix, why don't you go get dressed to play in the snow. We still have about a half an hour before dinner."

"Will you come out, Uncle Ewik?" Felix demanded. "We want to build a snow fowt."

"Please," Hazel pressed, her big, blue eyes, wide and imploring.

"I'll be out in a few minutes, and then we can build a fort, but right now I want to talk to your mother. She's my sister remember. I'm excited to see her, too."

"Okay," Hazel agreed.

"I'll wace you outside, Hazel," Felix dashed from the room.

Erik watched as Freya sat heavily down on her chair, her pale blue eyes, so like Hazel's, were ominously bright. For a moment, she covered her face with her hands. Then, exhaling loudly, she appeared to gather herself.

Erik sat down next to his sister and took her hand. "What's with the attitude from Hayden? You two were always so tight, and he's always adored the twins. What's going on?"

Freya nodded, nibbling on her lip. "I think it's a stage. Benji thinks so, too. You know Hayden had a tough time of it when he was little."

"I knew he was placed with you as a foster child because there were real issues with his birth mother, but I thought that all resolved when you adopted him."

"I did, too. Then I met Benji. We got married, and he loves Hayden. Next, came the twins. We were doing fine, even though it was a lot for Hayden to take in. This pregnancy," she swept a hand up to encompass her very swollen belly, "has him feeling insecure, like his place in this family is threatened. We think Hayden's afraid that there won't be enough of us for him with another baby coming."

"That's ridiculous," Erik protested. "You and Benji are two of the most loving people I know."

"We've talked with the counselor at school. She said that it's normal for a child to feel out of sorts with a new baby coming. We just need to find something that Hayden feels really good about to distract him."

"Makes sense. I'm no parent, but growing up I found the best way to stay out of trouble was to do sports. Hayden still skis right?"

Freya nodded, eyeing her brother warily. "Then there's the whole hockey issue," she continued.

"What hockey issue?" Erik asked. "Does Hayden want to play hockey?" He smacked his hands down on his thighs. "That's great. We can go to the outdoor rinks together, or maybe we can put a rink out back, right by the head of the trails. That's wonderful news! I never thought he had any interest."

"Oh, Hayden's had interest, but we haven't. Benji and I don't want Hayden to play hockey."

Freya's words fell heavily between the brother and sister. It took Erik a moment to process her words. "What are you talking about, Freya? You played hockey with me growing up. What's the problem with hockey? Benji and I've watched Minnesota Wild games together. He likes watching hockey."

"But not his son playing it," Freya replied pointedly. "I don't want Hayden to get hurt," she muttered, "the way you did."

Again, Erik was stunned into silence. This coming from his daredevil of a sister was a shock. "But that's crazy. Hayden can get hurt crossing the street or falling off a skateboard. He can get hurt skiing. You and Benji fly down the slopes going like ninety miles an hour when you downhill."

"We do more cross-country skiing now."

"Because you're pregnant. You're kidding me, aren't you, Freya. You're not truly afraid to let him play hockey?"

"I know all about hockey, Erik," Freya raised her hands up defensively. "I went with you and Mom and Dad to all of those emergency rooms. I saw you after the surgeries. I saw them sew your chin up multiple times." She took a tremulous breath.

"At least I have all of my teeth."

"Not funny, Erik. We are a cross country skiing family. No one hits you when you cross country ski. Neither Benji nor I want to see Hayden hurt."

Erik leaned back into his couch cushions. "I don't even know what to say. Hockey is a grand sport. Remember what Grandpa Ole always said, a kid on the ice is never in hot water. If I could go back and play one more game," his voice quivered a little on these words, and he looked down, composing himself. When he had gathered himself, he raised his head, his eyes intent on his sister's. "My hockey career may not have lasted as long as I wanted it to, but I wouldn't trade a minute of it. Hockey is fun."

Freya started to speak, but Erik raised his hand. "Hear me out, Freya. Don't get me wrong. I love what I do now, but hockey is pure magic. There's so much more to it than the checking, and there's less of that now than when I played. There's the camaraderie of the locker room, the learning of leadership skills, not to mention the thrill of facing a skater one-on-one on a penalty shot."

"You still have the bug," Freya remarked wryly, shaking her head. "After all you went through."

"I have the bug, but not the wheels," Erik admitted. "Still, it's a beautiful game. Freya, you should let Hayden try hockey. Maybe you'll get your wish, and he'll decide he doesn't like it. There are a lot of less productive ways for a kid to spend his time. There are many positives to it as well. Kids today need to be more active. You know that."

"Our kids are active," Freya replied tersely. "It's just we don't want Hayden to get hurt."

"You mean the way that I did."

Another arrival saved Freya from replying.

"Erik," a light tenor voice broke in. Benji Weber, Freya's husband, walked into the room, his arms extended to embrace his brother-in-law. The two men were a study in contrasts. Erik Engen stood well over six feet tall with the hard, muscled body of the lifelong athlete. His hair was dark and thick, his jaw, square and inevitably stubbled by mid-afternoon and marred with more than a few nicks and scars. His thighs and shoulders stretched his clothing despite excellent tailoring. Though his manners were polished and sophisticated, he still moved with the barely restrained power of a professional hockey player, a blood sport in which honor and loyalty remained crucial aspects of the game.

Benji was a head shorter than his brother-in-law. In fact, a little shorter than his wife. He was fit, whippet thin, with fine, blond hair combed straight back from a slightly receding hairline. His best feature was his green-flecked brown eyes behind his tortoiseshell glasses which reflected his active and curious mind. Benji kept a hand on the larger man's shoulder. "It's great to see you, Erik. Freya and I are so pleased that you've decided to spend this Christmas with us, though I must admit to some suspicion as to the reasons behind it."

"You, me, and everybody else in town" Freya put in.

"I've already gotten it from Freya," Erik groaned. "Not you, too."

Benji looked over to his wife who nodded in response. "Well, there will be plenty of time to discuss business. You're here for the entire two weeks of the festival, correct?"

Erik nodded.

"That's great news. How are your parents? Freya talks to them almost every day, but you've seen them recently?"

"Yes, we had dinner right before they left for their trip. It sounds like they're having a blast cruising the Caribbean."

"Mom's been texting me nonstop. She Facetimes me most nights, and I get the full breakdown on everything they did each day, their excursions, and what they ate." Freya explained. "Then she grills me all about what's happening here. I suspect she would much rather be here than be on that cruise ship for the holidays."

Erik sighed. "You know how that went down. The Board asked me to evaluate the Nutcracker Factory and its future with Engen Ornaments. Dad didn't think it was a good idea for him to be here while I'm putting together my assessment and proposal. That's why Mom and Dad went on the cruise."

"The kids are disappointed, too, that their grandparents won't be here," Benji affirmed. "But hopefully your parents can come for a visit after Christmas."

"It makes sense," Freya acknowledged. "I totally agree, but Mom and Dad have been here for the holidays every year for so many years. This is the first one that I can think of them missing."

All three settled back into the comfortable seating area. The fire crackled, emitting a pleasant pine scent, and Erik found himself extending his legs, feeling increasingly relaxed. "How are things at the university?" he asked. Benji was an English professor at the Noelle branch of the Wisconsin university system.

"Good, very good, actually. We're going to be getting a new writing center building in the next few years. The Board of Regents approved it. So, we'll be expanding, hiring new staff. It's an exciting time."

"And Benji may be the new head of the department," Freya put in proudly, patting her husband's thigh.

"That may be a bit premature, honey," Benji put in.

"Well, the current chair just announced his retirement," Freya explained to her brother. "Benji is the obvious choice to be the next chair of the English Department."

"I hope everyone on the hiring committee is as convinced of that as you are," Benji responded wryly. "But I did throw in my hat."

"Don't be so modest, Benji," Freya urged. "You've essentially been doing the job of the chair for months now. You've also had more papers published than anyone else in the department."

"True," Benji agreed, while pushing his glasses up his nose with a finger. "Now, Erik, I understand that you have become quite the corporate success. From what Freya's told me, Engen Ornaments has been enjoying a very successful year, and that's in no small part due to your efforts."

"It has been going well," Erik replied modestly. "It turns out that I do have some talent for something other than hockey. Hey, what's with Hayden? He seemed to be in a mood. Freya mentioned something about hockey."

Freya and Benji exchanged a look. "To be honest, Erik, it's rather complicated," Benji began.

"I've already told Erik," Freya explained, "about Hayden wanting to play hockey."

Erik leaned forward. "Benji, Hayden'll be starting late, but with some camps and working with a skating coach, we should be able to get him up to speed pretty quickly. Hayden's athletic." His voice trailed off as he caught the pained expression on his sister's face.

"That's not it," Benji replied.

Freya rested her hand on her husband's leg. "As I already explained to you, Erik, we don't want Hayden to get hurt playing hockey. Benji doesn't think that Hayden can catch up with other kids. We think it would be unsafe for him to play when he lacks the skills the other players have."

"The two of you go whipping down hills at over ninety miles per hour," Erik argued with his sister, "and you're worried about your son playing hockey? Freya, come on. That's crazy. You can't protect them all of the time."

"We feel that Hayden, who has real talent as a Nordic combined athlete, need not put himself at risk by playing hockey," Benji explained.

"Hockey is dangerous, but ski jumping isn't?" Erik shook

his head. "I can't believe I'm hearing this from you two. It's not like you'd be signing the kid up to play in the NHL, but let him play."

"There are only so many hours in the day," Benji protested. "With school and skiing and ski jumping, Hayden doesn't have time to make the commitment to a hockey team."

Freya shook her head. "Be honest, Benji, you don't want to see our boy get squished."

"Must we revisit this now?" Benji protested. "I thought you agreed with me, Freya."

"If you don't let him play, he'll always hold it against you," Erik observed.

"Kind of the way you do Mom for not letting you play football," Freya replied wryly.

"Touché," Erik acknowledged. "At least I know what I'm talking about."

"I appreciate your advice, Erik, but you aren't a parent or a coach," Benji pointed out.

"I am a hockey player, or I was one."

"Let me be frank with you, Hayden isn't a strong skater," Benji said this last bit softly, so that little ears wouldn't overhear it.

"He'll learn," Erik replied. "You two met downhill skiing, zooming down cliffs going faster than most cars do on the highway. That's much more terrifying than hockey. He's what, a squirt? Nowadays, there isn't any checking until bantams. Hayden can try it out before it gets rough."

Another look passed between Benji and Freya. Freya nodded and Benji exhaled loudly. "Maybe we need to revisit our decision, and with you here, this may be the time."

"I could take him to Pine Heights and see how he does," Erik offered.

Freya clapped her hands together. "That's a great idea, Erik," she agreed. "You can give us an honest evaluation of where he is and whether he would be safe playing."

Erik nodded. "I could do that. It'd be fun."

Benji met Erik's gaze and nodded slowly. "That does seem like a sensible plan of action."

"I'm glad that's settled," Freya rose ponderously to her feet. "I need go check on the twins. It's been quiet for too long. I'm worried. Who knows what they are in to?"

"I can go, Freya" Benji offered solicitously. "You stay here, and visit with your brother."

"No, I got it. I need to move around. I'll be right back."

"How does it feel to be back in town?" Benji asked Erik.

"Odd. Strange. Like I've never left and like it's been a hundred years. You'll never guess who I literally ran into on Anderson Street."

"Who?" Benji asked.

"Stella Larson."

"The art teacher at the elementary school? The kids really like her. She's quite a talented artist in her own right. You know she worked as a professional artist for years before taking the job at the elementary school. You should take the time to see the mural that she's working on in Sibelius Square. It's outstanding."

"I'll make a point of checking it out. I knew that Stella was an artist, but I didn't know that she'd returned to Noelle, at least until I ran into her car this morning."

"You ran into Stella Larson?" Freya repeated as she came back into the room.

Erik nodded. "It happened as I was pulling into town this morning. I bumped her car with the Hellcat."

"Within ten minutes of being in town, you literally ran

into the girl who broke your heart?" Freya questioned her brother.

Benji's eyes opened wide behind his glasses. "The art teacher broke your heart? You already know her?"

"Yes, a long time ago," Erik mumbled. "And she didn't break my heart."

"How did this happen?" Freya's eyebrows shot up. "You didn't do it on purpose?"

"Of course not," Erik scowled. "Give me some credit. It was completely accidental, and I was going maybe five or six miles per hour."

"Was she hurt?" Freya demanded.

"No, and her car wasn't damaged either."

"Good," Freya sat back slowly. "Stella is a reasonable person. I can't imagine she'll give you a hard time. Hayden and the twins love her, and she hasn't let your history with her affect our relationship."

"What history are we talking about?" Benji questioned, but brother and sister ignored him.

"Stella was dressed as a reindeer, for school, I guess." Erik mused, picturing his long-ago love as she'd appeared that morning. "She looked adorable. She didn't recognize me at first. When she did, let's just say things grew chilly. I wouldn't say she broke my heart, or I broke hers. We sort of grew apart or ended things because high school ended, and it was time to move on."

"Oh, that's right. You decided it was the right thing to do, ending things between you, before you left for college. Now I remember," Freya stated, rolling her eyes. "Typical. That's how you guys work."

"You jilted her?" Benji inquired pleasantly, amused by this

turn in the conversation. "I had no idea. Freya, you never told me."

Freya shrugged. "It never came up."

"It's not that simple," Erik explained, feeling somewhat embarrassed by the behavior of his teenaged self. "We were going to two different colleges. I was headed to Princeton. She was going to a design school somewhere. I didn't think the long-distance thing would work. I thought it best to end things cleanly. So I told her that at a graduation party."

Freya flinched. "You broke up with her at a graduation party? You never told me that."

"I thought I was doing the noble thing, the right thing. I was nineteen. I was stupid. What can I say? I didn't want to break up with her. We had a blast together, but I thought we were too young to be so serious. That's what everyone was telling me. All I could think about was hockey. The coaches kept telling us to not let a girl distract us from the game. So I did it. I broke up with her."

Benji chuckled, and then brother and sister turned to look at him. "It's funny when you think about it. You broke up with this woman a decade ago, and then you literally run into her when you return to town. I'd say it's karmic retribution."

"Not my best moment, I'll agree."

"I imagine the lady wasn't particularly welcoming," Benji observed.

"You are correct," Erik snorted. "But she did make a cute reindeer."

"Stella's a lovely person," Freya stated. "I always liked her. Far more than those plastic Barbies you paraded around after her while you were playing hockey and when you went corporate."

"Ouch," Erik replied. "Plastic Barbies?"

"I thought the term was *Puck Bunnies*," Benji remarked pleasantly.

Freya laughed out loud.

"It's not like I've brought any of my recent lady friends around the family," Erik defended himself.

"True and interesting," Freya remarked, narrowing her remarkable eyes at her brother. "Why not?"

"Let it go, Sis," Erik responded. "Is Stella married?"

"She's a miss, not a missus, so she's likely not married or not married right now. Then again, she may just go as a miss. But I haven't heard of her having a significant other," Freya answered. "But you leave her alone, Erik Engen," she shook her finger at her brother. "She's the art teacher at the kids' school. I don't want you causing any problems for them. You don't need to come into town, sweep Stella off her feet, and then vanish the way you do. That would make problems for us. You leave her alone."

"I don't think you have to worry about me sweeping Stella Larson off her feet," Erik muttered wryly. "She wasn't friendly at all. Clearly she wasn't happy to see me."

"Stella Larson's single," Benji offered, causing his wife to lightly smack him on the forearm. "She moved back here right after her brother died, so that she could be near her niece and her sister-in-law. Her parents, the Larsons, moved to Arizona a few years ago. You know she's a professional artist and a good one, too. When they couldn't find an art teacher for Leif Erickson Elementary, the school board president asked her to apply for the job, and she did. She is a certified teacher even though she didn't teach while she was travelling all over the world. To be honest, we were all surprised that she's stayed in Noelle as long as she has. She's been at the school for the past three years. She's an intriguing woman."

"How do you know all of this?" Erik questioned.

"Benji's on the School Board," Freya answered for her husband.

"You're sure Stella's unmarried?" he probed.

Benji nodded.

"I can't believe she never married," Erik considered. His stay in Noelle was looking more interesting by the moment.

"Well, you haven't married either," Freya observed. "Maybe you and Stella are more alike than you knew. Both of you left town to pursue your dreams, and now you're back."

Erik merely nodded.

"Oh, no, you don't, Erik Engen. I know that look," his sister protested. "The art teacher is off limits to you. I already told you that."

Erik was picturing Stella's full lips and emotive green eyes. Stella Larson had been an exhilarating handful as a teenager, and it appeared that like a fine wine, she'd become better with age. Maybe the next two weeks of the Noelle Nutcracker Festival wouldn't be such a drag after all.

CHAPTER 3

At the end of the school day and after the Holiday Celebration, the Leif Erickson Elementary School gymnasium looked like a Christmas maelstrom had swept through it. There were cookie sprinkles all over the floor, as well as gold and silver glitter, bits of wrapping paper, and bows that had fallen off presents. Stella, Jayda, Addie, and the other teachers pitched in so that the night custodian wouldn't be too overwhelmed with clean up. When most of the clutter had been removed, Jayda dusted her hands off on her thighs and announced, "That's it then. It's time to go home."

"It's been a long day," Stella agreed, raising her hand to cover a yawn. "Did Darius and Lyrique already leave?"

"I sent them home right after the celebration. Remember Lyrique was home sick today. Darius shouldn't have brought her. But as he said, she hasn't had a fever since before lunchtime."

"It's not like he set her down or let her play with the other children. He mostly held her, and she watched."

"Still, it hasn't been twenty-four hours. Lyrique needs a good night sleep."

"They both wanted to see you. That's dear."

Jayda smiled. "I know. They're sweet. I'm a lucky lady."

"Hey, Stella, Jayda, want to stop for some drinks at Ray's?" Jacob Meyer, the new fourth grade teacher, called out as he wound up a yellow electrical cord on his forearm.

Stella gave Jacob a tired smile. He was cute with his bow ties, overly coiffed light brown hair, and black oversize glasses. He was charming, too, with a keen wit. But the image of a brooding, scarred Scandihoovian with superhero muscles flashed into her mind. Jacob couldn't compete, but then few could compare physically with Erik Engen. Erik was a former professional athlete with the chiseled features of a Norse god. He was also smart and funny. It wasn't fair. She assured herself she wasn't still hung up on her first love, but he did throw some serious shade on her current prospects.

Stella banished Erik's image from her mind. There was no point in having it there. Erik had dumped her seemingly without a backward glance more than ten years ago. They'd both moved on with their lives. Jacob wasn't ultra-masculine, but he was nice, cute, and easy to be with, even though he did think a lot of himself. Still, being one of just three male teachers in an elementary school would have that effect on most men.

"Thanks, but no," Stella answered.

He looked crestfallen.

"I mean, I can't tonight. I'm coaching. I have hockey practice."

"Another night then?" he remained optimistic.

"Yes," Stella nodded, picking up her blue duffle coat from where she'd set it on the rolling chair rack. "I can't wait to get out of this reindeer costume. It's hot and itchy. Bye, Jayda, Addie," she waved to her friends. "See you all," she called to a few other colleagues, PTO members and their children who had remained behind after the event to help with clean up.

"I'll walk you to your car," Jacob offered, tucking her arm inside his. Immediately, the lemony scent of his cologne rose up around her. It was a bright, bracing scent, rather like its wearer. They passed through the first set of doors into the entrance vestibule. A student stood by the enormous fish tank, watching the giant goldfish swim about. Hearing the door slam, the student turned.

"Hi there, Hayden," Stella greeted the fourth grader.

Hayden swept his dark locks back from his eyes. "Hi, Miss Larson, Mr. Meyer," he replied.

"Are you waiting for your parents?" Jacob asked.

"Yeah. Dad went to get the car. See, there he is," he pointed as a shiny, black Suburban pulled up in front of the school. "I came back in because I forgot my hat." Hayden waved the green Minnesota Wild snow hat he was holding.

"Well, you have a good night, Hayden," Stella said as Jacob opened the outside door for her to pass through. It was at that moment that the darkly, tinted passenger window of the Suburban rolled down. Erik Engen gazed out at her, his sardonic features bemused. He waved at her. To Stella's immense dismay, her heart began to pound.

"Erik," she murmured his name without thinking.

"You know Uncle Erik?" Hayden questioned as he passed by her to the side of the vehicle.

"Yes, I mean, I used to," Stella whispered, rattled to be seeing Erik Engen for the second time in a day.

"See you tomorrow," Hayden popped open the back-passenger door and climbed in. Immediately, he started chattering away to his uncle and father.

Jacob inhaled sharply, then prodded Stella with his elbow. "Is that Erik *the Wall* Engen?"

She ignored him.

He gripped her arm. "Stella, do you actually know Erik Engen? Please introduce me," he pleaded. "I'm a huge hockey fan. I'd heard he was Hayden's uncle."

Stella shook her head. It would be too mortifying to introduce Erik to Jacob, like introducing a puppy to a mastiff. Jacob was either unaware or chose to ignore her cue. Releasing Stella's arm, he scurried right up to the side of the Suburban. "Mr. Engen? Are you Erik Engen who once played for the Northern Stars?"

Erik nodded.

To Stella's complete mortification, Jacob leaned in close to Erik. "Mister *The Wall*," Jacob shook his head. "I mean, Mr. Engen, could I please get your autograph? My father is a fan of yours, and he collects player autographs. He has this huge display set up in the basement family room. Your autograph would be the perfect Christmas present for him."

"Sure," Erik replied, his hooded gaze on Stella, though she refused to make eye contact with him. Instead, she stared out into the distance. Fortunately, it was one of those perfect, snowy winter nights that merited gazing at. It was dark and still, the sky heavy with lightly falling snow that hid the moon and the stars from view.

Jacob patted his pockets. "Darn, I don't have a pen or paper with me. Would you mind waiting a minute? I just have to run back to my classroom. I have some cardstock there. I'll be two minutes." He held up his fingers demonstratively.

Erik glanced over at Benji.

"We're not in any hurry," Benji shrugged. "We can wait."

"That's fine. What's your name?" Erik asked.

"Meyers. Jacob Meyers." He held out a hand, and Erik shook it. "This is just great. I can't believe my luck tonight. My father's Robert. That's who'd I'd like the autograph addressed to. Thanks, Mr. Engen, I really appreciate it. Give me two minutes."

"It's no trouble, and my name's Erik."

Grinning, Jacob tapped on the car door, then turned, and dashed back into the school without saying another word to the mortified woman beside him.

Stella wanted the ground to swallow her. She pivoted slowly and took a step toward the teacher parking lot.

"Bye, Miss Larson," Hayden called out to her.

"Bye, Hayden," she waved without looking back. She began to walk away.

"Aren't you going to wait for your boyfriend?" Erik called out in his silky baritone.

Stella's spine stiffened. "He's not my boyfriend," she couldn't resist answering. And he would never be now that he had mortified her in front of Erik. Why had she given Erik the satisfaction of answering him? A long time ago, Erik Engen had had a talent for goading her. Apparently, he had retained that ability. Despite the years that had passed, sparks still flew between them.

"Good to know," Erik replied, giving her a thumbs up. "I'll be seeing you around."

Stella rolled her eyes. "If you're staying in Noelle, I suppose it's inevitable. Well, good night." Gathering her dignity around her as well as her coat, she headed toward her car.

Erik watched her slender, elegant figure as she unlocked

her car door, tossed her bags in the back seat, climbed in, and drove away. Only then did he raise the car window.

Benji raised a curious eyebrow. "Some tension there. What was that all about?"

"Unfinished business," Erik offered with a wolfish grin.

"Between you and the art teacher?"

Erik glanced back at Hayden who was listening intently. "Let's just say she was the one who got away."

"So, is it game on?" Benji probed.

"It may well be," Erik admitted. "And I don't like to lose."

Bright and early the next morning, Erik pulled into the parking lot of the four-story brick building that housed the Engen Nutcracker Factory. The lot faced an unremarkable side of the building, just windows and an access door. After locking his car, Erik skirted two sides of the building to the front, which looked out over the Sibelius Square. Kitschy stores, coffee houses, and local drinking holes occupied the other three sides of the square. On this side of the Engen Nutcracker Factory building was a massive display window. As was the tradition for the holiday season, currently the display area was curtained off, though a wintery white window drawing of wind, swirling snow and evergreen trees covered the glass and drew the eye. Erik contemplated the red and green curtains. The display behind it would be unveiled on the twenty-third, the day before the night before Christmas, as a Christmas gift to the town. It was one of the special events of the Nutcracker Festival in Noelle. For a moment, he was that little boy he'd once been, excited because his parents had let him stay up late with his grandfather to watch the display reveal. Closing his eyes, he could recall the anticipation, the excitement of those moments right before the curtains drew back revealing more Christmas magic.

Erik's grandfather Ole Engen had started the Noelle traditions of the Nutcracker Contest, the Nutcracker Ball, and the display window reveal. For a moment, a swirling hodgepodge of countless Christmas displays filled Erik's mind. Two of his favorites had been a train-themed display and one modeled on the island of forgotten toys from the Rankin Bass Rudolph movies. He remembered gripping his grandfather's rough, callused, woodworking hands as the curtains drew back.

Theirs had been a special relationship of kindred spirits. Erik's grandmother, Agnes, had died when Erik was around two. After the loss of his wife, Ole Engen had devoted himself to his nutcracker factory and to his grandchildren, Freya and Erik. It was Ole who had taught Freya to ski. Ole was the one who had driven Erik to all his hockey practices. He had also taught Erik how to design and carve the nutcrackers for which Noelle was famous. Erik and his grandfather had been virtually inseparable until Ole had died when Erik was sixteen. After the loss of his beloved grandfather, Erik had drawn away from carving and the nutcrackers and even from Noelle. All of them were closely intertwined in his mind, and it had been too painful for him.

Erik had no idea of the theme selected for this year's display. Not that it really mattered. It was always exquisitely done and presided over by Miranda Fedie, his grandfather's and then his father's secretary. She was mostly retired but came back to the factory each year to work her Christmas magic during the holiday season.

Erik hadn't attended the events of the Festival since his grandfather's passing. When he was in high school, the loss had been too recent. He exhaled slowly. This year, however, he intended to take in the entire Nutcracker Festival, to be a part of it, so that he could make the best decisions for the Nutcracker Factory and for Engen Ornaments. Erik was ready for the challenge. It was what he'd been doing very successfully for the past few years with companies all over the world. The Engen Nutcracker Factory was just another company he was evaluating, exactly like so many others.

He sought to ignore the voice inside his head saying that this company, this situation was uniquely personal, special because Noelle was his childhood home and the factory was wrapped up with his memories of his grandfather and of his childhood. Oliver, his father, had admitted to the board that he couldn't be objective when looking at this particular branch of their global business. Erik had assured Oliver as well as the other board members that he could be. Now he wasn't so sure. It had seemed so uncomplicated back in Chicago, but here, in Noelle, memories and emotions ran deep. He took a deep breath, gathering himself, then he walked over to the double doors on one side of the display window and headed inside Engen Nutcrackers.

Once there, he savored the unmistakable aromas of wood shavings and varnish tickling his nose and his memories. He paused inside the doors, allowing the recollections of his childhood and visiting this factory with his grandfather to wash over him. These were good thoughts indeed. At a juncture in the corridor, he turned left and headed into the business offices, off to the side the factory floor. Here he opened another door.

"Can I help you?" A young, male administrative assistant whom he'd never seen before greeted him.

"Oh Justin, this is Mr. Engen, Erik Engen. Your boss. Erik, welcome," Miranda Fedie, the president's secretary for more than thirty years, bustled out from her office behind the administrative assistant's desk. Miranda was rounded and matronly with elaborate cat eye glasses, a bright smile, and hair that was always and unapologetically dyed bright red despite her more than seventy years of age. She was also sharp as a tack and more than a little opinionated.

"I suspected you'd be here bright and early, Erik. You always were an early bird." Miranda skirted around Justin at the desk, reaching for Erik with extended arms. Abruptly, she halted, hesitated, then she extended a hand to him for a handshake.

"Miss Miranda," Erik remonstrated. "You've known me since I was in diapers. I think a hug is in order."

She beamed, and the two embraced. "Well, Erik. Let's get you into the big office." She led the way into the wood paneled room from which his grandfather and then his father had run Engen Ornaments until the administrative offices had moved to Chicago. Oliver Engen still used this office when he worked from Noelle. The space was comfortable rather than ostentatious and very unlike the current office of the CEO of Engen Ornaments.

Erik's father's desk sat before an enormous picture window that overlooked the square below. The leather couch and armchair in the small seating area in front of the desk were worn and comfortable, nothing like the sleek, modern appointments in Erik's office in Chicago. He ran his fingers along the back of his father's green leather desk chair. Against his palms, the leather had the softness of well-worn gloves. The opposite wall remained covered in pictures of Ole Engen's family, his wife, Oliver and Meg, Erik and Freya as well as more recent shots of Freya and Benji and their children. Erik perused the pictures. There were shots of beach vacations to Lake Michigan, ski trips to Colorado, Freya downhill ski racing, and of himself in his goalie gear. He paused before one eight-by-twelve of himself as a gap-toothed eight or nine-year-old, helmet off, wearing the green and white of the Noelle Polar Bears travel hockey team, proudly holding up a zero patch. He swallowed the lump that formed in his throat. It seemed like a lifetime ago, and yet he could remember his feelings from that moment as if it were yesterday. They'd won the game in the Noelle peewee tournament. He'd felt like a superhero. Those were the golden days of hockey. He barely glanced at the pictures of himself in his pro pads from when he'd played for the Northern Stars. Those weren't entirely happy memories.

Erik took a seat in his father's worn leather chair behind the desk. The chair reclined to the right angle when he tilted it back. It was extremely comfortable. *I wonder if I could get another one of these chairs for my office.*

"It's good to have you back, Erik," Miranda avowed, taking a seat in one of the two chairs set in front of desk. "I want you to be truthful with me. With all the years we've known each other, you owe it to me to be honest with me. You're not here to shut down the Nutcracker Factory, are you? I'm not one to listen to water cooler gossip, but there is something odd about you being here for a full two weeks and your father not coming for the Festival for the first time ever. I'm on Facebook with your mother, so I know they are well. I thought I saw they were on a cruise."

"Of the Caribbean," Erik offered.

"Well, that sounds delightful. I'm sure your mother will enjoy it. But since we heard you were chosen to be the Grand Marshal, everyone has been wondering what your plans are for the factory. We know your reputation as a corporate fixer. I, for one, am very proud of your success. But the Nutcracker Factory is the heart of Noelle. You can't shut us down."

Contemplatively, Erik ran his fingertips over the sleek silver MacBook which lay closed on the desk before him. "I understand your concerns as well as everyone else's. I'm here on a fact-finding mission, Miss Miranda. Engen Ornaments has an obligation to its shareholders to consider how best to modernize so that we can better meet the needs of our shareholders and our customers."

"Oh, hogwash," Miranda, never one to mince words, replied. "What about your workers? If you plan on moving this factory to Thailand or Asia to save the almighty dollar, you're going to break this town's heart. You know that, Erik. Not to mention send this place into economic decline."

Erik exhaled slowly. "As I said, I'm here to evaluate. That's what I do, evaluate and then make suggestions to the board. Sometimes it's a matter of trimming the fat. Sometimes it's just reorganization. You should know me well enough to know I don't frivolously fire anyone. Besides, the Nutcracker Factory is profitable. I'm not here to close the factory, but I am here to put an objective eye on the situation. Things might be done better, more efficiently, and more affordably to ensure the future of the factory."

Miranda's lips narrowed. She huffed and then stood abruptly up. "Erik Engen, you come with me." She curled a finger at him in a way that Erik recalled from his childhood. Imperiously, she led him back down hall and paused at a door at the far end. Knowing what was coming, he inhaled deeply as she turned the knob. She stepped inside, not bothering to flip on the lights because of the way natural light from the windows flooded the large, corner room.

"My grandfather's workshop." He stepped inside. It had been more than a decade since he'd last entered this workshop. Oliver, his father, had locked Ole's workshop up right after Ole passed away. It appeared nothing had been touched in the ensuing years. It looked as if the room was waiting for his grandfather to return at any moment and pick up a piece of wood to whittle into a nutcracker.

Erik ran a finger over the table and then glanced at his fingertip. A combination of sawdust and regular dust covered it. His grandfather's tools lay neatly in rows on the workbench or hung from hooks above it, as if they had just been set down. Brilliantly detailed, colored sketches of nutcrackers that his grandpa had drawn and then brought to wooden life with his hands covered the walls. Ole Engen had been a true Geppetto whose wooden works had been filled with life and charm.

Erik walked slowly up to each of the sketches in turn. "They're incredible. Grandpa was an artist." He paused before the drawing of a nutcracker version of the one-eyed, Norse god Odin. The sketch displayed the carving from various angles. The detail work was remarkable, from Odin's muscled forearms, to the hairs of his beard, to the wrinkles in the skin around his eye, to the folds of his black cloak, to the great raven perched on his shoulder. Most impressive was how Odin's one eye seemed to follow Erik's movement about the room.

"Your grandfather always said designing the nutcrackers was the part that he enjoyed the most," Miranda acknowledged, her eyes suspiciously bright. "Running the business was never as important to him."

"We don't make nutcrackers like these now," he turned to face Miranda, gesturing at the sketches. "Each of these are works of art and worth a fortune, and we're talking about the sketches here. The nutcrackers are worth even more. If I remember correctly, most of my grandfather's nutcrackers are in private collections now except the ones the factory retained."

"There are a few in the Noelle Nutcracker Museum," Miranda acknowledged. "We have several examples from the American Myths and Legends series, including Ole's John Henry and Paul Bunyan. My personal favorites in the museum are the nutcrackers from the Trickster line. Those little leprechaun nutcrackers are precious, and I so love the trolls."

"The troll nutcrackers were one of Grandpa's most successful lines. I know we sold a bunch in Norway. Grandpa loved his folklore. Unfortunately, the Engen Nutcrackers we turn out today don't have this attention to detail and story line. I'm still proud of them, but they're more run of the mill, and they can be mass produced quickly."

"Of course they are," Miranda sniffed disapprovingly. "That's what happens when you automate and take the artistry out of the process." She pressed her sparkly framed glasses up her nose.

Erik resisted the urge to retort. Automation was a reality of twenty-first century life. His grandfather had done things differently twenty years ago. Lots of things were done differently then.

"Well," Miranda said. "I'll admit currently we don't have any artists with your grandfather's talent."

"Dad still does some designing. He was the driving force behind the Fairy Tale Nutcracker line we did several years ago."

"They were nice. I especially liked the Little Red Riding Hood Nutcracker. She was dear. I don't mean to be critical or disloyal...your father is a talented craftsman, but he isn't a true artist like your grandfather. There was only other person in your family who ever showed anything approaching your grandfather's talent." She arched a thin, pencil drawn eyebrow at Erik.

Looking down, Erik shook his head. "I haven't carved in years." His fingers involuntarily twitched at the thought. In his mind's eye, he pictured himself sitting on this same bench at this worktable with his grandfather, learning to hold the carving tools, making his first, tentative strokes with his knife. Ole Engen had been a slighter man than Erik or his father, with a lean build, except for a belly which revealed a fondness for Grandma Engen's Swedish cookies and his home brewed beer. Ole had been a quiet man with a gentle spirit, but he'd also had a wicked sense of humor that he shared with his grandson. His booming laugh was contagious.

"I could carve," Erik admitted. "But I never could draw the way Grandpa did. His work told a story about each of his nutcrackers. His designs were filled with real emotions, and that's what made them so special." He swallowed hard, pushing down the lump that had risen in his throat. He inhaled through his nostrils, savoring the scent of wood, really of trees, that still lingered in the workshop, transporting him back to happy times long past. "Doesn't anyone use this workshop now?" he finally asked Miranda.

In response, she clasped her hands in front of her waist, a small smile curving her bright red lips. "No, your father never wanted anyone else in here. Besides nowadays, as you know, the nutcrackers are designed on computers by the creatives, and machines do most of the carving. Only the painting and the fine finishing work are done by hand. This workshop is all yours for as long as you are here. I thought you would want to see it. I know how close you were to your grandfather, how special this room was to both of you."

"Right." Erik glanced again at the colored sketches covering the walls. He picked up a fine chisel, closing his eyes as the weight settled into his palm, feeling so foreign and yet familiar. When he opened his eyes and met Miranda's gaze, it was with a wry expression. "So many memories in this place. I remember carving my own nutcrackers while waiting for Grandpa to get done with work."

She chuckled. "I can still see you sitting there over by his desk. You stayed for hours. I was always scared to death you were going stab yourself with one of those sharp tools he let you handle. What was Mr. Engen thinking letting a little boy handle all of those sharp tools?"

Erik nodded. "I remember asking you for more than a few band aids."

"I kept a bottle of peroxide in my desk for your visits. Do you remember when you were about ten, and you were using that new knife he'd gotten you for carving, and you cut yourself?"

"I about took my finger off, and I still don't have any sensation on the palm side," Erik chuckled, holding the finger in question up. "The blood shot out of my finger as I ran around this room and then down the hall."

Snickering, she pressed a hand to her lips. "I remember. There was blood all over the walls. It looked like there had been a massacre in here."

"It's vivid in my memory, too. Mom was not thrilled about another emergency room visit. Dad was more worried about getting blood on the upholstery of his new car."

"Your grandfather always said that you were the most gifted, natural woodworker he'd ever trained. You really don't carve at all anymore?"

"No, I don't have time for that with my job and all of the travel that it involves."

"Well, that's a shame."

"It takes weeks to create the nutcrackers in the old way. With the machines, we reduce the entire process to hours."

"And you lose the unique, one-of-a-kind artistry that made the Engen nutcrackers so special," she reproved him.

"Miranda, you know how things work today. Every Target and Kohl store has their own nutcrackers, fifty of the exact same at any given store, all for less than twenty dollars. Engen Nutcrackers can't compete with that."

"Why would you want to?" Miranda reproved him. "Engen Nutcrackers was never about assembly line and mass manufacture. It was about artistry, craftsmanship, one of kind works of art. There is still a place for craftsmanship in today's world. I'm afraid we've lost our way. Your grandfather created art and holiday joy. This factory has always been about more than the bottom dollar."

"You mean Dad and I have lost our way? Miranda, I appreciate your concerns and thoughts, but I have to think about what is best for the company. Engen Ornaments is a successful company. We look out for our shareholders and employees."

"That doesn't mean it can't be improved on, young man."

There was a knock at the door, interrupting the conversation. It opened to reveal a tall, extremely good-looking man in his early thirties with dark skin and pale golden eyes. "Hello, Erik, I heard on the floor that you'd arrived. I went looking for you, and someone mentioned you might be in here. I don't know if you remember me from that corporate retreat in Kohler last year. I'm Darius Watkins. I'm the general manager here at Engen Nutcrackers."

"Yes, Darius, of course. It's good to see you again." Erik extended his hand in a warm greeting. He remembered the young manager as clever and innovative but with a practical bent. Erik and his father had identified Darius as a possible accessory to their envisioned transformation of the Nutcracker Factory into a more modern, more profitable entity better suited for its role in the Engen Ornaments empire.

"Are you ready for a tour? Afterwards, we can talk in my office or in yours, whatever you prefer," Darius offered. "As long as you and Miss Fedie are done in here?" he questioned, glancing from Erik to Miranda.

"Yes, we're finished, Darius," Miranda agreed, moving to the door. "It's good to see you back in Noelle, Erik. It will be good for you to be a part of the whole Nutcracker Festival and see how important it is for this town. We can catch up later." She headed out the door.

Erik's eyes followed his grandfather's former secretary. Other than Freya, Miranda was the first Noelle resident to voice her opposition to any potential changes at the Nutcracker Factory, but he was confident she wouldn't be the last.

Darius waited, sensing some residual tension in the room. Having been employed at the factory going on five years, he was aware that Miranda was not one to withhold her opinion. He suspected that she had brought up some of his shared concerns regarding Erik's appearance in Noelle. As for Erik himself, Darius wanted to like him. He certainly liked what he'd heard and seen of him at that corporate retreat, but he was also worried about his own family's welfare, the factory, and indeed, the town of Noelle. He planned on treading softly in his interactions with Erik, but at the same time defending all that he considered important.

Then he caught sight of Ole Engen's nutcracker sketches on the walls. Transfixed, he walked over to study them slowly, one at a time. "Wow, I knew about this room, but they've always kept it locked. I've never had a chance to really see your grandfather's work." He whistled low, standing before one wall filled with sketches of Santa Clauses from all over the world. The figures looked like they could step out of their drawings. "He was the Faberge of nutcrackers."

"I agree." Erik moved to stand beside the other man, so they were studying the sketches together.

"You realize that these sketches are amazing?" Darius asked, glancing over at Erik.

Erik nodded.

"But you're leaving them here in this abandoned workroom?" Darius pointed out. "Don't you think these should be seen? Not forgotten in here?"

Erik gazed at Darius. "Maybe you're right. These should see the light of day."

"They're inspirational. They should be framed, then placed throughout the factory, in the boardroom and on the factory floor. We could use glass that would protect them from sunlight. They're part of the heritage of the company."

Erik eyed Darius. "You are passionate about nutcrackers, aren't you?"

"We had several of them when I was a little boy. I always

associated them with the joy of the season. Yes, I am very enthusiastic about our products."

"That's a great quality and one I appreciate as your boss. Truthfully, I hadn't even considered what to do with my grandfather's sketches. I'd forgotten about them, but I will consider them now. Your suggestion sounds good. We'll see what we can do. So," Erik rubbed his hands together, "are you going to take me on the tour?"

"Yes, absolutely," Darius replied. "But I imagine you already know everything about this factory. I sent you all the financial information several weeks ago. You've seen the three-year plan, and I also forwarded you the designs that our creatives are working on. I believe you must have a pretty complete understanding of our enterprise here."

"I do," Erik admitted, "but I'd like to see it through your eyes and through the eyes of the other people who work here. I know what I think and believe, but I need to take it all in before—" he paused.

"Before what?" Darius probed.

Erik patted him on the shoulder. "Darius, relax. Right now, I understand exactly where you're coming from. I appreciate your commitment and your loyalty. Have some faith in me. Let me see what you're fighting to protect. Take me on the tour. I'm sure you have a great deal you want to show me. The truth is I haven't spent much time in this factory for more than a decade. After my grandfather died, it was hard for me to be here without him. Now I'm ready to take it all in."

"All right then, let's go," Darius nodded with resolution. "This is an amazing place, and we have great people working here."

"Show me," Erik agreed. "I'm excited to see everything."

The day passed quickly. With his keen eye for detail, Erik absorbed more information concerning the functioning of the Engen Nutcracker Factory. He asked questions of the employees and took notes on the yellow legal pad he took with him everywhere. He planned on transposing those notes into something comprehensible later that evening. At the end of the day, Darius pressed Erik to discuss his reactions and thoughts. Erik didn't yet feel he was ready. He was concerned that his view of the workings of the factory remained somewhat superficial and rudimentary, and he had yet to speak with the designers. He knew the nuts and bolts of the operation, but he wanted to put names to faces and get a sense of the feeling of the place, the esprit de corps. Only after he had fully immersed himself into the world of the Nutcracker Factory would he offer his thoughts and evaluations.

He had successfully employed this same process in evaluating companies all over the world, and he didn't intend to let sentiment and personal connections shade his thoughts and conclusions in this case.

Later that evening, Erik was hanging out in the living room of the Weber house, chatting with Freya and Benji, while the twins played with toys on the carpet.

"How did the day go?" Freya asked. "What do you think?"

Erik took a deep breath. "Well, there's a lot to process."

Benji glanced over at him. "For example," he prompted, "are you closing the factory, downsizing, or laying people off? What other options are there?"

Freya inhaled sharply. "Be straight with us, Erik. I know you were coming here to evaluate how things are at the factory, but you and Dad aren't considering shutting it down, are you?"

"The factory remains profitable," Benji announced. "I researched it today."

Erik closed his eyes, considering his response. "I'm not here to evaluate whether we are profitable right now. All anyone has to do is look at the financials, and that answers the question. My focus is on the future. Is there a long term for the Nutcracker Factory? If there is, what does it look like? What changes do we need to make to ensure that we get there? Does that make sense?"

"You're really here to see how to ensure its survival?" Freya nodded with approval. "I feel much better knowing that. You could have told me that. I wouldn't have hassled you."

"That doesn't mean preparing for the future won't be painful or challenging. Business moves so fast these days, and trends are here today and gone tomorrow. I'm tasked with making our nutcrackers appealing now and for twenty years from now. Or, if they don't have enduring appeal, with developing a plan for downsizing the factory so that we hurt as few people as possible. Engen Ornaments employs so many people now, we must protect them by critically evaluating each entity within the larger corporation. It's the right and ethical thing to do."

"That makes sense," Benji conceded.

"When you put it that way," Freya admitted wryly, "I feel guilty for giving you a hard time about it. Do keep us in the loop about what you observe and what you conclude. You must do what's best for the corporation. I understand that. Is there is anything I can do to help you?"

"Darius Watkins has been taking me around and

introducing me. He is clever, diligent, and I believe open to innovation."

"He's smart," Benji agreed. "I know him through Chamber of Commerce functions. He's also a heck of a golfer. We play in the same league during the summer," he explained.

"Hey, Mom and Dad," Hayden burst into the room, interrupting the conversation. He was layered up for the outdoors with black snow pants, a Carhartt jacket, and a stocking cap. "Can I go to the outdoor rink? Jocho is going to meet me there. Can I go, please?"

"It's getting late," Freya hesitated.

"There's no school tomorrow. Mom, please?" he prodded. "It'll be super fun."

"Are you planning on a snow day?" Benji asked.

"No, it's a teacher workday. Kids don't have to go," Hayden was euphoric. "Can I go skating, please?"

His parents glanced at each other, neither wanting to relinquish the warm comfort of their living room.

"I'll take him," Erik offered.

"For real?" Hayden asked enthusiastically.

"Yeah, it'd be fun," Erik agreed, getting to his feet. "It'll feel good to move around after talking, eating, and sitting all day."

"You have your hockey gear here?" Benji questioned.

"I think some of my old pads are tucked around here somewhere, probably down in the backroom of the basement or in the garage. I have some skates in my car. I'd rather skate out anyway. No one wants to play goalie on the outdoor ice."

"You did," his sister pointed out. "When your Uncle Erik was a kid, Hayden, on Saturdays, he'd put on his gear and spend the whole day on the outdoor rinks, taking shots."

"Those were good times," Erik sighed. "Hopefully, I can still skate. I haven't skated yet this winter."

"Erik, do you have a helmet with you?" Freya asked. "They do make you wear those now."

"I don't think I brought one," Erik began.

"Oh, don't worry about it," Hayden interrupted, waving his hand dismissively. "They have like a hundred helmets there for people to use."

About a half an hour later, Erik and Hayden turned Freya's minivan up the long drive sheltered by towering pine trees to the outdoor skating rink which was situated on city land behind the elementary school. Erik was driving his sister's car because Hellcats weren't designed for transporting hockey gear, especially hockey sticks. He didn't pull directly into a parking spot. Instead, he paused facing into the lot, taking in the oh-so-familiar scene.

It hadn't changed at all since he'd been there as a teenager. At one end of the snow-and-ice covered parking lot, there was a dark brown, wooden, warming house and, beside it, the brilliantly lit outdoor ice hockey rink. The floodlights reflected off the white boards. The figure skating rink, situated on the other side of the warming house, was not visible from where they currently parked.

"Come on, Uncle Erik. The guys are waiting," Hayden prodded.

Lost in memories of countless winter nights spent skating under the moonlight at this very rink, Erik was slow to respond. "Oh-okay," he agreed. "There are a lot of cars here tonight," he observed.

"Some nights, hockey teams practice here," Hayden related with awe in his voice.

"Oh, you mean the in-house hockey teams. I'd forgotten about that. They still have outdoor practices?" Erik asked, the corners of his mouth quirking up, as he remembered outdoor hockey practices from his own youth.

"I think so," Hayden agreed. "I've only ever been on the skating rink, but I've seen teams practicing out here with real jerseys and socks and hockey sticks and stuff. We're not allowed to have sticks and pucks on the skating rink, which kind of sucks, I mean, stinks."

"Back in my day, if there was a practice going on when we wanted to skate, we asked the hockey coaches if they wouldn't mind us messing around down at one end of the hockey rink. They were usually fine with that. There's no reason to go to the skating rink."

Just then, the door to the warming house burst open. A boy stood in the back lit doorway, waving at them.

Hayden waved jubilantly back. "That's Jocho, Uncle Erik. Let's go." He scrambled out of the car and tugged open the minivan's sliding door. He juggled his skates and his stick, trying to get them under control in his arms.

"Whoa, Hayden. Skates are much easier to carry if you put them on your stick," Erik observed.

"What do you mean?" Hayden asked, confused.

"You put your stick through the blades," Erik explained, gesturing with his hands to illustrate his point. "It makes it easier to carry them."

"Oh, I get it. That's how all the hockey players do it," Hayden enthused while pushing his stick, a cut down adult one they'd scrounged up from the dark recesses of Freya's and Benji's basement, through his skates.

"You head on in. I have to get my stuff together," Erik directed, wanting a few moments alone to take it all in. Ice had once been his life, but he hadn't been on skates in a long while. "Go on, get your skates on. I'll be in shortly."

"Are you sure? I mean, Mom wouldn't like it if I ditched you to hang out with a friend." Impatiently, Hayden bounced from one foot to the other.

"Nah, I'm good. I want a minute out here."

"Why?"

"Memories."

Hayden looked perplexed.

"It's a grown-up thing, Hayden," Erik patted the boy's head. "I'll meet you in there."

"Okay." Hayden pulled the handle of the sliding door again, so that it closed. He eagerly headed over to join his friend, his battered, old stick and skates proudly held aloft on his shoulder. The two boys connected under the lights of the warming house and headed inside, chattering all the way.

I have to get him a decent stick, Erik reflected. *I'll stop at the Bike and Skate Shop tomorrow at lunch time. Ronnie should have something for Hayden. Kid can't play with that log in his hands.*

Erik opened the car windows, closed his eyes, and inhaled deeply. There it was…that olfactory concoction of frigid air and car exhaust that was unique to an outdoor ice rink in the middle of winter. He associated the aroma with excitement, friendship, and fun. His nostrils flared wide when he caught the whiff of a log fire in some house beyond the circle of evergreen trees surrounding the rink.

In his opinion, there was no better scent in the world, and it took him back to that long ago, magical time when Erik's world was full of hockey, dreams, and Stella Larson. All three were jumbled up in his memories of those halcyon days of high school hockey when he'd been the town star, dating a beautiful and amazing girl, and his future had appeared golden and full of promise. He shook his head. Life had a way of beating that kind of optimism out of you.

Tonight's winter air still tasted of hope in a way it hadn't for Erik in years. True, his hockey dream hadn't ended as he'd envisioned it would, but he wouldn't trade those days and that passion for anything. In the end, it had all turned out as it was meant to. Today, he genuinely enjoyed his job, selecting and selling unique collectibles associated with specific holidays from all over the world. He enjoyed meeting the crafts people and then formulating a plan to take their creations global in an economically feasible manner. He appreciated working at Engen Ornaments, the traveling and the deal making, and he liked the people he worked with. But at this moment, it felt right to be back in Noelle, Wisconsin. There was no place else he would rather be.

Finally, he emerged from the minivan, pulled his own stick and skates out through the rear access door and strolled over to the hockey rink. It hadn't changed in the decade since he'd last been here. There was the usual assortment of players out puck handling and shooting at the net. There were the little water bugs, fast skaters zooming around, chasing after each other. There were some stiff-legged college students who could barely skate. There were also the serious hockey players, a few teenagers, a girl and several boys who could really move and stick handle and who were making a game of it on one far end of the rink over by the net. The hockey team practice that Hayden had mentioned was not yet taking place.

Erik lingered there, soaking it all in, the brightness of the overhead lights reflecting off the ice, the sounds of skates cutting into the surface, and of pucks bouncing off frozen, wooden boards. Some of his best childhood memories involved pickup games with whoever was at the outdoor rink.

The players' ages had never mattered. All that had mattered was the game, and they'd all played for hours for the joy of it. Seemingly, this place was unchanged, frozen in time, even though to Erik those long-ago nights felt like a lifetime ago. He turned and walking flat-footed and penguin-like because of the ice patches on the dirt of the parking lot as he, too, headed into the warming house.

Upon swinging the heavy, wooden door wide, the overwhelming stench of hot air, sweaty, young bodies, and cloyingly sweet hot cocoa assailed him. There was nothing of the freshness of the out-of-doors here, not a hint of a log fire or frost on the air. It was also loud inside the warming house, with a cacophony of young voices shouting over each other, and dueling strains of music pouring forth from portable speakers linked to cell phones.

Erik entered the main room of the warming house where players sat to tie their laces on wooden benches that lined each wall. A hallway led to another smaller changing room with an attached bathroom where recreational skaters or moms with small kids generally went. It was the quieter side. On the rowdy side, a passel of nine or ten-year-old kids wearing skates were laughing, chatting, and throwing gloves and hats at each other. The rink attendant, who looked like he was a junior or a senior in high school, sat behind his desk wearing a sound canceling headset and staring at his laptop screen, completely oblivious to it all. There was no sign of Hayden and his buddy. Suddenly, a damp wool hat hit Erik squarely in the face.

"Hey," he picked up the offending black and red Chicago Blackhawks knit hat off the ground. "Whose is this?" he growled, glaring at the four offenders who'd been tossing the hat about and were now staring at him in some concern.

One boy with a straw yellow flow of hockey hair stepped forward reluctantly. "It's my hat, mister, but I didn't throw it at you. I was trying to get it back. They took it from me," he pointed at the other kids.

"Tattle tale," one of the accused muttered.

"Were you boys bullying him?" Erik demanded, flicking a thumb at the boy in question.

"No," a scrawny, freckled brunette replied, stepping forward indignantly, seemingly outraged at the question.

"'Course not," said another. This one had chipmunk cheeks and long, brown bangs.

"They weren't," the first boy announced. "We're friends. We were just messin' around. They weren't being mean or nothing."

"Well, here, take your hat then," Erik tossed it back to him.

"Sorry about that, mister," the hat owner stated.

The scrawny brunette took a step closer to Erik. "Hey, aren't you—?"

Hayden appeared in the doorway between the two rooms, interrupting the other boy's question. He glanced at the group of hockey players and then at his uncle. Nervously, he made his way over to Erik's side, avoiding jostling or making any kind of eye contact with the other kids. "Hey, Uncle Erik, you ready to go?" he whispered, tugging on Erik's coat sleeve.

"Let me get my skates on." Erik sat down on a bench, setting his stick against the wall and extending his legs. He set his skates between his feet and began to adjust the stiff, dried out laces. His fingers moved with easy dexterity.

"You mean in here?" Hayden nervously muttered. "There's more space in the other room. We can spread out."

Perplexed, Erik glanced over at him. "All of the hockey

players get dressed in here. In my day, the other room was for recreational skaters and moms with little kids."

"That's it," Hayden explained in a whisper, blushing red. "This room's for hockey players. I'm not a hockey player."

Erik waved his hand. "Neither are half of these characters. Some of those teenagers out on the hockey rink can barely skate. It's all about confidence…swagger. We're playing hockey today, and we're going to get dressed in here."

"Hey, mister." The scrawny brunette boy materialized before him. There was something oddly familiar about the shape of his brown eyes and the freckles across his nose. The kid's eyes turned up a little at the corners.

I wonder if I know his mom or dad? Erik considered.

"Hi, Hayden," the boy said. "This your uncle?" he asked Hayden, indicating Erik.

"Yeah, Sam, he's my uncle," Hayden answered with some pride.

At least he likes something about me, Erik reflected.

The brunette whispered something to Hayden behind a raised hand.

Hayden shook his head in response while biting at a fingernail.

"Come on, Hayden," the other boy tugged at Hayden's arm. "I bet you he won't mind. Players never do."

"Fine, ask him yourself," Hayden retreated to the bench, nothing in his demeanor or expression providing any clues to Erik as to how he should proceed.

"Mr. Engen," the boy with the freckles stepped right up to Erik. "You're Erik Engen, right? The goalie? Erik *The Wall* Engen? From the Northern Stars?"

Erik nodded.

"I've seen you play," the child enthused with a gap-toothed grin.

"Aren't you a little young to have seen me play? You're about what, ten?"

"I'm nine, actually, but me and my dad, we're big hockey fans. We used to watch all these old-time hockey games on YouTube. And the fights, too. I know all the great ones, Gretzky, Lemieux, Lindros, all those old guys. My dad liked to watch your videos especially 'cause he said he went to school with you. He showed me the videos of when you stood on your head at the World Juniors."

"We lost, you know?" The passion of this diminutive hockey fan mentioning a game that had been played probably before he was born bemused Erik.

"I know, but it wasn't your fault," the child patted him reassuringly on the forearm. "My dad said you played your heart out."

"We lost in a shootout, so it sort of was my fault."

"Well, if your skaters had scored, you wouldn't have lost."

"What's your dad's name, kid?" There was something familiar about this boy.

"Elias Larson."

Erik studied the earnest face before him, the name sounded familiar, but dredging through all the names and faces of the guys he'd played with over the years, he couldn't make the connection. "You tell him hi for me, okay?'"

The child continued to stare at him earnestly, big, brown eyes fixed on his face "Could I get your autograph?"

"Sure. Of course," Erik agreed. "What do you want me to sign?"

"Oh, shoot," the child glanced around fiercely. His eyes

caught on the attendant. He dashed over to him. "Hey, Ryan, can I borrow a piece of paper?"

Removing his headset, the attendant, Ryan, glanced over at the child with some irritation. "Sam, all I have is notebook paper."

"That'll be fine."

Rolling his eyes, Ryan tore the page out and handed it to Sam.

"Can I borrow your pen, too?" Sam prompted.

"Fine," Ryan agreed, grudgingly handing over his ballpoint pen.

Sam dashed over, handing his prizes to Erik.

"Who do you want me to write it to?" Erik asked, falling into autograph-signing mode.

Biting his lip, Sam considered. "Could you write it *To my buddy, Bam Bam?*"

Erik's hand froze in the midst of writing a word. "Bam Bam Larson is your dad?" he asked Sam. His mind's eye was filled with the image of his left winger from his junior year of high school, a lanky kid with brown eyes turned up at the corners, a big smile, endless energy, and a mischievous streak. Bam Bam Larson had been two years older than Erik but one year ahead of him in school. He was also Stella's older brother.

Sam nodded eagerly.

The door to the warming house opened letting in a gust of cold air. A tall female figure appeared in the doorway. Eyeglasses that immediately steamed up in the moist heat of the warming house obscured her face. A coat, snow hat, and hockey breezers completely covered the woman as she teetered precariously on hockey skates. "Samantha, boys, the rest of the team is already on the ice. We only have forty-five minutes of ice time tonight, and we have a lot of drills to do. You need to shake a leg." Demonstratively, she waved a handful of printouts in the air. Erik thought he glimpsed the familiar shapes of hockey drills on the pages.

"We're almost ready, Aunt Stella," Sam replied.

"Samantha?" Perplexed, Erik glanced down at the child before him whose winter gear and hockey apparel had concealed that the fact that he was, in fact, she. "Stella?" Erik recognized the voice emerging from under the layered winter clothing and hockey gear.

"Erik, what are you doing here?" Removing her glasses, she glared at him. Back in their high school days, he couldn't remember her narrowing those green eyes at him. They'd had the usual teenaged spats, but they'd gotten along well. Apparently, this had changed in the past decade as well.

"Aunt Stella's our coach," Sam announced, stepping forward. "I'm coming. You done with that yet, Mr. Wall?"

"Stella's your coach?" Erik repeated incredulously, glancing over at Stella. Without providing any explanation, she simply nodded as he finished signing his autograph and handed it to her niece. Sam tucked the autograph into her pocket, then turned about, picking up her hockey gloves and stick.

"Manners, Samantha," her aunt prodded.

"Thanks, Mr. Wall," she called back to him before she and the other hockey players filed out the door. Stella held the door wide as her troop preceded her outside. She saluted Erik with her drill papers and allowed the heavy door to swing shut behind her.

"Sam is Stella's, I mean Ms. Larson's, niece?" Erik questioned Hayden. He was missing something. Why would

Stella be coaching her niece's team instead of her brother Elias? To Erik's knowledge, Stella had never played hockey.

Hayden nodded. "Sam, I mean Samantha, is one of the best players on the Rockets. She's fast. She's in my class at school, and so are some of the other players, too."

"Her father was fast, too. But why is Ms. Larson coaching? If I remember correctly, she could barely skate. I know. I took her skating a couple of times on dates. She swam and did cross country back in high school." Erik snapped her fingers. "Samantha is playing on a boys' team. I get it. Stella is helping her brother out because her niece is on the team, acting as a female role model?"

"Nope," Hayden shook his head. "Sam's father is dead. He died a long time ago, like when we were in kindergarten."

Hayden and Sam were third graders now. That meant Elias had died about four years ago. Erik felt his heart sink into a deep pit. *That little girl lost her father at such a young age. Do you even remember your dad when you lose him in kindergarten?* For a moment, he struggled to reconcile the image of the cocky, grinning, fast skating, teenage boy with the knowledge that he was deceased, leaving behind a daughter. He hadn't thought of Elias Larson in years, but now his former teammate appeared vital and alive in Erik's memories. *Elias Larson dead. It didn't seem possible or right.* Elias had had the fever for hockey if not the hands or the vision, Erik recalled. For a moment, he imagined Elias showing his little girl YouTube videos of himself and other hockey players. He felt sad for the little girl and her aunt.

"Ms. Larson is the coach of this hockey team?" Erik interrogated his nephew.

"The Rockets. Yes, she is," Hayden explained. "She's our art teacher, too. She's nice even though she doesn't skate very well. Will you tie my skates, Uncle Erik," he asked, oblivious to Erik's turmoil.

"Hockey players tie their own skates," Erik replied automatically, his mind still grappling with the Larsons' tragic loss. Repeating the saying was automatic. *Hockey players tie their own skates* was a mantra he'd heard repeated in countless locker rooms from countless coaches throughout his childhood.

"Well, I'm not a hockey player," Hayden replied hotly. "My mom usually ties my skates. Please, Uncle Erik, I don't think I can get them tight enough. If they're loose, I skate really bad."

"You might not be able to get them tight enough today, but if you try to tie them every day, you will improve. One day, you'll be able to do it. Hockey player should tie their own skates. It's kind of a rule, like carrying your own hockey gear. Always be suspicious of a player whose mom or dad carries his or her gear. They're likely cake eaters."

"Cake eaters?" Hayden scrunched his nose. "But I like cake, especially with chocolate frosting."

"Cake eater is an expression," Erik explained. "Haven't you seen *The Mighty Ducks*? I used to think the expression came from that movie, but it turns out that it was originally ascribed to Queen Marie Antoinette of France."

"Huh? Queen Marie," Hayden shook his head, not following his uncle's perambulations.

"Forget the Marie Antoinette stuff, but every kid should watch *The Mighty Ducks*. Geez. Freya needs to step up her classic sports movie game. As a kid, I watched that movie so many times I can do almost all the dialogue for that movie and *The Miracle*, too."

"I've seen *The Miracle*." Hayden glanced disconsolately down. He thumped his heels against the base of the bench.

"My mom and dad don't like contact sports. They don't want me to get hurt. It stinks. All of the other kids play tackle football and hockey, and I just ski."

"Actually, skiing is very cool. I wish that I could do it well. I never had time for it growing up, but it's something I always planned on pursuing once I got settled somewhere." Erik gripped his nephew's chin and tilted it up. "Trust me, Hayden. We'll get something worked out with respect to hockey."

"For real?" Hayden asked, his face lighting up.

"I'm not promising anything except that I will talk with your parents. Now, give me your foot. I'll tighten your laces this one time, but you watch so you can do it next time. Put your foot here," Erik squatted down in front of Hayden, his fingers moving over the laces with easy familiarity and strength. After he finished with one skate, he set the foot down and inquired, "How does that feel?"

"Too tight," Hayden replied, frowning as he wiggled his ankle up and down. "Yeah, I can barely move my ankle. It kinda hurts."

"Good. That's the idea. You don't want to be sloppy in your skates, an ankle bender. Now give me your other foot."

"Help!" Erik thought he heard a muffled call from outside somewhere. No, it must have been his imagination, he decided. Hayden didn't appear to have heard anything. No one else responded or reacted in the warming house, so he continued with the lace tightening.

"We're going out onto the figure skating rink, right?" Hayden prodded.

"Help me!" the call came again, this time, louder and clearer.

"Did you hear that?" Erik demanded.

"I heard *Help*!" Hayden nodded.

Erik glanced over at the rink attendant, but he had on a headset and couldn't hear anything. So Erik stepped around the bench and pushed the door wide.

There, flat on her back with her skate tucked up under her in a clearly uncomfortable and awkward position, was the subject of his musings, Stella Larson.

"Hey, are you okay?" he questioned, standing over her and staring down at her.

Stella scowled at him. He'd forgotten how her pretty nose turned up at the end. "Honestly, Erik, do I look okay? Don't just stand there. Do something."

"How can I help you? Why can't you get up?"

"My skate blade is somehow hooked on my coat. I slipped on a patch of ice and fell, and then this happened." She wiggled slightly, demonstrating that she could not extricate her skate from underneath her. Her leg disappeared under her three-quarter length black winter coat. "I don't want to tear it. It's a new coat, and frankly I can't move. My thigh is killing me. None of my kids heard me calling over the sound of pucks hitting wood and the blades on ice." She groaned. "It would have to be you seeing me like this. I give up. I've lost all semblance of dignity today. First, the reindeer costume, then this. Get me out of this, please."

Erik squatted down beside her. "I'm going to turn you on your side and pull the blade out of your coat, okay? I'll do my best not to tear it."

Stella bit her lip but nodded. Erik grasped her by the hip and shoulder and turned her gently onto her side. He saw the problem. The skate blade had punctured her coat and was hooked into a seam in a layer beneath. "Is the blade cutting you?" he queried anxiously.

"I don't think so, but my quadricep is about to rupture, so

please pull the skate out, but be careful with the coat. It's Columbia and new."

Erik eyed where the skate blade had punctured through a seam. He tried to work it free with no success. Stella's efforts to extricate herself from the position had pulled the blade deeper into the material. He raised his hands in frustration. "I'm not sure I can avoid tearing the coat. It's really hooked in there."

"Darn. I just got this coat for coaching. It's good for subzero weather. It was my birthday present to myself. I really like it."

"I'll get you a new one," Erik growled. "You lying out here in freezing temperatures because you are afraid of tearing your coat is ridiculous. I thought you had more sense than that, Stella," he remonstrated. "What would you tell your players?"

Stella gritted her teeth. "Actually, it was more about not wanting you to see me in another embarrassing moment than worrying about the coat."

"It's not like you haven't seen me in embarrassing moments," Erik chuckled.

"You saw me in a reindeer costume," Stella pointed out.

"For the record, you make an adorable reindeer."

Stella felt a blush suffuse her cheeks and was glad that Erik was busy trying to figure out how to extract her skate so he wouldn't observe her reaction to his words. She was very aware of his hands on her hip and side as he studied her predicament. "Fine," she muttered.

"Fine what?" Erik questioned.

"Fine, tear it," Stella replied, closing her eyes. "You don't have to buy me a new coat. I'll get this one repaired, or I'll order a new one."

Erik grasped both sides of the coat around the skate blade and tore them back. He saw that the blade was also hooked into her black, overall snow pants underneath. With a jerk, he tugged the skate free and then gently and carefully straightened Stella's leg.

She grimaced as she slowly sat up while massaging her thigh. "Thanks. I guess I'm not meant to be on frozen water, but you already knew that, right?" she commented, offering him a sheepish grin.

Erik felt a punch in his gut as those green eyes met his own. His eyes travelled the elegant lines of her cheekbones dusted with cinnamon freckles, those deliciously full lips. *This woman is trouble* was the thought that immediately struck him. Stella Larson had been hard to leave once. He imagined it might be worse trying to do so a second time.

"You always did better with water in its liquid form." He stepped back. *Should I pick her up?* he wondered. Figuring she wouldn't respond well to that gallantry from him, he offered her a hand instead. She studied his face for a long moment, then took his hand and rose shakily to her feet.

He gripped her arm, steadying her. Stella smelled of cherry blossoms and peach. Resolutely, he resisted the urge to lean closer to her. She held fast to his hand and arm as well, their eyes locked on each other. The moment held. Stella's breath caught, as did Erik's. Irresistibly, chemistry, moonlight, and memories began to draw them together. Abruptly, the warming house door slammed open. Stella and Erik took a step back from each other.

A flustered Stella examined the damage to her coat. "It's not that bad. I think I can fix it. Thank you, Erik," she gave him a half smile, her lips, parting only slightly. The expression in her eyes was troubled and vulnerable.

Erik's body went still and on high alert. He closed his eyes and took a deep, steadying breath, resisting the urge to step forward and sweep her into his arms. *I have to take this slow,* he counseled himself. *She's still angry with me.* He offered her his arm which she took. He guided her along the path toward the ice rink. "Let me walk you out there, Stella. Then skate around a little bit to get the blood flowing in that leg. How is it now?"

She shook the leg out. "It's getting better," she nodded. "Part of the problem is that I did a super intense barre workout this morning. I'm physically wrecked tonight which is probably why I couldn't get out of that position. I'm glad the kids didn't see me like that."

Erik chuckled. "Hayden tells me you're coaching?" He gestured out at the hockey rink where her diminutive players were gliding around under the bright lights.

She nodded. "We're one of the in-house teams, the misfit one. Noelle Youth Hockey had enough players for four squirt in-house teams. They had real hockey players, three dads and a mom, who volunteered to coach the other teams. At first, we thought Samantha was lucky. Jim Severson picked her for his team."

"But you had no goalie," Erik guessed.

"True, but that wasn't the real problem. Jim thought he could have the kids take turns playing goalie until someone decided that they liked the position."

Erik nodded his approval. "I remember Jim. He's a great guy, and he knows hockey. He's coached forever. He was in the organization when I was coming up."

"Exactly, and he's a third-grade teacher at the elementary school, too, so he can handle kids. But then at one of the very first practices, a kid skated behind Jim. He didn't see him, and he fell. To avoid landing on the child, he landed on his elbow instead, shattering it. I usually drive Sam to hockey practice, so I happened to be here that night. Anyway, Jim had surgery a couple of weeks ago and is out for the season. I spoke with his wife, and she said he's still too uncomfortable to be out here for practice."

Erik nodded. "I imagine a shattered elbow is painful."

"Yeah, but he's doing better every day. Anyway, the coaches were set for the other teams, and there were too many kids to cut it down to three teams, so Jim asked me if I would coach. I'm here anyway, so what could I say?" Stella held up her hands. "Hockey is so important to Sam, and I teach all of these kids. I couldn't say *no*," she concluded. Sensing Erik's disapproval, she continued. "Jim prints out all of the practice plans for me. That's the story of how I ended up being a hockey coach."

"But... but, no offense, Stella, you don't know a thing about hockey. It would be like me teaching art."

Stella nodded. "I know. You're not telling me anything I don't know. There wasn't anyone else, and I do know how to manage kids. I'm a teacher remember. I can run drills, though I'm not always sure what certain things are supposed to look like. I watch a lot of videos. We're not that bad, even though we have lost every game. Our other issue is we don't have a real goalie. Like I said, we rotate a player at goalie." Her eyes brightened. She gripped his arm. "Erik, you're an unbelievable goalie, the best Noelle ever saw. You could train a goalie for us. You could help us! Please," she implored.

"No, no." Erik held up his hands. "I'm busy at the factory, and I'm only in Noelle through the holidays." They had arrived at the gate to the boarded ice rink.

Stella's green eyes narrowed at him suspiciously. "Oh, so

you're here to pull some corporate raider action at the Nutcracker Factory? That's what people have been saying around town."

"Who's been saying that? Who even knows that I'm in Noelle, and why does everyone suspect the worst of me?" Erik demanded. "First Freya, then Miranda, and now you." He found himself becoming defensive because there was a kernel of truth to her comment.

"It's hard to believe that you came for the festival, Erik," she had the audacity to wink at him. "You haven't stayed for it since high school." Stella had always been sassy and direct. These qualities were some of the things that had most charmed him about her. She hadn't been impressed that he was the son of the richest man in town and the star hockey player on the high school hockey team. Added to the fact that she was downright beautiful with more than a passing resemblance to Blake Lively, Stella Larson had been virtually impossible to resist.

Erik ignored the pounding of his heart and simply stared at her, took her all in. She had tousled waves of hair, an All-American smile, and a Bohemian charm. "Remember...I know you well," she shook her finger at him "You don't do anything without a reason, Erik Engen. The clues are obvious. Suddenly, your father who has been a fixture at the festival is out of commission, and then corporate Boy Wonder, you, makes an appearance. It's clear something is up at the factory. You know how this town depends on the Nutcracker Factory."

"I'll tell you the same thing that I told Hayden a few minutes ago...trust me a little."

"Why are you here, Erik?" she asked more softly, tilting her head back to meet his gaze. "You can't sweep into Noelle and turn this place upside down. That's always been your way. You are single minded, and you don't take time to consider who becomes collateral damage as you pursue your goals."

"You knew me a long time ago, Stella," he uttered. "People change, you know. They mature. I've matured, and you were never collateral damage to me. I can't tell you how hard it was to leave Noelle and you."

"But you managed to do it." She eyed him wryly. "No, you're still the same Erik Engen I knew years ago. Too serious, too sure-of-yourself, and too driven."

"And you're the same Stella Larson. Hot headed and quick to judge and condemn when you don't know the whole story."

Her lips narrowed. He'd angered her. "It was your own words which condemned you in my eyes back years ago, and now you aren't giving me the whole story. You say *trust me,* but you don't reciprocate. I think our conversation here is done." On stiff legs and with a little hitch in her stride, she glided out onto the rink. Once in the middle, she blew into her whistle, calling the players to her.

Watching her, Erik felt remorseful. He hadn't meant to hurt her or be critical of her. Her explanation of how she came to coach this youth hockey team moved him. Stella had been a decent enough athlete back in high school, but her artistic nature had always come first. It was who and what she was. Stella had also always been kind and thoughtful, so he wasn't entirely surprised that she had become a teacher. He guessed that having an interested if inexpert coach was better than a lot of other options for those kids out on the ice now.

"Hey, you comin', Uncle Erik?" Hayden called to him as he poked his head and shoulders out through the warming house door.

Taking one last, lingering glance at Stella Larson, the girl he still considered the one who'd gotten away even though he had been the one who'd broken up with her, he headed back to the warming house.

"You ready, buddy?" he asked Hayden.

"Yup," his nephew nodded eagerly. "Don't forget your stick," he gestured toward the tall hockey stick that Erik had left propped up in the corner. Erik picked it up.

"That's not a goalie stick," Hayden pointed out.

"Yes, back when we were kids, more often than not when we went to the outdoor rinks, I played out. I only played in net if there were a bunch of us planning on meeting here. Your stick is kind of rough there," Erik observed, eyeing it. "We're going to have to get you a new one."

"I think it's one of your old ones cut down." Hayden explained. "I've never gotten a real hockey stick of my own."

"Let me see that," Erik took Hayden's stick in hands. Leaning into it, he flexed it against the ground, testing it. "This stick is too stiff for you. You can't shoot with this. We're going to have to get a lighter and whippier one. It'll be fine for tonight though."

Hayden nodded eagerly and turned toward the door.

Erik stepped over to the rink attendant. "Hey, do you have any soft pucks?"

He nodded and tossed Erik one of several that were set out on the desk in front of him.

Uncle and nephew headed back out into the biting cold of the winter's night. The two moved cautiously along another rubber matted path leading to the skating rink. This area was lit also, though not as brightly as the hockey rink. Erik stepped onto the ice. He pushed with one leg, allowing the minimal effort to carry him out over the ice. Hearing a shout of laughter behind him, he turned to see Hayden seated on a plastic chair and gripping the sides while a friend pushed him forward. Digging his skates into the ice beneath him, the child's legs moved seemingly as fast as they could go.

Observing that Hayden was content, Erik closed his eyes, savoring the feeling of the motion. He recalled an old expression, something about how one can never go home. But in this place, out skating on an outdoor rink, hearing the shouts and the laughter of children and the boom of pucks hitting wooden rink walls, in this spot where he had spent countless hours as a child, he felt truly home for the first time in as long as he could recall. It was pure winter magic.

He began to skate. It was like riding a bike. Your body never forgets the motion though your muscles might regret it later. Here, on the ice, life had been so much simpler. He hadn't had to worry about the family business and how changes to it might impact the people who lived in Noelle. Erik hadn't been back on the ice much in recent years, not since that final surgery that had precipitated his premature retirement. And he'd been a goaltender, not a skater. After reassuring himself that Hayden was still having fun, Erik lost himself in the motion and in the moment. He picked up speed. It felt like flying. Around and around. At some point he obtained a puck. He danced around deking past phantom opponents, having fun in a way he hadn't in so long. Finally, thoroughly winded, his legs nearly trembling from his exertion, he took a puck-less shot at an imaginary net, then skated abruptly to a stop. He stood there, his sweating face steaming in the cold air.

Happening to glance over at the hockey rink, he saw that Stella Larson was watching him. She didn't pretend otherwise. Acknowledging him, she raised a hand in salute.

The white ice under the lights illuminated her beautiful face. She'd always been so lovely that she'd taken his breath away. With the benefit of hindsight, Erik recognized the truth that at the end of high school, he'd broken up with Stella at that graduation party because she'd been too much. He'd had dreams and ambitions, and he'd been afraid that she'd make him want to remain in Noelle with her. But after that miserable summer night, she'd been the one to leave town first to attend a design school out east. After that, he'd heard, she'd travelled all over the world.

Deliberately turning her back to him, Stella raised her coaching whistle to her lips, calling her players back from their drills. The sound broke the spell that had momentarily linked Erik to her. Turning away, he observed that Hayden's friend was heading into the warming house, leaving Hayden alone, stick in hand, circling slowly about on the ice. Erik skated over to his nephew. "Hey, let's pass the puck a little. You can show me what you got."

Hayden's face, which had been a little crestfallen at his friend's departure, lit up. "For real?"

Grinning, Erik nodded.

The two passed and skated for the next hour. They were having so much fun that they didn't even notice when Stella and her players headed back into the warming house. A college-aged couple remained, skating about holding hands, and then they, too, went inside leaving only Erik and Hayden out on the ice of the figure skating rink. Finally, the attendant came out and shut off the lights, but still the two skated, the moonlight providing more than enough illumination for them to play hockey by.

The spell was finally broken when Hayden commented, "My phone's ringing. I can feel it vibrate in my pocket. It's probably my mom." He pulled off his leather chopper gloves and dug into his coat pocket. His cheeks were ruddy from the cold and the exertion. He rubbed his dripping nose with his coat sleeve after he swiped on his cell phone to answer it. "Hi, Mom... Okay, I'll tell him. Can't we stay for a little longer? No, I didn't know it was that late. Okay. Bye."

"Your mom wants us back home?" Erik asked.

Hayden nodded.

Erik pushed up his sleeve and looked at his Apple watch. "Wow, nine-twenty. I had no idea it was this late. We should get going."

Predictably, the warming house was mostly empty when they went in to take off their skates. The attendant was out on the hockey rink, pulling in and chaining up the nets.

On the ride back to Lingonberry Lodge, Hayden was a transformed child, all adolescent angst and sulkiness gone, replaced by bright, sparkling enthusiasm. "Uncle Erik, do you think that I could be a hockey player?"

Erik considered. "Well, I'll be honest with you, you are starting late at nine. You have a lot of catching up to do in terms of skating and stick handling, but you're athletic and strong. You'll get the hang of it. I can give you some tips while I'm here. If you work at it, you'll be fine."

"Awesome. Uncle Erik, do goalies have to be good skaters?"

Erik sensed where this was heading. It was clear to him that Hayden was considering being a goalie like Erik had once been. "Some coaches will tell you that goalies are the best skaters on the ice."

"Oh," Hayden murmured, crestfallen. "I'm not a good skater like Sam."

"Sam is an exceptional skater. I was only ever a decent

skater myself. My skating was something that I really had to work on. Hard work pays off in hockey and in life."

"And you made it to the NHL," Hayden observed.

"I played a couple of exhibition games," Erik acknowledged. "I think a good goalie has to be quick, tough, and willing to throw themselves into the line of fire. That's what coaches are looking for in their goalies. That and size and skill," he shared. "Most importantly, a goalie has to have a short memory."

"How come?"

"They have to be able to get over a goal that is scored against them."

Hayden was quiet for a moment, and then he asked, "Do you think I could be a goalie?"

Erik gazed at his nephew. "I think you could."

"Uncle Erik, can you please talk to my parents about letting me play hockey for real?"

"Of course, I will," Erik tousled Hayden's hair. An aberrant thought struck him. It was convenient that Stella's hockey team needed a player in the goalie position. Coaching Hayden to be a goalie for her team might provide him with the opportunity he realized he desired to spend more time with the girl who'd stolen his heart so many years before. He didn't investigate it too closely, but he liked that idea very much.

After hockey practice, Stella went home, showered, changed, and then headed over to Ray's Place, a small, local pub off Hans Christian Anderson Street which hosted a weekly Trivia Night. This was a regular faculty outing for some of the teachers of Leif Erikson Elementary School.

As Stella headed into the bar, she hit the usual wall of musty, heated air scented with beer. Ray's Place was simple, unassuming, and welcoming. Neon beer signs decorated the wall behind the bar. The small, round tables before the bar were already filled with people gathered for Trivia Night. The only concessions to the season at Ray's Place were a rather haggard looking rope of silver garland looped along the front of the weathered, oak bar as well as an artificial Christmas tree set up in the corner beside the Pac Man arcade game. Red bows and white lights decorated the sad looking tree that appeared as if it could use a good dusting. People sat along the long, wooden bar. For Trivia Night at Ray's place, the crowd was little different from other nights. More young millennials were in attendance, all eager to dominate at Trivia.

Stella's team, Team Mischief Management, was already in attendance. The team included Jacob Meyer, Addie, Jennifer, a thirty-something member of the kindergarten team, Jody Adler, a third grade teacher in her early fifties and her husband, Max, who taught at the high school, as well as Jessica Kong, the new second grade teacher. Stella pulled off her coat and hat, tucked the hat into her pocket, and headed over to the table to join her friends. She hung her coat on the back of a chair and took a seat. "Hi, everyone," she waved. "Sorry I'm late. I had hockey practice. Have we started?"

"No worries." Addie shook her head. "Trivia doesn't start for another fifteen minutes. You're good. We're just glad you made it. You crush on art." She and Stella fist pumped. "Jayda texted that she and Darius wouldn't be able to make it tonight."

Jennifer, who sported a hippy aesthetic from her long, straight blond hair to her eclectic apparel, gestured at another table. "The Agatha Quiztees are here tonight," she stated ominously.

"Who?" Stella asked.

"The Agatha Quiztees," Jacob whispered behind a raised hand. "That team is made up of the librarians from the Noelle Public Library. They're legendary at every bar within a fifty-mile radius that hosts a trivia night. They destroy the competition every time they compete."

"It doesn't seem fair that all of the librarians in town are on one team," Jessica commented.

"But I thought we were the best trivia team in Noelle," Stella observed, eyeing the multi-generational crew over at the other table. The Agatha Quiztees appeared both scholarly and edgy. Stella recognized several of the team members from the Noelle Public Library. She waved a tentative hand to Lena, the youth librarian whose short, brunette hair sported a purple streak and who wore a golden hoop through one nostril. Lena waved back, but she didn't smile. There was a competitive set to her features. "We've been doing okay lately, right?" Stella questioned.

"Not exactly," Jessica replied, shifting on her chair.

"Well, you've missed a bunch of recent trivia nights, Stella," Addie explained. "Since Thanksgiving, the Agatha Quiztees have been unbeatable. We've been a distant second."

"We were saving up our winnings for a holiday staff party, but we may have to dial it down if we don't start winning again soon," Jacob observed. "By the way, how cool is it that you know Erik Engen? It was great that you could introduce me. I didn't realize you're into hockey. Hey folks, you aren't going to believe this, but Stella knows a professional hockey player."

Addie, who had been sipping her beer, snorted and blew it out through her nose.

"Are you okay?" Jody Adler patted Addie solicitously on the back. "I always swallow down the wrong tube, too."

Addie and Stella exchanged a glance.

"This guy actually played in the NHL, a few games, I'm pretty sure," Jacob rambled on to everyone and to no one in particular, "and Stella knows him."

"You mean Erik Engen?" Max Adler, the trivia team's resident sports expert, put in. "I think Erik played mostly in the IHL, I watched him play in high school. His senior year, Jodi and I were in our second or third year of teaching, and I did crowd control at the hockey games. Erik Engen was exceptional. He carried his team that season. I'll never forget that sectional final against Rock Lake. He saw like fifty shots, and he stopped them all. I don't think the Noelle Chill had many shots on net at the other end, but it didn't matter. Erik was outstanding. They made it to State that year. They lost the first game at State, a one-goal game, and Erik was the goalie of the year and player of the year. Watching him was worth the price of admission."

"I actually met him," Jacob Meyer put in eagerly. "He came by the school to pick up Hayden Weber. Hayden is his nephew. Stella introduced us. He gave me an autograph for my dad. My dad is going to be thrilled."

Addie laughed out loud. "He doesn't know, does he?" she asked Stella.

Stella simply shook her head. "He doesn't need to."

Jacob glanced between Addie and Stella. "I don't need to know what? Come on. Don't hold out on me."

"Stella, may I?" Addie questioned.

"Oh, go ahead and tell him," Stella muttered. "It's not like it's a secret, and it is ancient history."

Addie, who knew that Jacob had a more than friendly interest in Stella and who liked to stir the proverbial pot, leaned forward, resting her elbows on the table. "Well, Erik Engen and Stella were the *It* couple of Noelle's class of two-thousand and eight."

"You're kidding me. You dated Erik *The Wall* Engen?" Clearly, Jacob hadn't considered that possibility. "But you're an artist, and he's a hockey player," he sputtered. "You couldn't have had much in common."

Stella could almost see the gears turning in Jacob's head. "It was a high school romance. It ended. I haven't seen him or thought about him in years." *That was a blatant lie.*

"Oh," Jacob replied dolefully, leaning back in his chair.

The bar door swung open letting in a blast of cold air. Everyone automatically turned to look at the new arrivals.

Benji Weber emerged from under a ski cap and a hooded, winter coat. Behind him loomed the much larger shape of Erik Engen. He tipped his Chicago Blackhawks ball cap back and unzipped his jacket. As he and Benji made their way to the bar, he nodded to Stella, his gaze immediately seeking out hers.

To Stella, it felt as if Erik drew all the energy and attention of the small crowd to him, like a human magnet. Erik was a big man, and energy seemed to vibrate in the air around him.

"Speak of the devil," Addie muttered under her breath.

"The game's about to start," Jody broke in. "Team Mischief Management, are we ready to play?"

In her defense, Stella tried to focus throughout the trivia game. Fortunately, the other members of the team were more *on* than she was and competitive enough not to notice that she was distracted. The problem was that Erik sat by his brother-in-law at the bar within her line of vision. There should have been nothing fascinating about what they were doing. The two men were chatting and sharing a pitcher of beer. They weren't doing anything remarkable or noteworthy. Still, Stella found herself wanting to look at them or more particularly at Erik. He had been a very good-looking boy, but he was an even better-looking grown man. She realized she remained hopelessly attracted to him. It wasn't fair.

She forced herself to study Jacob's more bland features. It took only a moment or so for her to acknowledge that Jacob Meyer didn't make her heart beat faster. She had considered dating him, but now realized it was a no go. Unfortunately, most men paled next to Erik Engen. *Erik and I have history, not a future*, she scolded herself.

Erik and Benji left before the end of the trivia game. As they passed by, Stella pretended to be completely riveted by the trivia questions. After they were gone, she did find it easier to concentrate. She even managed to answer a few, but the evening had lost its zest for her once Erik Engen headed out the door of Ray's Place.

CHAPTER 4

While listening to Darius go over the Nutcracker Factory's financials, Erik leaned back from his laptop and linked his fingers behind his head. It was lunchtime, and he had been working since before seven that morning. He turned his seat to stare out the picture window at Sibelius Square below. For a moment, he contemplated where he could find a quick meal down in one of the restaurants. He thought he glimpsed the boxy shapes of some food trucks on the other side of the evergreen trees on the opposite side of the square. *An interesting option,* he pondered, *and one that is new to Noelle* in his experience.

It was a picture-perfect winter's day with bright sunlight reflecting off the snow. The square was fully adorned with Christmas decorations and buzzing with folks finishing their holiday shopping. He noticed a particularly large crowd had formed on the far right corner of the square, over by the old Livery Bar and Restaurant. *What's going on down there?* he wondered. He thought he glimpsed a familiar, tall, elegant shape sporting a thick ponytail. *Is that Stella Larson? What is she up to?* He leaned closer to the window, trying to make out what was happening through the treetops. Unfortunately, some were large evergreens which made them impossible to visually penetrate.

"The Nutcracker Factory's profit margin is currently fifteen percent which is higher than the average profit margin for comparable companies," Darius related.

Turning his attention from the holiday cheer in the town square below him, Erik glanced at the other man. "I'm familiar with the factory's financial status, Darius. I'm looking for something else."

Taking off his tortoise shell glasses and rubbing at the points where they perched on his nose, Darius took a deep breath. Thinking of Jayda and Lyrique, he decided that the time had come to speak up. *Sometimes you have to fight for what you believe in,* he reflected. He would forever regret it if he didn't speak candidly now for the sake of his family, his fellow factory workers, and the town. "Mr. Engen," he began, "What are you looking for?"

"It's Erik. Mr. Engen is my father."

"You can't dismantle this factory. The Nutcracker Factory is vital to this entire town. It's a major employer, but more importantly, it's part of the identity of Noelle, Wisconsin. The Nutcracker Festival is significant to this town in terms of traditions and because of its economic impact. People flock here from the Twin Cities, Madison, and even Chicago because of our two weeks of holiday events. The crowning event is the Nutcracker Ball which follows the selection of the season's winning nutcracker design, the one that is then released as a limited edition."

Erik shook his head. "I know all of this, Darius. You forget...I grew up here. I know all about the festival.

Remember, I'm here this week to serve as the Grand Marshal."

"Can I speak to you frankly, Mr.... er, Erik?" Darius challenged, his expression, unrelenting.

"I expect nothing less."

Darius swallowed, for he was aware what he risked. "For the past twenty-some years, your father has served as Grand Marshal of the Nutcracker Festival, and before that, your grandfather, Ole, was the Grand Marshal, correct?"

Erik studied Darius with a bemused expression. He suspected he knew where this was leading. "All of that's true."

"Naturally, there are a lot of questions about why, this year, you are here."

"I can shed some—"

Darius held up his hand. "No, with all due respect, Erik, let me speak my piece." He waited until Erik nodded for him to proceed. "You have the reputation of being a corporate fixer. We've all heard how you've gone into various companies that are part of the Engen Ornament empire and cleaned things up, either trimmed the fat or chopped things up and sold the pieces outright. I keep getting questions from our employees. That's what all of us here at the Nutcracker Factory want to know. It's not right to have your employees worrying about whether they are going to lose their jobs right before Christmas. Erik, are you here to dismantle us or sell us off?"

Giving Darius his full attention, Erik leaned forward toward the other man. "You know it's a tough economic climate for affordable luxury goods. Our entire company is facing some serious challenges now that so many people prefer to shop online or from Amazon. We've had to evaluate each one of our corporate holdings in order to determine which ones we want to continue to invest in and develop and which ones we need to eliminate. We have an obligation to our employees and to our shareholders that we assess all our product lines so that we can continue to be a profitable company. Doing so is in our employees' best interests."

"You are going to shut us down?" Darius appeared stricken.

Erik shook his head. "I certainly hope not. I love this factory. I think I'd forgotten how much. I've been away for so long. This trip is the longest I've been back in Noelle since I left for college years ago. I learned to love the holidays and holiday ornaments here at the Engen Nutcracker factory, at my grandfather's knee."

"Okay, but are you are considering closing us down?" Darius prodded.

"You said it yourself...the factory is profitable right now. I'm good at fixing companies, Darius. I make them better, more successful. I believe I can do that here. You've spent the past few days showing me all that you know about this factory. You're doing a good job here, Darius. You take pride in your work. I can see that. The question facing the Engen Nutcracker Factory isn't really a *today* one. It's more about a vision for the future. I've listened to all that you've told me. I've looked at the financial information you've shared, and, yes, today, I agree the Engen Nutcracker Factory is performing respectably. But you haven't provided me with anything that convinces me that we have a plan for the future."

Darius paused, considering. "Did you look at the designs for next season's nutcrackers that I forwarded to you? Erik, you must admit, they are attractive and can be created affordably. That's been our goal in recent years, to produce a quality product that is economical for consumers."

"Yes, I saw those designs. They are," he paused, "nice," he finished. "But they're not significantly different from what you could find at any other ornament store or online."

Darius looked frustrated. "I don't know what you want to see."

Erik stood up, rolling his shoulders back. "I know what I'm asking is hard. I want you to visualize beyond the here and now. Try to predict the future. I have a clear vision for the future of Engen Ornaments. The question remains how that vision syncs with the future of the Nutcracker Factory."

"Whatever you want, Erik, we'll do it," Darius implored.

"This isn't meant to be a guessing game, Darius, and I'm not trying to be a cipher. We have to achieve a synergistic vision. I've found that when people creatively collaborate, they come up with the best solutions. Let's proceed down this road a bit further and see where it takes us. Of course, I have my ideas, but they may not be the right ones for the company or for this factory. Let's give ourselves a little time to process all we've discussed."

Defeated, Darius slumped down in his chair.

Erik stood up and patted him on the shoulder. "Let's take a break. I'm going to get something to eat and walk around the square for some fresh air. We can tackle all of this in an hour. It'll keep. I've found moving around improves my thinking. Get some food, Darius. Clear your mind. We'll reconvene in an hour." He checked his watch then turned to gaze wistfully down at the square below. Even with having worked essentially a desk job for years, he still struggled with being inside all the time. "Have you ever eaten at any of the food trucks down there?" Erik asked.

"My wife, Jayda," Darius nodded, "she loves Food Truck Fridays. On Fridays is when you get the biggest selection of food trucks, but it looks like there are a good number down on the street right now, considering it's not a Friday. It's likely because of the festival and all the tourists in town. Jayda makes sure we stop down there for supper. Then we walk around the square and look at the holiday window displays. Last Friday night, the weather was perfect, above thirty with no wind. It was a good night," Darius concluded, nodding.

"Do you have any food truck favorites?"

Darius grinned, his smile revealing strong white teeth. He seemed to relax a little, the tension of moments before melting away. "The pizza place, That's Amore, is really good. For Asian or stir fry, there's the Happy Wok. There's also the Hmong egg roll spot. Mine and Jayda's favorite food truck is Opa Opa Gyros. The tzatziki sauce is unbelievable there."

"Then gyros it is. Thanks. You want to join me? My treat," Erik offered. "You have to eat sometime."

"Jayda always packs a lunch for me," Darius explained. "I know. I'm spoiled. But remember, she's a Phy Ed teacher, so she's always pushing the healthy stuff. Tons of raw vegetables."

"Yes, but it's nice to have someone think about you," Erik reflected.

"Yeah," Darius agreed. "I'm a lucky guy. Jayda and Lyrique are the best parts of my life," he announced proudly. "How about you? You have a special lady in your life?"

Erik shook his head. It seemed a little sad and lonely when he thought about it. He truly didn't have a special someone in his life currently. "No, no one in particular. I work a lot, and I travel a good amount."

"Oh, well, not everyone is inclined to the domestic life, but it suits me." Darius turned to the door. "I'll see you in an hour?" he called back over his shoulder.

"Sounds good," Erik agreed. Darius left the room while Erik put on his coat, scarf, hat, and gloves. He headed out of the office and then the building, and down into Sibelius Square. He pondered Darius's words. It wasn't that he wasn't inclined to the domestic life. It's just that the situation hadn't presented itself. First, hockey had been his life. He'd focused on it with all his passion and drive, to the exclusion of relationships. Hockey had come first. It was why he had broken it off with Stella so many years before. It was why he'd kept his relationships since brief and insignificant. A coach had once told him that girls are a hockey player's greatest downfall, and Erik had believed him.

Looking back, he wondered at his own foolishness. He'd broken up with a girl he'd truly cared about because he'd been worried that she'd detract from his hockey career! But Stella had never been one of those girls who suck a boy's soul dry and demand all his attention. Back in high school, she'd been committed to following her own dreams. Maybe they would have worked out despite being physically separated, independent, and ambitious. Erik admitted he regretted the decision to end their relationship more than about any other he'd made in his life. He'd never found another girl with whom he'd clicked as much as with Stella. The two of them had fit together in a way he'd been too young to appreciate. No other woman had ever made him want to settle down.

When he lost hockey, he'd had a huge hole to fill. He'd filled it with work. Being busy had blocked out the pain of loss. In time, he'd come to enjoy the business of negotiating on behalf of Engen Ornaments. Since then, he hadn't taken the time to slow down long enough to make lasting, meaningful relationships. Perhaps that was something he wanted to change about his life now.

As the window had promised, it was a beautiful winter's day outside. The air was fresh and crisp, and there was no wind. As he'd seen from above, the sidewalks were crowded with Christmas shoppers. In the small park at the center of the square, a circular skating rink had been set up. Garlands adorned the streetlights, and Christmas carols played out over speakers. But none of this holiday paraphernalia distracted him from his mission. Erik was hungry. He spied the hulking food trucks lining the two sides of the square opposite his current location. He made his way in their direction. Upon locating the silver food truck with the blue and white sign labeled Opa Opa Gyros, he crossed the street right by the crowd that he had observed from his office window.

His interest piqued, Erik turned away from the food truck and followed the milling people. He was a tall man, so he could easily see over folks. The area in front of one side of a brick building was cordoned off, and a crew of artists was working on a massive mural that adorned that entire side of the building. Upon seeing the mural, Erik sucked in his breath. It was amazing. In bold colors, the dominant, central image depicted two Viking warriors, one with a baby secured to his chest, as they skied on old fashioned, wooden skis through a winter forest landscape. The images around the outside depicted several distinct scenes, all involving a blond princess and her baby. One peripheral image showed her holding hands with a kingly looking warrior. The two gazed at each other with smitten expressions. On another corner, the beautiful princess was carrying red, hot objects in her hands, her face, anguished. Another part of the mural displayed this same young woman, with the baby in her arms, dressed in winter gear, conferring with a group of Viking warriors, including the two from the largest central image. The final image was of the mother, now beatifically smiling and reunited with her baby, over whose head floated a crown.

A horde of painters of all ages, wearing smocks over their winter gear, worked on the massive mural. Long, plastic tubes connected to whirring and humming heaters blew warm air up on the wall. Three scaffolds were set up to various heights so that the painters could work on a variety of levels. There appeared to be some sort of time urgency to the installation as so many people were working simultaneously. It was also apparent to Erik that the public was expected, even encouraged, to observe, comment, and thus be involved in the creation of the mural.

One familiar looking artist was poised precariously on a three-step ladder that looked to Erik to be perched on a patch of ice. The ladder was shifting dangerously. Meanwhile, this artist, who was directing the other artists, seemed oblivious to the unsafe nature of her position. She had a thick, dark blond ponytail spilling out of the back of her knitted hat. *Stella.* Holding a paper draft of the larger mural in one hand and gesticulating with the other, she was engaged in an animated discussion with a middle-aged male artist below her who was working on the shadow filled forest surrounding the primary image of the two Viking warriors skiing with the baby.

"What is this?" Erik turned, questioning a stout, older woman wearing a black coat and a red hat with a jaunty sprig of mistletoe fixed to it covering her snow-white hair. She stood beside him in the crowd of observers.

"It's a public art installation, a new addition to our annual Nutcracker Festival," she explained pleasantly. "The City Council solicited proposals for the mural from artists back in

September or October. This one was selected. It's grand, isn't it," the lady continued, clasping her hands together. "I do love folklore, and this story is so appropriate, given our town's connection to cross country skiing as well as the heritage of many of Noelle's founding fathers and mothers."

"Folklore?" Erik puzzled. "Heritage?"

"Well, young man," the lady's alert, blue eyes fixed on him. "Today Noelle has people from all over the world, but it was founded by Norwegians. This mural depicts the story of Inga and Prince Haakon of Norway."

The story sounded vaguely familiar to Erik. He knew he'd heard about it from someone, most likely, Freya, especially given the cross-country skiing connection. He was still rifling through his memories when he froze. As he watched with concern, while still engaged in a conversation with the painter, Stella was leaning precariously to one side. The ladder started to slide under her. Erik saw the danger and acted. Without thinking, he pushed through the crowd. He was beside the ladder when it fell. He caught Stella as it clattered to the frozen ground.

"Oof." Stella's expression panicked. Her face was mere inches from Erik's, her eyes huge.

The crowd behind them broke into spontaneous applause at the rescue.

"Well done, young man," the lady with whom Erik had been speaking before called out.

Erik grinned, enjoying the weight of this woman in his arms. Her scent of cherry blossoms and peach blended with the paint and cold air to create a heady and unique perfume. "Here you go, falling for me again," he teased.

She smiled, revealing one of her dimples. "You do have a way of saving the day."

"Call me Dudley Do-Right."

"Thanks, Dudley," Stella reached up to touch his stubbled cheek. "My posterior appreciates your intervention. You can set me down now," she commented, but she didn't break the connection between their eyes.

With reluctance, he set her down. Still, he kept his hands on her hips. For a moment, he lost awareness of the crowd around them. It was only the two of them, in the moment. Her hands were on his shoulders. Her green eyes sparkled with mischief and magic and enchanted him in the same way they had when he was eighteen. Stella had always had power over him. It would feel so right to kiss her right here and right now. Recognizing the intent in his eyes, her breath caught. She leaned closer to him. Erik was lowering his head to hers when a voice broke in.

"Ms. Larson… Ms. Larson. We're almost out of the pine tree green paint for the darker, shadowed areas. Can you mix some more?"

Stella pulled back from Erik and turned to face a teenage girl with dark eyes, a red, knitted head band that protected her ears, and thick, shiny black hair that fell almost to her waist.

"Gaonha, I've premixed all of the paint colors used in the mural," Stella replied. "Remember we left them in the heated trailer, so the paint doesn't get thick from the cold. I believe that shade is green fourteen. You should find a can labeled with that number in the trailer. Here are the keys. I'll be there in a minute to help you. You can go ahead, and start stirring the paint."

"Okay," the teenager replied, taking the proffered keys and then heading on her way.

"Erik, I got paint on your nice coat," Stella pulled a paint splattered rag from her back pocket and began to dab at a spot on the shoulder of his black, cashmere coat.

"Don't worry about it. It adds character. It looks like your crew has things well in hand. Could you take a break? Maybe have lunch with me?"

"I can't leave the mural. The team and I need to get a good chunk of work done today. We must finish up before the end of the week. I can't leave the site. It's my responsibility."

"That's fine. I'd planned on getting food at one of the food trucks. I've been told the gyros are especially good. We can stay here, eat, and you can watch your painters."

"Actually, that sounds great. I'm starving. I haven't eaten in hours."

"I'll go get the food." Feeling lighter hearted and more enthusiastic than he had in as long as he could remember, Erik hurried over to the line in front of the Opa Opa Gyros. To his relief, he found it moved quickly. While waiting his turn, he glanced over at Stella. She was continuing to direct her workers, moving all around in front of the mural, pointing out changes that needed to be made or areas requiring additional work. She was amazing.

"What can I get you?" asked the young man working the cash register in the food truck.

"Two gyros with everything and two orders of fries." Erik held up two fingers, and the worker nodded. "And please give us two bottles of water as well."

Moments later, his hands filled with aluminum foil wrapped food and with water bottles tucked under his arms, Erik headed back to where Stella continued to work.

"Stella," he called.

She glanced over at him with relief. She led him over to a picnic table off to one side of the mural. The snow had already been swept off, and two enormous, black, plastic, restaurant sized, hot beverage dispensers had been set there as well as a stack of insulated paper cups. There was room for both of them on the bench in front of the table.

"Would you care for a hot cocoa?" Stella asked. "I'm not sure how cocoa goes with gyros, but it is good cocoa. Topped Off Coffee House donated it to support the public art display." She poured them both a cup, handing one to Erik.

In return, Erik gave Stella her fries, sandwich, and water bottle. He unrolled his own sandwich. Steam rose from the hot meat as it hit the cold air. "This smells so good. Why is it that food smells and tastes better when eaten outside?"

"Too true." Then Stella groaned, closing her eyes as she bit into her gyro. "These are incredible."

For a few moments, the two sat in companionable silence, eating and watching the painting. "Tell me about this." Erik gestured at the mural. "I mean, I'm guessing it's your work, but why are all of these other people working on it? Many of these people don't look like professionals. Some appear really young."

"It's actually a neat idea," Stella began eagerly. Erik sat back and realized that he enjoyed watching her. He always had, even though he'd forgotten that fact as well as so many others over the years. Stella Larson was pure magic. "It's a public art display. The City Council is all about the beautification of the downtown. As you know, the holiday season is when the big tourist dollars come into Noelle. The idea is to extend the festival longer and build in mini events that keep people engaged. This," she waved at the huge painting, "is part of it. Back in October, the tavern on the other side of this wall sponsored a mural contest," she explained.

"The Livery," Erik offered. "I've eaten there a few times."

"I've heard it's all fresh, local foods but pricey. Anyway, the owners approached City Council and asked for proposals for this space. My mural was selected."

"I'm not surprised," Erik commented. "Your design is amazing."

"Thanks. Personally, I think the selection of my mural may have had more to do with them wanting to choose a local artist than my particular vision."

Erik snorted. "You've always been an incredibly talented artist, and you incorporated the Norwegian heritage of the town and cross-country skiing, a favored pastime. Seems to me, you hit on all cylinders."

Stella blushed. "Well, once my work was selected, I put out a request for artists to apply to work on the project. That's where all these people came from," she waved her hand at her crew. "They submitted portfolios from which I selected my crew. To be honest," she whispered behind her hand, "I took everyone who applied. I can find something for about anyone to do. Many of them are high school students. A friend of mine teaches at the high school. I think he promised extra credit to those who worked on the mural," she admitted. "Some of others are artist friends, and we also have a whole crowd of retired people who don't have much experience with art but who want to help out. We have four eight-hour days to complete the entire mural. That's part of the whole deal. We are on day two and a half. I think we should finish up most of it by tonight. Then tomorrow will be for touch ups and detail work. That work crew will be significantly smaller."

"Amazing," Erik acknowledged, taking it all in. "How does it work? I mean, do you give all these people your design? I'm sure that there are artists of varying abilities here."

She nodded. "I completed the original design as a large oil painting on canvas. I divided the painting into quadrants. Then I sketched it to scale on the brick wall here. If you'd seen the mural a day ago, you would have seen the lines marking out the quadrants. They're covered with paint now. You see that awning up there? We extend it down and cover up the work at night, to keep it dry. Those tubes are blowing warm air on the wall because paint doesn't dry well below a certain temperature. I assigned numbers to each of the colors. The lead painters whom I selected were allocated blocks of the painting."

"I get it," Erik asserted. "It's like a giant paint-by-numbers. Clever."

"Exactly. We assigned areas on the painting based on the level of difficulty and the skill of the painter," she whispered this last bit behind her hand. "The whole point of a public art project is the participatory element. The mural is meant to be both an event and an art object. It's festive and promotes town pride."

"I think it's amazing that so many people are working on it with you. Quite an undertaking. I always thought that art was something that you do alone." Erik took another bite. "Mmm," he said, closing his eyes, chewing slowly, and savoring the flavor.

Stella watched him with amusement. "That tzatziki sauce is to die for, and the meat is so tender."

"I don't think I've ever had a gyro this good," Erik eyed the aluminum wrapped sandwich ruefully. "Who would have thought I'd have it in Noelle."

"Noelle has come a long way in the past ten years," Stella

observed between mouthfuls. She had a smudge of the white sauce on her lip. Erik handed her a napkin. "Thanks," she grinned. "It's becoming quite the artistic community. Of course, there's the Nutcracker Festival over the holidays, and there's the whole artists' collective over at the Artisan Studios, and the music festivals in the summertime. Noelle is developing into a mini-Portland."

"It makes sense that you came back here. You always wanted to be a professional artist. You achieved your dream."

She nodded, taking a sip of her cocoa. "I'm a professional artist. I've done murals in cities all over the world. When I was in college, I realized that art can be a shared experience. I majored in Visual Arts and Art Education. After graduating, I traveled for years doing contract mural work. I sort of stumbled into the whole participatory public art thing. I was working on a mural in Mexico City. That place is filled with incredible street art. The sponsors of the project had the idea of involving some local students, and it took off. I ended up doing several similar projects. So when this contest came up, I was excited. I've had this story of the amazing journey of Inga and Prince Haakon in my head for so long, and this was the right place to tell it. I already have an idea for next year's contest. I'd like to approach some local Hmong artists about collaborating on a mural based on a Hmong story cloth, to honor their traditions and heritage. But this year, I'm thrilled to be sharing the legend of the Birkebeiner."

"Slow down," Erik grinned. "Legend of the Birke...? What?"

"Seriously," she shook her head incredulously. "Your sister Freya is a topflight cross-country skier, and you don't know the legend of the Birkebeiners?"

"I know there's a long cross-country ski race in Hayward,

but I don't know about the legend. To be honest, I didn't get to watch Freya ski much back in the day. Cross country skiing and hockey seasons overlap."

Stella studied her mural. "I'm not a historian, and I wasn't going for total historical accuracy, but I don't want there to be any glaring errors. I wanted the work to have a legendary, dream quality to it."

"That it has," Erik agreed, also studying the work in progress. "The snow and the mist connecting each of the areas of the mural enhance that feeling."

"The story goes," Stella explained, "the king of Norway died suddenly. The country was divided in a civil war between two groups, the Baglers and the Birkebeiners. The king's heir, Prince Haakon, was a toddler. The Birkebeiner warriors—they're named that because of their birchbark leggings—helped the prince and his mother, Inga, escape the Baglers by skiing from Lillehammer to Trondheim. At one point, Prince Haakon and his mother had to separate so the prince could travel more swiftly. He went with the two best Birkebeiner skiers. The hope was that Inga and the others would follow and hopefully distract their pursuers. The two warriors skiing with the prince, that's the segment there," she pointed to where the two Viking warriors, one with a child strapped to him, battled the wind and the snow as they skied through a forested landscape. "They were successful. In the end, Prince Haakon became King Haakon."

Erik nodded. "It's amazing how you make people feel the energy and the emotion of the characters in your painting."

"That's the goal," she acknowledged, looking pleased.

"What's happening in that corner? That's Prince Haakon's mother again, right? Inga?" He pointed to where the blond woman stood before a tribunal. She wore a simple white dress, her hair braided back, and strange objects in her hands. "What's she holding?"

"That part of the mural isn't yet complete," Stella explained. "Inga didn't have an easy time of it. Later, when her son was older, she had to prove his right to the throne by undergoing a trial by ordeal. Those are hot irons she's holding. She passed the ordeal. I wanted to celebrate Inga as well because Prince Haakon would never have succeeded to the throne without her bravery. The mural is meant to honor strong women, like Inga." She studied her creation through the narrowed eyes of the work's creator. "I did a ton of research, but it is a legend, so I took some license with it. For example, I'm not sure what the landscape looks like from Lillehammer to Trondheim. The mural is supposed to have a local flavor, so I chose to use the landscape around Noelle. Last winter, I went out on my skis and took pictures to lend authenticity to the setting. That segment there," she pointed, "is a juncture of a ski trail not far from here. Freya recognized it right away."

"She would know," Erik agreed.

"The legend of the Birkebeiner has inspired many cross-country races in Norway and in this country. The Birkebeiner race in Hayward is one of the famous ones. We have our own Prince Haakon races here as an event of the Nutcracker Festival. I imagine that I'll have to do some work on the facial features tomorrow afternoon, but there are some other people here who are excellent on faces as well." She exhaled with determination. "We'll get it done on time. We have to get it done before they close all of the streets on the square for the ice sculpture contest and the Nutcracker Contest."

"You're amazing," Erik observed. "Here I worried you'd given up your dream by becoming a schoolteacher."

Stella leaned back, stretching her long legs out in front of her. "Me? No," she shook her head. "I'm too stubborn, you know that. I'd already gotten into doing public art displays and away from focusing on my own standalone work when Elias got sick," she explained. "To be honest, at the time, I was getting a little tired of the constant traveling, of the living out of a suitcase. Now I have a home base, but I still do some contract work during the summer. I get to work with kids, which I always wanted and enjoyed, a definite plus, and I'm here for my niece and my sister-in-law." She hesitated for a moment and then gazed directly at Erik. "You know about Elias's death, right?"

He nodded. "I'm so sorry. Hayden told me. Elias was a great guy."

Stella sniffed and swiped at a suspicious brightness in her eyes. "It happened. There's not much else to say. It doesn't make sense, but there it is. Thank you for lunch, Erik. It's been nice talking. We even managed to have a civil conversation. After our last interaction, I would have sworn that was impossible."

"You mean when I rear ended your car or when we broke up?" Erik dead panned.

"I was referring to when you dumped me at a graduation party," she replied archly.

Erik's brow wrinkled as if he was deep in thought. "That's not how I remember it. You were leaving to go to college, too. I thought we mutually agreed."

"Nope," Stella interrupted him. "That's not how it happened. You told me you thought it would be better if we ended things before college. I may even have thrown some cake at you. I remember feeling well satisfied with that," she wiggled her eyebrows.

"Oh yes," Erik acknowledged with a mischievous glance over at her through his sinfully thick eyelashes. "I do remember the cake. It was a marble with vanilla cream icing. What a waste."

Stella laughed. Several of her painters turned at the sound. She took another sip of her cocoa and began to clean up the aluminum wrappings from lunch. "It's good being able to laugh with you again," she admitted.

"I agree," Erik smiled.

"Seriously, Erik, how did things turn out for you? I mean, I know you're a big success. I heard you played pro hockey for a while, and now you're a bigwig in your family's company." She paused, a serious frown on her face. "But are things good?"

Erik stared at Stella's mural. "I think so. I wouldn't say I'm a huge success. There's not much to my story. I played hockey through college. Afterwards, I was playing in the minors. There was one injury and then the next. My hip wouldn't last. When I was facing the third surgery in eighteen months, I decided it was time to move on. I entered the corporate world, and here I am."

"Now it's my turn to say I'm sorry," Stella began, genuine sympathy on her expressive features.

Erik held up his hand. "Don't be. It's unnecessary. I got to play the game far longer than most people do. I made it through college and then two years in the pros. I met a lot of interesting people, went a lot of places, and had some amazing experiences. I wouldn't trade it for anything. But then, it ended. I wasn't cheated. Fortunately, I have a knack for what I do now, and I enjoy it. I consider myself blessed that I like my second parachute."

"Second parachute?" she questioned.

"When you're a rookie in the pros, you have to attend all of these meetings about planning for your life beyond hockey, your *second parachute*." He made quotation marks with his fingers. "Most people don't take those meetings seriously because we're all going to play forever. Fortunately I did. I was also lucky to get involved in my family's business. A business that I genuinely care about."

"I can't imagine giving up art," Stella reflected sadly, studying his face with her incredible green eyes. "You must miss hockey so much. Oh, I shouldn't have said that. Open mouth insert foot. I'm sorry." She covered her mouth with her fingertips. "I still haven't developed a filter."

Erik considered for a moment. "Of course, I miss hockey. The camaraderie with the guys, the times in the locker room. All of that was unforgettable, but the best times for me with hockey were those nights out on the outdoor ponds, skating in the moonlight with my buddies. I remembered that the night I took Hayden out skating when we ran into you and your team over at the outdoor rink."

"I wish I felt that way about the outdoor hockey practices," Stella remarked ruefully. "It's so cold, and the hour seems to last forever. I'm freezing the whole time. It's miserable."

"I give you credit for taking on the coaching."

"I can tell the kids to do drills, but I don't know if they're doing them well or badly," she admitted.

Setting her rubbish down on the table beside her, she impulsively reached for his hand. His fingers were bare and hers, covered with funny, fingerless gloves, but at her touch, he could have sworn sparks shot up his arm. "Erik, would you please come out, and help me coach the Rockets?" she implored.

He'd always had trouble saying *no* to her. "Stella, I'm only here for two weeks," he pointed out.

"Help me for a couple of practices while you're here...to get a handle on things. I'm a quick study. I think the kids are becoming disheartened with me coaching them. They know I'm clueless. Having a real pro like you come out would make all the difference. Please, for my niece, Samantha. She hasn't stopped talking about you and how you knew her dad. Hearing you remembered him at the rink the other day meant the world to her."

He was a goner. He almost reached out and brushed back a strand of Stella's honey blond hair that had escaped her white, knit cap. In his mind's eye, an image of a hockey locker room from back when he was in high school popped into his head. He pictured Elias *Bam Bam* Larson holding forth in front of a troop of boys. Bam Bam's eyes had been brown, unlike his sister's, but very much like his daughter's. *This is for you, Bam Bam,* Erik thought. "Okay, I'll do it."

"You will!" Stella squealed with excitement. "Sam will be so excited."

"I have two conditions."

"They are?" Stella questioned suspiciously.

"That you go with me to the snowmobile races on Thursday night. You should be done with the mural. Correct?"

"I have to be, but—"

"My other condition is that Hayden will come with me to the practices. He wants to try hockey. Are those terms acceptable to you?"

"Of course, we'd love it if Hayden would join our practices. As far as us going to the snowmobile races together, I don't know if that's such a good idea."

"And dinner. A date. The whole enchilada," he insisted ruthlessly. Erik knew he had the upper hand in this negotiation, and he wasn't willing to give it up.

"Okay," she finally agreed, staring at him. "If that's what you want. I can handle that."

"Ms. Larson. Ms. Larson, I'm not finding that color in the trailer," Gaonha, the young Hmong girl who had spoken to Stella before about the green paint had reappeared, a frustrated look on her face. "I'm sorry for interrupting you, but I can't find that color. Would you please come help me?"

"I'll be right there, Gaonha," Stella agreed.

"We have a deal?" Erik prompted, his hand extended to her.

"Fine. Yes," Stella agreed, taking his hand and shaking it.

"Where can I pick you up?"

She patted her pockets. "I don't have my phone on me. My business card is right over on that table," she pointed to another picnic table on which design sketches were spread about and held down by objects like rocks and empty paint cans so the wind couldn't pick them up. There was a stack of business cards set there as well. "My cell phone number is on the card. Grab one. Text me your number." She followed Gaonha who immediately engaged her in conversation. "Erik," she paused. "Thanks again for lunch," she called over her shoulder. "I'll send you our practice schedule."

Erik nodded, feeling a thrill of victory. If he had to coach a couple of kids for a few hours in order to spend time with the woman of his dreams, so be it. *The woman of his dreams.* It was true, he realized. He hadn't stopped dreaming about Stella Larson in the years since he'd seen her last. Feeling more excited and energized than he could recall feeling in a long time, he tossed the lunch wrappings in a nearby garbage can, then stood and studied Stella's mural for a few more long moments. *Stella is an amazing woman.* Erik glanced at his watch. It had only been about twenty minutes. He still had some time until he'd planned to rejoin Darius. He picked up one of her business cards from the table, tucked it into his pocket, and headed with quick strides back to the Nutcracker Factory. There was something that he wanted—no—needed to do.

Once inside, he didn't return to his father's office. Instead, he nodded to Miranda as he passed by her desk. "Don't get up," he waved her down. "I have an idea."

Miranda chuckled. "I can remember your grandfather, with that same determined look in his eyes, telling me much the same thing."

Erik headed straight to his grandfather's studio, flipped on the lights, and closed the door behind him. He unzipped his coat but didn't bother taking it off. He was too impatient and too excited by his intentions. He grabbed a leaf of sketching paper, shook the dust off it, grabbed a pencil, and set to work. An image had formed in his mind that was so clear and vivid, but his out-of-practice fingers couldn't keep up. It had been so long since he done more than doodled. After a few strokes, he studied the lines he'd drawn in dissatisfaction. He tore up his first sheet of paper and tossed it into the nearby wastebasket. He did the same with his second attempt. His vision only began to take shape on his third try. Slowly and painstakingly, he sketched the image that had come to him while lunching with Stella and watching her mural take shape. About halfway through this sketch, his phone vibrated. He pulled it from his pocket. There was a text from Darius. "Are you back in the building?"

Erik's fingers flew. "I'll meet you in my father's office in fifteen minutes. I'm finishing up something," he texted.

Darius sent a thumbs up in return.

Erik set his phone aside and considered his sketch. Immediately, he saw where it lacked detail and could use more effort. He set to work on it again. Finally, about ten minutes later, he put his pencil down, exhaled, and studied the sketch. *It's only a first draft,* he reassured himself, *but it's not bad. In fact, it's decent and has promise.* He needed to set it aside for a little while, to allow it to marinate in his mind. That had been the practice that his grandfather had taught him. After some time for reflection, he'd fine-tune it. The drawing was good, but he still didn't know if he could carve this nutcracker, for that was what he'd drawn. He didn't know if he had the talent or even the ability anymore. It had been so long. Still, he intended to try.

He had a week until the Nutcracker Contest. His nutcracker, drafted from this sketch, would be ready by then, he decided, as would his plan for the Engen Nutcracker Factory. His vision for the future of the factory, like the sketch on the table before him, was crystal clear to him. He wished his feelings for Stella were as well. Emotions and relationships were far more complex than creating nutcrackers or running companies, he concluded.

CHAPTER 5

The next two days, Wednesday and Thursday, were busy ones for Erik and Darius. The two of them put in long hours developing and refining their shared vision for the future of the Engen Nutcracker Factory. At first, Darius was hesitant, but as Erik revealed his ideas, Darius's enthusiasm for the project nearly outpaced Erik's.

At about five-fifteen Thursday evening, Darius checked his messages on his cell phone. He leaped to his feet. "Shoot, I'm in the doghouse. I turned off sound and vibrate on my phone earlier, so I wouldn't get distracted. I missed all of Jayda's messages, and there are at least five of them," Darius commented wryly.

"Everything okay at home?" Erik asked with some concern.

"Yes, but I have to get going. Jayda needs me back home by five-thirty. I totally lost track of time. I'm sorry, but she has a yoga class tonight. It's a regular thing that she attends each week with some girlfriends. It's important to her, and I promised I'd be home to take care of Lyrique. I can come back here afterwards," Darius offered.

Erik shook his head. "Of course not. I'm burned out anyway. It's been selfish of me to keep you so late these past few evenings, especially with the holidays coming up. I'm sorry, and please apologize to your wife for me."

"No worries. It's been exciting to be a part of this, and Jayda knows it's short term."

"Get going, Darius," Erik waved him out. "There'll be plenty left for the two of us to work on tomorrow. One bite of the elephant at a time. That's all we can take. I appreciate you keeping all of this," he gestured with his hands toward the conference table which was littered with spreadsheets and charts as well as their pair of laptops, "confidential until we get the plan fully fleshed out. I know that you've been coming under a lot of pressure from your coworkers."

Darius nodded, one corner of his mouth turning up. "You're not kidding. Can you blame them? The employees are all worried about their livelihoods and about Noelle's future. The Nutcracker Factory is critical to both. It's about killing me keeping it from my friends and especially from Jayda. I know. I know," Darius nodded. "You don't want anyone to know our plan until the night of the Nutcracker Ball, two days before Christmas."

"The day before the night before Christmas or the twenty-third, to be exact." Erik stretched his arms back behind his head, and his face lit up.

"What?" Darius asked.

"Aw, it's nothing," he replied.

"Don't hold out on me. You look amused."

"*The Day before the Night before Christmas* by the Carolers was my grandfather's favorite Christmas carol. He had one of those big, wooden record players that are like pieces of furniture in the living room at Lingonberry Lodge. He had a bunch of vinyl records of Christmas carols that he would play in the evenings heading into Christmas. Pretty much from Thanksgiving on. Man, I'd forgotten how much Grandpa loved that song. Did you know he was the one who came up with the idea for the Nutcracker Ball?"

"No, I didn't," Darius replied while gathering his papers together.

"I have to remember to ask Freya where she put Grandpa's record player. It's probably out in her storage shed or her basement."

"If she's not using it, you should bring it into the factory. It may be an antique, and it's at least vintage. Vintage is in right now, Jayda tells me. Your grandfather's record player would be a cool addition to the showroom floor."

"That's an excellent idea, Darius," Erik acknowledged. "I'm looking forward to the night of the Nutcracker Ball. It can't get here soon enough."

"We still have a lot of work to do," Darius observed, "but I'm excited, too.

"Most of the board members will be here for the ball. I—or rather we—will already have presented our plan to them. If all goes well at the board meeting, we can make a public announcement at the ball."

Darius whistled low. "Very dramatic."

"We want to get as much press attention as we can," Erik elaborated. "That's part of the plan. It will help promote the factory and publicize the new mission and vision. At first, all the scrutiny that the people of Noelle were giving me was overwhelming and annoying, but now I see real potential to it."

"People are afraid of change. They need time to process it. It took me a little time to understand and see the genius of your plan," Darius commented. "I gotta get going. Jayda's spin class is on the other side of town. I'll see you tomorrow."

"It's our plan, Darius. I can't do it without you. Good night," Erik nodded and waved, turning back to his work. It was still and quiet in the office once the other man left. Feeling stiff from being bent over a laptop for most of the day, he rolled his shoulders, recognizing that he was tired, and his ability to concentrate was fading. His phone vibrated on the desk before him. He flipped it over and saw he'd gotten a message from Stella. It read: "I've scheduled an extra outdoor practice for the Rockets tonight at seven. Can you make it?"

His heart soared. Sitting bolt upright in his chair, he pumped his fist into the air. Then he counted to ten in his head and texted back, "Yes, I can do that."

"Please bring Hayden."

"Sounds good. I got him a stick today. We'll cut it down before practice." He hesitated briefly before continuing to type in his message. "Are we on for tomorrow tonight?"

"Tomorrow?" she echoed.

"Date night... Snowmobile races."

"I thought you were kidding."

"A deal's a deal."

"Fine." She sent him the winking face-tongue out emoji. "Be at the rink tonight at seven. I'll tell the parents and kids you're coming. Thanks."

"No problem," Erik grinned, tucking his phone back into his pocket. Eagerly he stood up. Excitement and anticipation filled him. After working at a desk for most of the day, getting outside and moving around sounded perfect. Seeing Stella would be the icing on the cake.

It was a few minutes before seven when Erik emerged from his car in the parking lot of the outdoor rink which he eyed with satisfaction. It was a beautiful night. Dark, nearly pitch black. The moon and stars were behind some clouds, but even with the wind, the temperature was over twenty degrees. It was another perfect night for skating.

Hayden slammed the passenger door on the other side of the car. He looked rather woebegone and nervous, his forehead furrowed. He put his hockey stick through his skates and then drew it up on his shoulder, the way his uncle taught him to do. "Are you sure that the other kids, I mean, the Rockets, know I'm coming? This is a real team practice. I'm not sure they'll want other people here."

Erik turned to his nephew. "Hayden, you want to try playing hockey? This is your chance. I explained that Ms. Larson, I mean, Coach Larson invited you specifically. I even showed you her text. You have nothing to worry about."

"Uncle Erik," Hayden's voice was tremulous. "What if I stink?"

"You have to stink," Erik explained, "before you can become good at something. I wasn't any good at skating when I first tried it. My grandpa, your great grandpa, used to tease me because I only pushed with one leg when I started out skating."

"Is that true?" Hayden asked.

"Yeah," Erik nodded. "Hayden," Erik put his hands on his thighs and leaned down so that he and his nephew were face to face. "Those kids are your classmates. They will be happy to see you. Don't you get along with them at school?"

"Yeah, but we're not at school, and they're hockey players. I'm not," he mumbled miserably.

"You will be, too, after tonight. Let's go." Erik pressed the button on his car remote, locking the door on the Hellcat. The vehicle chirped in response. He picked up his stick and skates, and uncle and nephew made their way over to the warming house.

Erik opened the door, but then a gust of wind caught it and slammed it open against the wall. Inside the warming house, everyone looked up at the newcomers.

Sam, Stella's niece, walked right up to them. "Dude," she began, addressing Erik. "You look like Paul Bunyan," she murmured with awe. "I thought you were big the other night, but you're huge."

"Excuse me?" Erik replied, glancing at Stella in consternation. Stella was squatting before another diminutive skater tightening his skates. Her cheeks flushed charmingly.

Catching his gaze, she rolled her eyes. "Sam, please leave Mr. Engen alone, and get your gear on."

"I'm just saying," Sam replied. "Doesn't he look like Paul Bunyan?"

Stella looked bemused, snorted, then burst out laughing. "Come to think of it. You do."

Erik glanced down at his apparel. *What was wrong with what he was wearing?* He had on brown leather work boots, some heavy fleece sweats and a sheepskin-lined, red, checkered jacket from his high school days that he'd unearthed while searching in Freya's basement for one of his old hockey helmets. "What?" he demanded defensively.

"They're all third graders, and they're doing the logging

unit in Social Studies right now. That's why Sam is all about Paul Bunyan," Stella quipped. "Any big guy in checkered flannel is going to look like a lumberjack to them."

"Except he doesn't have a beard, just stubble," Sam observed. "Paul Bunyan has a big, black beard. Well, maybe not when he was young. You're not that young."

"Samantha Larson," her aunt stood up, placing her hands on her hips.

"What did I say?" the brown-haired cherub demanded.

Samantha Larson is just like her dad, Elias. Erik was sure he saw a familiar twinkle in her eyes. He scratched at his jaw line, "Maybe a beard would be in order for my time in Noelle. It would complete the look. All right, I'll stop shaving for the time being, Sam. I should have a full beard by the end of the week. I'll really look like Paul Bunyan. I gotta tell you, Samantha, you remind me of your dad."

Samantha stepped closer and patted him on the forearm. "That's what my mom and Auntie Stella say, too, that I'm a chip off the old block." She nibbled on her lip.

"And?" Erik prompted, sensing that Sam wasn't completing her thought.

"When they say that, I'm usually in trouble, so I'm not sure it's a good thing."

Erik winked at her. "Trust me, Samantha, your father was the heart and soul of any hockey team he ever played on. If you're like him, well, that's a very good thing in my book."

Samantha beamed.

"This is a far cry from your corporate business suit," Stella looked Erik up and down. He could almost feel the touch of her eyes. "You look more like the guy I remember from high school."

"It wasn't all bad then? I thought maybe you remembered

things between us differently than I do. I thought we did well together. We had some good times."

Stella stilled and tugged at her earlobe, avoiding meeting his eyes. Finally, as if firming her resolve, she exhaled. "No, it was very good. That was the problem."

Erik felt something shift inside. *Maybe there was some hope for him and Stella.* He felt more like himself than he had in years. He enjoyed his corporate life and where it had taken him, but now he recognized that it had been too far from frozen ponds like this one, too far from the people whom he cared about. It felt great being back in Noelle, back with Stella as well as his family.

"Hey, Hayden, Aunt Stella said you're skating with us today," Sam addressed Hayden.

Hayden nodded, his eyes wide, while glancing anxiously at the rambunctious hockey players who were putting on their gear throughout the room.

"That's cool. We gotta hurry up," Sam prompted.

Continuing their conversation in more muted tones, Sam and Hayden made their way over to a bench by some other players. Erik and Stella were left sort of alone, their attention wholly focused on each other.

"Thanks for coming," Stella began. "I wasn't sure you would."

"I told you I would. You know I keep promises. I always have. Besides, Hayden really wants to try hockey. I talked Freya and Benji around. They're going to let him try it."

"I'm really glad you both came."

"Me, too," Erik replied, his voice roughening. The moment took on an element of intimacy between them, but Hayden calling his uncle's name broke the fragile spell.

"Uncle Erik, can you help me tie my skates?"

"How old are you, Hayden?" Erik replied automatically.

"Nine."

"That's old enough to tie your skates. That's what my grandpa always told me."

Stella's jaw dropped, and she glanced over at Hayden with some concern. "But shouldn't we, I mean, I always help the kids tie their skates. It kills my fingers doing all of them, but they can't tie their skates tight enough."

Erik scowled. "You're tying skates for nine and ten-year-olds?" he repeated incredulously. "Kids," he called out.

No one listened.

"Do you want me to get their attention?" Stella asked. "I have this rhythmic clap that I do at school."

Erik shook his head, reached into his shirt, and pulled out a rusty, silver whistle on an old, weathered, formerly white, now gray skate lace. He blew one sharp blast.

"Rockets?" he called. There was no answer though he had the kids' attention. They eyed him expectantly.

"Here's how this works," Erik began, his deep, coaching voice booming out in the small room. "When you hear the whistle, you listen up. When I say Rockets, you say, *Yes, Coach.* Got it?"

A chorus of assents rang out. "Rockets, you are nine and ten-year-olds," he began.

"I'm eight," a pale, towheaded child called out.

"That's Uriah," a taller, version of the towheaded boy explained. "He's my brother. I'm Ezekiel. My parents wanted both of us on the same team, even though he should still be a beginner mite," Ezekiel complained.

"Listen up, Rockets. You all are going to try and tie your own skates. They may be loose the first few times, and Coach Larson or I may have to retie them, but you have to try and do them yourselves first. If you're a hockey player, you should be able to tie your own skates."

"Really?" Stella questioned. "I mean that would be great if they could. My fingers are about falling off after every practice because of tying all of the skates."

"You don't really tie all of their skates every time, do you?" Erik muttered, shaking his head disapprovingly. "That's not right."

She nodded.

"They have to learn to tie their own skates," he offered in a soft aside to her. "Rockets?"

"Yes, Coach," the kids replied, maybe not all together but in a fashion that showed they had been listening to him and had good intentions.

"We'll meet you out on the rink after you've tied your skates. You have five minutes."

"I can't skate if my skates are loose," a stout, dark-skinned boy with glasses announced.

"Well, then you will have to pull harder on your laces," Erik replied. "Coach Larson and I will help you only after you have tried it yourself first."

There was a chorus of groans, but then the kids set to work.

"You think this will work?" Stella whispered to Erik, her fingers brushing against his. "If you can get them to tie their own skates from now on, my life will be so much easier."

"Don't you have them take care of their school supplies or art supplies or whatever when you have them in school?" Erik questioned.

"Yes, of course," she asserted. "They have to learn to take care of their own materials." She flushed sheepishly. "I guess I didn't think that applied to sharp objects like skates." She threw her hands up in the air. "I don't know what is age-appropriate with hockey."

"It's not your fault. You don't know what you don't know, right? You have to let them do what they can do for themselves."

"Teachers refer to that as a gradual release of responsibility," she shook her head ruefully. "I should have known better."

Not able to resist the impulse, Erik reached down and squeezed her hand. "That's why I'm here." He winked at her.

Their eyes locked again.

Stella's smile faded. Gently tugging her hand away from him, she addressed her players. "Who wants to play goalie today?" She reached behind the bench and pulled up a netted bag filled with hockey pads.

No one stepped up to take her offer.

"I was goalie last time," a boy whose name, Brady, was written in black sharpie on hockey tape right on his helmet, put in.

"I remember, Brady. Come on, kids. Who hasn't taken a turn?" She eyed the children before her. "Connor, I don't think you have."

"Aw, come on, Ms. Larson. I su... stink at goalie," replied a chipmunk cheeked blond who was a bit taller than the other players.

"Miss Larson," Hayden called softly from where he sat on the bench. "Could I try it? I mean, I know I don't play on the team or anything, but the Rockets need a goalie. I want to play goalie, I think." Hayden gazed at his uncle with what could only be described as pure adulation.

Erik felt something melt inside him. Something that he hadn't even known was frozen. He didn't know what to say.

In all those years of signing autographs and meeting enthusiastic fans, he had never felt so moved as when his nephew asked to play his position.

Sam grabbed the bag from her aunt. "Come on, Hayden. I'll help you put the pads on."

"That would be great, Hayden. Perfect, in fact," Stella replied, giving Erik *the eye*, expecting him to say something to his nephew.

Erik cleared his throat, his eyes, suspiciously bright. "Three minutes until you're all out on the ice," he pivoted, picked up his stick and skates, and headed outside.

"You big softie," Stella mumbled to herself. Surveying her crew, she announced, "You heard Coach Erik. Rockets, we'll see you on the ice."

In surprisingly short order, the Rocket players trooped out of the warming house and onto the rink. Stella lingered behind to help Hayden put on the goalie pads. Finally, Sam, Hayden, and Stella joined the team on the hockey rink.

To Stella's amazement, Erik had the Rockets lined up with military precision on one end of the ice. He stood in front of them. Hayden and Sam rushed to join the lines of skaters.

"Hockey position," Erik shouted, demonstrating the desired stance and slamming his stick on the ice for emphasis. The little cherubs obediently mimicked him. There was none of the usual pushing and shoving and chitchatting that was, in Stella's opinion, part and parcel of hockey practice. Somehow in the few minutes that he'd been out with her players, he had worked a minor miracle. They were listening to him.

"Okay, now left leg push, together, push. The length of the ice. Go." Erik smacked his stick to the ice, clearly the signal to go. The Rockets set to work performing the desired movement. Erik skated with the Rockets giving instructions, shifting a child's position, offering encouragement. When one child started to run amuck and deliberately crash into other players, Erik blew his whistle, went and addressed the player, and then continued the drill.

He led the players through several more drills. The kids were working hard. Stella was relieved to see that Hayden was doing reasonably well. Despite the cumbersome nature of the goalie pads, he was able to skate, though slowly. He held his hockey stick awkwardly, more like a ski pole, but he appeared ecstatic. Sam was, as usual, the fastest kid on the ice. Stella was pleased to observe her niece come back to encourage Hayden several times.

Stella skated over to Erik. He turned toward her but didn't look away from the players.

"How did you do it?" she whispered.

"What?" he asked.

"This," she sputtered. "They're being so good."

"You're surprised by this?" Erik inquired. "You're a teacher. You know kids are cooperative when they want to learn something and they think you may know what you're talking about."

"Exactly." Stella rolled her eyes. "That's my problem out here. I have no credibility. They're all good kids. I mean, they're good for me at school. But out here, they're all over the place. Sawyer is always crashing into other kids, taking out their knees." She gestured at the boy in the Maple Leafs jersey.

"Sawyer's the drill wrecker?" Erik gave her a lopsided grin.

Her eyes hungrily lingered on the muscular column of his neck. "Drill wrecker?" she questioned, amused.

"There's one on every team," he explained. "The kid who

doesn't listen to directions or watch the demo, so he messes up every drill."

"That's Sawyer," Stella agreed, nodding.

"The key to dealing with drill wreckers is to send them to the back of the line. That way they watch the drill a bunch of times before they do it, and there is no audience if they mess it up. Thus, they're no longer drill wreckers."

"Well played," Stella approved. "How do you know all of this? I mean, I went to school for education, and I'm a teacher."

"And I'm just some broken down old hockey player," Erik teased with a wink. "I played hockey, and I coached kids at camps through college. I've also volunteered with some youth hockey teams over the years. Kids are kids, and coaching is coaching. Certain things work with kids, especially when those kids are motivated."

"You do it well," Stella praised him. "I can't get them to behave this well out here. They must sense I'm insecure. I don't have these problems in my art room."

"The trick is to keep them moving and to keep your eyes on them. Bad things will happen if you look away."

"Hayden's doing well," Stella observed.

"Yes, he is," Erik noted with pride. "But he's just skating now. We'll see how he does when they take some shots on him. That's the true test of a goalie."

"Goalies don't really need to skate well, do they?" Stella inquired.

Erik snorted. "I'll have you know I'm an excellent skater. The best coach I ever had in the pros told me that the goalie is the best skater on any team."

"That doesn't even make sense," Stella dissented. "They

only scoot from side to side," she squatted down and demonstrated shuffling awkwardly sideways.

"Is that what you've been teaching these kids?" Erik groaned. He pulled his chopper glove off and stroked his beard. "It would be great if it was that easy, but there's a lot more to goaltending than that."

There was a sudden crash from over by the boards. The two adults turned. It appeared that Sawyer had skated into several of the players in his line and brought them down.

"You can't look away from them for a second," Stella acknowledged as both skated over to untangle the players.

For the rest of the practice, Stella stayed by the boards and watched as Erik coached. She observed the drills, saw how they were meant to look, and she took note of how Erik managed the ice and the players. To be honest, even though she was seeing him in a whole new light, it was hard to focus on his excellence as a coach. Instead, she just wanted to watch him, to take him in. There remained something so irresistible to her about Erik Engen. He was joyful and passionate about his chosen sport, and he communicated those feelings to the players. After about half an hour of working on skating and other skills with the kids, he devoted some time to his nephew. With Hayden, he went over the goalie stance and gave him some rudimentary instruction. Finally, he skated over to Stella and handed her his whistle. "We're going to do the French drill now," he declared.

"What? What's that?" Stella asked, staring at the whistle in her hand. "I don't know what that is."

"Blow the whistle," he directed, gently pressing her hand with the whistle toward her mouth.

Stella's eyebrows shot up. "I don't recall seeing a *French Drill* on the list of drills that the other coaches gave me." She grabbed her clipboard off the boards and flipped through the pages fixed to it. "No, there's nothing like that here."

Erik shot her a broad grin that stood out against his swarthy skin and bearded cheeks. "Put the clipboard down, sweetheart. That means we're going to scrimmage. We're going to play. Right, kids?" he called out.

The Rockets cheered.

"But there are more drills to do," Stella protested. "That's what the other coaches told me. No one told me to have the kids scrimmage."

"Drills are fine, but the kids also need to have fun and apply the skills they're learning in game situations. Scrimmaging is always the best part of practice."

"Yeah, and we never get to do it with Miss Larson," Sawyer grumbled, having come up behind the coaches. Then, he oofed as Sam elbowed him.

"Hayden, you're in that net," Erik directed his nephew to the one that was closer to them.

"Me?" Hayden raised his thumb to his chest. "But...but what do I do?"

"Stop the puck," Erik replied.

"Okay, I guess," Hayden turned to skate over to the net.

"Hey, Mister Wall, we still only have one goalie," Sam pointed out while tugging on his jacket.

"You have two. Me." Erik turned to head to the other net. As he skated away, he heard Sam say, "That's sick! We get to shoot on a pro goalie."

"Erik, you don't have one of those helmet, mask things," Stella protested. "That doesn't seem safe."

"You mean a goalie mask? These kids can't lift a puck yet anyway. I'll be fine," Erik responded. "Divide up the players into teams."

"And then what do I do?" Stella questioned.

"You drop the puck for the face off, and blow the whistle if things get out of hand."

"Out of hand?"

"Relax, Stella. You won't have to do anything. Just drop the puck. We're going to have fun. Go get the biscuit, I mean, the puck."

"I *do* know that *biscuit* is another word for puck. Come on, Rockets. Let's go to the middle circle."

"Center ice," Erik corrected with a grin.

Stella divided up the players, dropped the puck, and then stood back and enjoyed the ensuing chaos. The kids were flying all over ice, shouting and calling to one another. Everyone was having fun. Sam got the puck on her stick, zoomed through most of the rest of the players, and shot the puck right over the shoulder of Hayden, who flailed backwards and then fell over. But when Stella went to help him up, he waved her off grinning. "That's was awesome," he announced. He smacked his stick on the ground and called out, "Try that again, Sam. I'm ready for you this time."

Erik beamed with pride. Stella dropped the puck again. This time, Uriah got it. He passed it to his brother who took a low shot at Erik. He easily swept it away. The man moved with a grace and ease of movement in the net that was breathtaking. Memories transported Stella back to all those high school hockey games she'd attended when they'd both been at Noelle High School.

Despite her brother Elias's passion for hockey, Stella had been so caught up in her own activities that she hadn't attended many games. That is, until her junior year of high school. That September, both Stella and Erik had returned to school transformed. Stella had grown into her long lines and developed curves. She had a mane of hair and no braces, and boys were noticing her for the first time. As for Erik, a summer of weightlifting and hockey training had irrevocably altered his tall, lanky frame. He'd remained lean, but he'd developed some hard-won muscle as well. They'd checked out each other more than once at school but never really spoke. They'd been aware of each other, but both were too shy to act on it.

One snowy December night, right before the Nutcracker Festival, Stella, Jayda and couple of other friends had decided to attend a hockey game. Elias was finally playing varsity as a senior in high school.

That night, the Noelle Chill had triumphed over their archrivals, the Icedogs, from nearby Forest Lake. It had been one of those rowdy games where the fans of both high schools dressed up. The Noelle fans had been in blaze orange, and the Forest Lake students in White Out. The fan groups had chanted back and forth tauntingly at each other throughout the game. The Noelle pep band had added to the excitement and energy of the event by playing rousing tunes during intermissions and goals.

After the game, the triumphant Noelle students had milled about in the lobby, waiting for their players to emerge. Stella had made up her mind that she was going to talk to Erik that night. She'd shared her plan with Jayda and Amy, another friend of theirs. Before the game, the girls had made signs for their favorite players. First, Stella had made one for Elias. Next, she made Erik one, though she hadn't had the nerve to hold it up during the game. She'd drawn a cartoon picture of a brick wall with hands and feet wearing a goalie helmet and a jersey with Erik's number one on it. The sign read *Erik Engen —His Goal is to Deny Yours*. She'd signed her name on the bottom corner and replaced the A in her name with a red heart. Now she worried that the heart was too much. Nervously, she'd kept the sign tucked behind her legs while she waited for Erik to come out. Elias was already out in the lobby surrounded by a posse of friends. Minutes passed, a half hour, she peered around the other players, willing Erik to emerge.

Finally, he came out of the locker room. Like many of the other players, he was wearing a dark pea coat over his formal, game day apparel. Fresh out of the shower, his cheeks remained flushed from the game, and his wet, dark hair lay slicked back. He'd worn it longer then, nearly shoulder-length. Stella knew from Elias that long hockey player hair was referred to as *flow*. Students from Noelle High School lined both sides of the narrow corridor leading from their locker room into the lobby. Erik smiled and acknowledged the accolades as the students patted him on the back and congratulated him. He was leaning a little forward against the weight of his blue and black goalie gear bag which was slung over one shoulder. His sticks were in his other hand.

"Stella, come on. There he is," Amy, who was petite, blond, and confident, had pushed Stella from behind when Erik was nearly abreast of them.

Stella stumbled into his path. She noticed how tall he was. Erik paused. "Hey," he'd said, his voice, already deep enough to give her the shivers.

"I, ah, made you a sign." Sheepishly she held it out to him.

He looked at the sign, taking in the message, and her drawing. He grinned. "That's really cool," he observed. "Thanks."

She smiled back at him, still holding the sign out. "It's yours. I mean, take it." She practically shoved it at him.

His hands were full, but he adjusted his bag further back on his shoulder, put his sticks in the same hand, and took the poster from her. "Thanks, Stella."

He knew her name. At that point, Stella had sort of dissolved back into the crowd. Her heart was pounding. She hadn't looked back at him. She'd been too blown away by the moment, bemused by her own boldness at finally addressing him. Only later, had Jayda told her that Erik had stood watching her as she'd walked away from him.

The next day at school during seventh hour, Stella was in the library where she went to avoid seventh hour Study Hall. As was her custom, she sat on the couch over by the windows, her feet up on the table in front of her. She'd been reading the horoscopes in the local paper, the Noelle Gazette.

"Hi. What's up?" a familiar, deep voice asked.

"Erik?" Surprised to see him, she'd stared up at him.

"Can I sit down?" he'd asked.

"Yeah. I mean, sure," she'd replied, pulling her legs off the table and scooting over on the couch.

"You two kids keep it down back here," Mr. Kohls, the librarian, had teased, shaking his finger at them as he passed by.

Once they were seated side-by-side on the coach, neither said a word for a minute or two. Both felt self-conscious.

"That poster you made me was awesome," Erik began.

"Thanks. I like to draw."

"I know. I mean, I've seen your drawings in some of the art shows. I guess everyone knows you're a good artist. You've always been like the best artist in our class. I like to draw, too. Wood carving is more my thing. My grandpa taught me how to carve, but I draw a little, too. It's good to get your ideas out on paper before you start carving."

"Really? You draw?" She was dubious. Erik was a hockey player, a total jock. They'd been at the same school since kindergarten, but she couldn't recall ever hearing that he drew or carved anything. Obviously, he was using the art angle to make a move on her. It was flattering.

"You don't believe me. Here let me show you." He pulled a black notebook from his backpack. He hesitated before handing it to her. "You won't laugh or anything, right?" His eyes flickered with some concern. "I mean, I haven't shown anyone my drawings since my grandpa died."

"Of course not," she'd replied, reaching for the notebook. He allowed her to take it from his hand.

She took a deep breath and opened it. The first sketch was of a deer in a wooded grove. The next of a fisherman on a boat at sunset. Both works were done in pencil—black and white. You could tell the time of day in the boat picture because of Erik's sophisticated shading and how he'd drawn the sky. The detail on both drawings was exquisite.

"Grandpa always wanted me to do more sketching of people," he rambled nervously on. "He said that my nutcrackers can only ever be as good as the pre-carving sketches. I prefer the actual carving part, but I get what he's saying. You need the sketches in order to create a decent carving. Now I kind of like drawing. When I am sitting in class, I doodle."

"Me, too." Mesmerized, Stella flipped through page after page of Erik's artwork. She'd never expected him to be talented, but the sketches, many involving nature, proved to be both skillful and creative.

"Well, what do you think?"

"You're really good. How come you draw deer so much?"

He blushed and looked down, allowing his forelock to cloak his dark eyes. "Can you keep a secret?"

She nodded.

"A bunch of my buddies like to hunt. We did hunter safety together, and we go every year. I go with them, but I really don't like shooting deer. They're too pretty. I try to miss, and I spend my time in the deer blind drawing the deer I see."

Stella giggled. "Yup. I won't tell anyone. You would definitely lose some of your fan base around here if they knew you didn't like hunting."

"I know," Erik smiled at her bashfully.

"I get it," Stella turned the page of his notebook. "Deer are beautiful, and you are really talented. You know, it doesn't seem fair, you're good at hockey and you can draw." She was studying his sketch of a Labrador retriever rolling in the snow when she felt the touch of his fingertips on her forearm. Awareness of contact with him shot through her. "Is there anything you're not good at?" she teased. She recalled commenting to Jayda and Amy that Erik Engen *pissed excellence*. Apparently, the joke was on her. The cute hockey player she might kind of like could prove to be a better artist than she was.

"No, there's nothing," he'd responded with a straight face.

"What?" she questioned incredulously. "You're kidding, right?"

"There's nothing that I'm not good at," he joshed. "Right now, I'm hoping I'm good at impressing a certain girl." Then he leaned a little closer and casually dropped his arm around her shoulders. She was completely charmed. "I spent hours last night working on that drawing of the dog so that I could show it to you. That's our dog, Harley."

"You did? For me?"

He nodded.

And so, it began. Erik and Stella started to hang out together during their shared end of the day study hall. With time, the interaction between them become more natural, less stilted. They went on dates and eventually transitioned into a true couple. Their relationship had proven magical for the remaining year and a half of high school. Then when high school ended, Erik had broken up with her, ravaging her teenaged heart.

A line appeared between her brows at the memory. Stella shook her head, dismissing the bittersweet thoughts and the still lingering hurt that the breakup had inflicted on her. *It's all ancient history.* Instead, she focused on her current reality of a team of nine and ten-year-olds skating around on sharpened blades and swinging sticks at one another.

As the scrimmage continued, the play was even, and there were only a few shots taken. Stella could see that the kids were having a blast. In what seemed like no time at all, the rink attendant in his blue Parks and Rec jacket called out to her, "There's an adult broom ball game scheduled for nine. You all are going to have to clear off the ice. Sorry."

"It's almost nine?" Stella dug around inside her pocket with her gloved hand until she encountered her phone. She pulled it out, used her teeth to remove her glove, and then checked the time. *Shoot. It was getting late.* Putting Erik's whistle in her mouth, she blew hard. "Come on, kids," she called out in her teaching voice, waving her arm, gesturing the players toward the gate in the boards where she stood. "We have to get off now."

"Aw," Connor protested. "But we're having fun."

"Come on," Brady muttered, smacking his stick to the ice.

"Nope," Erik appeared at her side. His dark eyes were

bright and sparkling with energy and pleasure against his cold reddened cheeks. "You heard what Coach Larson said, and there's no whining in hockey."

Without another complaint, the children trooped into the warming house.

Slack jawed, Stella stared at Erik. "Is that true?"

"What?" he replied. He had enjoyed himself during the hockey practice. *Life is good.* He leaned on the knob of his hockey stick, cocked a hip forward, and studied Stella. *Stella Larson is easy on the eyes. Maybe prettier now than she was as a teenager, and she'd been a knockout then.*

"You said there's no whining in hockey. That's pure magic. I wish I could say the same in art class, but I don't think the kids will go for it. For most kids, art class doesn't have the same panache as playing hockey."

"I don't know. There are some bad ass artists. I can think of Van Gogh, Picasso, and Gauguin, not to mention Frida Kahlo and Georgia O'Keefe."

"Impressive." Stella observed. "Whenever I think I can write you off as a dumb jock, you prove me wrong."

"My grandpa wouldn't have it any other way, and back in high school, I dated this girl who was really into art," he teased.

"Did she teach you all you know?" Stella countered, taking a careful step to move past him and onto the rubber matted walkway. He steadied her by gently gripping her elbow.

"Yes?" She turned and blinked up at him.

"I think she could still teach me a few things."

"Maybe," she agreed with a coy smile. "Maybe indeed."

"I'll plan on picking you up tomorrow night at six. Will that work for you? For dinner and then snowmobile races afterwards? I hope you don't mind going to the track, but I have to give out the trophy for one of the races."

Stella didn't reply immediately

"We had a deal, remember?" he prompted. "You got me as a coach, and I get you for dinner and a date tomorrow night."

"Are you being sincere?" All traces of humorous banter vanished from her voice. "Where are we going with this, Erik?" She worried her lower lip with her teeth.

The heavy door to the warming house swung open, and Sam, Stella's niece, appeared. She had one skate in hand, one still on her other foot. Most of her brown hair had worked loose from her ponytail. "Aunt Stella, would you please untie my skate? The lace is stuck in a knot. I tried to undo it, but it's wet and cold, and I can't get it. I know Coach Erik said we have to do our own laces, but it's stuck, for real. Can you help me please?"

"I'll be right there, Sam."

"I'm completely sincere. Text me your address," Erik mumbled, heading past Stella and into the warming house.

The locker room was too loud and hectic for them to continue their conversation. Parents came to pick up their players, and Stella and Sam left before Hayden was fully changed out of his gear. In short order, Erik and Hayden were loaded up in the Hellcat. On the way home, Hayden was super excited and chatty, but Erik was distracted.

"Did you see me stop Justin's shot? And he's good. I mean, he beat me between the legs another time, but—"

"Five hole," Erik corrected.

"Yeah, he beat me five hole. That's between the legs, right? Yeah, well, I kicked at the puck the next time, and it didn't go in. Can we go skate with the Rockets again another time? Can you ask Miss Larson? She listens to you. I mean, I'm sure if you asked, she'd let me. Would you? Please? Ask her?"

"What do you mean Stella listens to me?" Erik questioned, glancing over at his nephew.

Hayden giggled, giving his uncle a wise glance. "She gets all googly eyed and watches you. I've never seen her do that at school. Some of the kids are afraid of her. I mean, they like her and all, but she doesn't put up with kids messin' around. She's different around you, more like a girl. Do you like her?"

To his amazement, Erik felt a flush rise into his cheeks. He was suddenly glad it was dark in his car. He reached over and tousled Hayden's hair. "Ms. Larson just wants me to help her coach her team. I knew her brother, Elias, Sam's father, back in high school. We played together. That's why I'm helping her and because I want you to have the chance to play some hockey and see if you like it."

"But you do like her, don't you?" Hayden crowed. *The kid is too sharp. He isn't going to be distracted from his focus.* "It's okay if you do. She's nice and pretty...one of my favorite teachers, and I don't even like art. Will you talk to Mom and Dad about me joining the team? I mean, the Rockets still need a goalie, right? You could train me. You're going to be here until after Christmas. We could go to the outdoor rinks every day." Hayden continued to babble on. Erik nodded, pretending to listen, but his mind was on laughing green eyes, a dusting of freckles across a pert nose, and full red lips. In that moment, he realized he felt happy, simply uncomplicatedly happy for the first time in as long as he could remember.

CHAPTER 6

S tella glanced down at the cryptic text message on her cell phone. It read, "Dress warm." Of course, she was going to dress warm. *It's winter in northern Wisconsin, Erik Engen.* But he needed to give her more of a clue on what to wear than what was in this text. Stella was most concerned about footwear. She knew they were going to the snowmobile races, but she could wear cute boots to that. If they were going on a snowshoe hike over at Whispering Pines or ice skating on the lake, well, that would suggest very different footwear—real snow boots.

Both possibilities would be romantic and something that she could imagine Erik having in mind for them that evening. Were they going to a restaurant first? That could impact her plans, too. Still, having lived in Noelle for a good portion of her adult life, Stella knew how to dress for the outdoors while looking cute as well.

She'd gone for a white faux fur vest with gray leggings and a matching hat. The outfit had a definite artistic flare and reminded Stella of Tonya Zhivago's outfit in the classic movie

Dr. Zhivago that the character worn on her return to Russia. The outfit had been pink and had involved real fur, but it had the same whimsical, extravagant feel Stella imagined her own vest possessed. She'd last worn this same outfit to an outdoor art installation with an ice castle in St. Petersburg, Russia. Tonight seemed like the perfect occasion to wear it again. Maybe she did want to impress a former flame.

Her doorbell rang, interrupting her reflections. She glanced at the digital alarm clock on her bedside table. *He's a little early, but I'm ready.* After doing one final check on her appearance in the hallway mirror, Stella opened the front door.

Erik stood there, dwarfing the arched doorway of her little house. He was dressed in outdoor winter gear as well, all in black, which looked amazing on him. Erik had always been ruggedly handsome, but with his black knit toque, his beard, and his huge shoulders filling a Columbia jacket, he was breathtaking.

"I just need a moment. Did you have any trouble finding my house?"

Erik shook his head. "You look beautiful, Stella," he replied with a big, bemused grin.

"Thank you for the compliment, but why are you smiling?" she queried. "Why do you look like the cat that ate the canary?" She placed her hands on her hips.

"It's not you. It's your house, or rather your yard art. You were correct, your house is on Third Avenue, and it is a cute gray Cape Cod with burgundy shutters and a chimney in the middle of the roof. But you neglected to mention the headless, winged statue of a woman in your front yard or the gargoyles clustered on your front porch. I would never have missed those. They pretty much scream artist. Very different from the chainsaw carved bears and eagles that some Noelle locals put out in front of their houses."

Stella looked pleased as she tucked a strand of hair behind her ear. "I'll have you know that statue is a copy of the Nike of Samothrace. Her name is Winged Victory."

Erik snapped his fingers. "You mean Nike, like the tennis shoes. I knew I'd seen that sculpture somewhere before."

Stella smothered a grin. "That's my personal reproduction. The real Nike of Samothrace is one of the most famous sculptures in western civilization. She's at the Louvre in Paris. A couple of years ago, I was playing around with sculpture. My Nike is the result. She's smaller than the original, and I took some liberties with the folds of her garments. Mine isn't an exact replica, but I still like her. When I bought this house, I could finally take her out of my parents' storage unit. So, there she stands. I'm not sure if many people notice her anymore, though she caused quite a stir when I first put her out. Now she's part of the scenery on Third Avenue."

"Are the gargoyles yours, too?"

"No, just some fun lawn art. I've always liked gargoyles, and I have more in my back yard. I also have some more modern pieces back there, too."

"I would like to see those sometime. I didn't know you did sculpture."

"It's not my usual medium," Stella clarified. "I'm far more comfortable with murals. But sometimes you need to challenge yourself as an artist. Maybe I should take up chainsaw carving to better blend in with the neighbors."

Erik chuckled as he gazed around her living room, taking in the bright, colorful space with approval. Throughout the house, white walls served to showcase the eclectic and colorful artwork on the walls and on the furniture. She clearly had a passion for textiles and other natural materials. Her furniture was all wooden and rendered cheerful and comfortable with cushions and other accessories. Whimsical pillows of all shapes and sizes made in a wide variety of fabrics covered her red futon couch. Her coffee table was a window shutter that had been stripped down to the natural wood, sanded to a smooth finish, and set on legs. Off to one side of the coach and separating this room from the kitchen stood a ceiling high bookcase filled with books, brightly colored pottery, and family pictures. There was a sleek leather Scandinavian reclining chair as well as a wicker chair opposite the couch. Across the back of the reclining chair was a fringed, crocheted blanket in creams and other earth tones. "Your place is charming," he admired.

"Thanks," Stella blushed. "I like it. It's home."

Erik walked to the reclining chair and ran his fingertips over the afghan. "Do you knit?"

"No, my grandmother made that. My Poppy loved to watch football games, and my Nana loved my Poppy. She crocheted her way through about forty years of football games. All of us, me, my parents, all of Nana's children and grandchildren, have trunks filled with afghans. I don't know if or when we will ever use them, but we can't bear to part with them. They remind us of her."

"You mentioned your parents. How are they doing?"

"They're great. They live in Arizona now, but they come back here for the summer, and they rent an apartment at one of the university dorms. Dad likes to golf, and Mom likes to be out of the cold weather. Also, we visit them for spring break. It's turned out to be a good arrangement all around."

"It sounds good," Erik replied.

They stood for a moment, the silence becoming somewhat extended and awkward.

"I, ah, brought you a little something." He reached into his pocket and pulled out a small, silver paper wrapped box. He handed it to her.

"What's this?" she inquired, taking the box.

"I remembered you didn't like cut flowers, and I didn't want to bring a living plant out in this weather. I thought the cold might kill it. I brought you this instead."

Stella pursed her lips. "I didn't expect…" Her eyes glinted. "Thanks, Erik. This is very thoughtful of you," she stumbled over the words.

"You're welcome," Erik beamed. "Open it. I'm dying to see what you think of it," he prompted.

With slightly shaking fingers, Stella carefully pulled apart the silver paper. Inside was a small, white perfume box, the three-ounce size, that bore the label, *Jicky* as well as *Guerlain* and *Paris*.

"It's a perfume," Erik stated the obvious. "I was on a transatlantic flight about a year ago, and you know how they have those in-flight magazines?"

Stella listened as she removed the packaging.

"Well, this magazine had an article about the great perfumes of the world."

"And you read it?" An amused Stella challenged him. "You're kidding me, right?"

Erik adjusted the lapels of his jacket. "It was a long flight. I was going to Hong Kong. I'd seen the movie before." He shrugged, the corner of his eyes, crinkling. "Anyway, the article proved to be interesting. It shared the origin stories of famous perfumes. The article mentioned how the perfume *Joy* was created after the Wall Street Crash, and *Chanel Number*

Five was based on Empress Alexandra of Russia's personal perfume."

"Jicky?" Stella read the label aloud. "I've never heard of it," she studied the elegant bottle with the cork stopper.

"I vaguely recall it being one of the oldest synthetic perfumes. The bottle is supposed to look like a medicine bottle with a champagne cork stopper."

Stella went to the small hall mirror and, after removing the packaging, un-stoppered the perfume bottle. She put a dab on her wrist and then sniffed at the scent. "Lavender, citrus with a musky, woody base. A hint of vanilla. Wow," her eyes opened appreciatively. "It's potent."

"It's strong. People either like it or hate it. The article explained that the Guerlain Company saw perfume as performance art. I thought that you, as an artist, would appreciate that and the story as well."

"It's amazing. Different. Earthy. What's the story that goes with it?"

Erik didn't answer right away. "I read a review of the perfume that described it as a scent of summertime sadness, a fading dream."

"That reminded you of me?" Stella questioned softly. "Wow."

"That and the story of the perfume."

"You haven't told me the story yet," she pointed out.

"I'll tell it to you over dinner. I promise. You'll enjoy it. It's romantic."

"I'll hold you to that."

"Where's your coat?"

"It's in the closet." Stella opened the closet door and was reaching for her thigh length, black winter coat when Erik took it from her and held it up for her so that she could slip her arms inside the sleeves. As he did so, he sniffed a little at her neck where she had dabbed the perfume.

"It smells great on you. The lady at the perfume counter said it takes a special lady to wear Jicky."

Stella was aware of her heart fluttering. "I can't believe they sell an exotic perfume like this in Noelle."

"I bought it in Paris." Erik confided as he stepped back outside, holding the door wide for her.

"You bought it in Paris? For me? But... but when?" Stella stuttered, not understanding. "We haven't spoken in years."

He lifted his chin. "I had a hunch. You'll understand when I tell you the story of the perfume," he rejoined enigmatically. "That's what all great art does, right? Tells a story? I remember someone telling me that once."

Not knowing how to respond, Stella smoothed down her coat. He'd repeated her own words to him from a conversation that had taken place more than a decade ago.

Erik took her arm and led her out to his car. He used his remote to unlock the car door and opened hers for her. Once he had taken the driver's seat and buckled in, she asked, "Where are we going to eat?"

He gave her a wry look. "I was hoping you wouldn't mind going to the Wiley Cat. I mean, unless you would prefer a fancier place."

"That's the place that's right over by the ice oval," she clapped her hands together. "The Wily Cat sounds great. The food is good there, and the service is fast. The fried pickles and cheese curds are to die for."

"It's convenient to the ice oval, and I have to give away that trophy after the amateur snowmobile race at nine. Do you mind?"

"Of course not." She cast him a sidelong glance. "The Wily

Cat will be hopping tonight with the races. Lots of people are likely to see us there together."

"And?" Erik began to back his car out of her driveway.

"They may jump to conclusions if they see us there... together," Stella finished. "We may stir up some gossip."

"I don't have a problem with that," Erik answered. "Do you?"

Stella considered for a moment, then settled back into the heated, leather seat. "No, I guess I don't."

The Wiley Cat Restaurant and Bar was lodged in a log building that was backlit by the brightly illuminated snowmobile oval rising behind it. A mist of exhaust haloed the restaurant. As they got out of the car, they could taste the winter cold exhaust in the air. They could hear the roar of the racing snowmobile engines from the oval.

"Smells like winter in Noelle," Erik practically shouted, leaning close to Stella so that she could hear him.

"I kind of like it," Stella replied.

"The snowmobile exhaust?" he questioned, raising an eyebrow.

"Mm-hmm," Stella beamed, excitement on her features. "I'm looking forward to seeing the races tonight."

"Me too."

In addition to the usual SUVs, Arctic Cat and Polaris snowmobiles were also parked outside the bar. *I'm not in Chicago anymore*, Erik contemplated. He'd grown up in the winter culture of northern Wisconsin, but returning as an adult, he was seeing it with fresh eyes.

They stepped through the door and then made their way to one of the industrial metal tables. Blond wood covered in snowmobiling paraphernalia, the usual sports teams' banners, and neon beer signs paneled the walls of the Wily Cat. An antique snowmobile hung suspended over the bar. In addition, mounted on the wall across from where they were sitting was a display of hockey jerseys. There were several jerseys from the boys' high school team, the Chill, as well as the girls' team, the Noelle Force. In the center of all of them, framed and hanging in prime real estate was a dark blue Northern Star jersey.

Once they took their seats at one of the metal tables by the roaring fire in the flagstone fireplace, Stella gestured up at the jersey. "Isn't that jersey from the team who drafted you?"

Eyeing the menu and not looking up, Erik nodded.

She glanced at it again and then at Erik. "That's your jersey, isn't it?"

Meeting her shrewd gaze, Erik set down his menu, a flush rising up his neck.

"You really have stayed connected to Noelle all these years. I thought you couldn't wait to get out of town. Did you give that jersey to the owner?"

"Erik Engen," a fit, bald man wearing black glasses and white chef's apparel appeared. He held his arms wide for Erik who stood. The two men embraced.

"Chue, it's good to see you," Erik replied.

"You should have told me you were coming," Chue remonstrated, waving his finger at the other man. "Erik and I go way back. We met in kindergarten and have been friends ever since," he told Stella.

"I went to Noelle High, too," Stella pointed out. "I'm sorry, but did we know each other?"

"I moved away in eighth grade to California, but I moved back after culinary school. I missed the winters," he joked. "Actually, I came back to be with family. My sisters and their families and my parents all live in Noelle."

He rubbed his hands together in anticipation. "Now, what can I get you two? I have some new features on the menu that I would recommend. We try to locally source our food, but given the season and the weather, we do have to bring in some of our items," he finished. "I always recommend the poutine with the pulled pork, and our fish tacos which are served with a Korean hot sauce drizzle is also very popular."

Erik set his menu down, closing it.

Chue laughed out loud and shook his head. "You are a creature of habit, Erik. I'm assuming you want the usual?"

Erik grinned. "Yup, the Farmer's Market Burger with cheese curds."

"The usual?" Stella questioned with a raised eyebrow. "I didn't realize you were in town enough to have a usual here."

"I try to stop by here when I'm in town," Erik explained.

Chue patted Erik on the shoulder. "As a half owner, it's good he keeps an eye on things."

"Half owner?" Stella repeated.

"I'm sure your poutine is delicious, but you know that I come here for the cheese curds, Chue," Erik explained, seeking to shift the discussion away from himself. "You make the best cheese curds in northern Wisconsin. I can't find a restaurant in Chicago that comes even close."

Chue grinned. "It's because of the secret ingredient."

"And you still won't tell me what that is?" Erik prodded.

"Nope. Now, miss, have you had a chance to look at the menu?"

"It's Stella, and I think that I have your daughter Mabel as a student. She's a kindergartner, right?"

"Yes, Mabel, that's right. Mabel is our oldest. You're the art teacher, Ms. Larson," Chue tapped a pen to his notepad. "My son, Tyler, will be going to school next year. He's a handful."

"Well, Mabel's adorable, and I look forward to getting to know Tyler as well. I've not had a chance to look at the menu, but I think I'm going to go with the fish tacos you were telling us about."

"What am I thinking?" Chue smacked his hand to his forehead. "I haven't even taken your drink orders yet. Forgive me, but I was so excited to see Erik here. What would you like to drink?"

"I'd like a Spotted Cow," Stella replied.

"Make that two, Chue," Erik held up two fingers, "and an order of deep-fried pickles. Thanks."

"I'll be back in a minute with your apps. You two enjoy yourselves, and if there is anything you want or need, don't hesitate to ask," Chue finished before making his way to the door at the end of the bar that led to the kitchen.

"You're a restaurateur," Stella observed, gesturing with her arms to take in the whole scene. "I had no idea. You really are a businessman."

Erik nodded, resting his forearms on the table. "Chue is a sharp guy. I knew that he would make a success of this place. He has another one in Hayward. It was a low risk investment."

Stella clasped her hands and turned to further take in the surroundings. She'd been into the Wiley Cat before but seeing it as Erik's restaurant transformed it.

The fine line of Stella's chin to her neck drew Erik's eyes. He remembered her slender elegance so well. Truthfully, it had haunted his dreams. He realized that he didn't intend to simply walk away from Stella this time. His challenge was to convince her to give him a second chance. He needed a comeback and tonight's date was his first move.

"I've been here so many times," Stella commented. "I had no idea that you had any connection to this place."

Erik snorted. "You probably wouldn't have come here if you had."

"I wouldn't say that," Stella dimpled. "Apparently, there's a lot I don't know about you." She set her forearms on the table. "The perfume. You were going to tell me about the perfume, Jicky."

"That's right. Let's see if I can remember the story. Jicky is one of the oldest continuously produced perfumes. It's like a hundred years old. Aime Guerlain was the nephew of the founder of Guerlain's perfumes. From what I recall, Guerlain makes some high-end French perfumes."

"Yes, that's correct. Guerlain makes Shalimar and Champ Elysees."

"Back then, the place to study the science or the chemistry of making perfumes was in London. While in London, Aime met a girl with whom he fell in love, or so the story goes. I can't remember if she jilted him or what happened in terms of the relationship, but he made the perfume for her, though he never told anyone her name."

Stella's eyes were suspiciously bright. She patted her hand to her chest. "That's so romantic. You always did have an artist's soul, Erik. Thank you for the perfume. I will treasure it."

"You're teary-eyed. You always were a romantic, Stella. To be honest, I wasn't sure about the actual scent. It's different than any perfume I've ever smelled before, but I thought you might like the story."

"I do," she reached across the table and took his hand, "and I like the scent as well. It's floral but also exotic. It may be my new signature scent, but I still don't understand why you bought it for me. We haven't spoken in nearly a decade. What's happening here, Erik?"

"Wishful thinking, I guess." He set his other large, warm hand on top of hers.

Startled by his response, Stella's eyelashes fluttered down, cloaking her eyes and her thoughts.

"I'll come clean," he continued. "There was no reason for me to think that I would have the opportunity to give you the perfume, but something compelled me to buy it. I've never really been able to put you out my mind and my heart. You were always there, throwing shade on any girl that I met. The memory of what I had with you was always better than any current relationship. I hoped, and I had faith that an occasion would present itself, and it did. What can I say? I'm an optimist."

"Here are your Spotted Cows," Chue set the two tall, chilled glasses of the amber hued beer on the table. "And your deep-fried pickles. The rest of your order will be up shortly. Can I get you anything else?" Chue directed his question to Stella, who had drawn back from Erik at Chue's interruption.

"No, this is fine. Thank you," she responded, unable to look away from Erik.

"I'm good, too," Erik replied, holding up a hand.

"Well then, enjoy," Chue said.

Erik took a sip of his beer and then held it up to the light, contemplating the shade of liquid. "Try the pickles," he encouraged Stella.

Hesitantly, Stella picked up one and bit in. Her eyes went wide.

"Dip it in the ranch dressing," he said.

The first taste was of ranch, then she encountered the fried coating, and finally she broke through to the dill interior. After chewing and swallowing, she reached for another, raising her eyebrows demonstratively.

Erik chuckled. "Told you they're good."

"They're incredible," Stella acknowledged. She nibbled on a few more pickles as did he. "Erik, let's put our cards on the table," she leaned closer to him over the table. Both were aware of a nearly electric pull between them. "You broke up with me all of those years ago. I haven't heard from you since. Now you ask me to dinner, and you bring me a gift and tell me you've never gotten over me. What's going on here? What do you want to hear from me?"

He didn't hesitate before responding. He met her gaze straight on. "We were eighteen. I was young and stupid. All I wanted to do was play hockey or be with you. I thought I couldn't do both. You were talking about studying art out east and then travelling all over the world as an artist. I didn't know how *us* would work, given that we were going to be apart. I thought I was doing the right thing for both of us by breaking it off," he finished. "I didn't plan on having this conversation tonight. I wasn't sure you were ready to hear it. Things are different now for both of us than they were back then. If that wasn't the right time for us, maybe now is."

"You broke my heart," she replied. "Why would I ever trust you with it again?"

He picked her hand up, squeezing it gently. "Sweetheart, what you don't understand is that I broke my own, too."

"Erik Engen," a familiar voice shattered the tender moment. Pulling apart, both Erik and Stella turned. Miranda Fedie was bearing down on them. A much shorter, almost colorless, balding man trailed along in her wake.

"Miss Miranda," Erik greeted his father's bejeweled, seventy-year-plus secretary once she was at tableside, "and your husband," he paused searching for the name. The man looked familiar, but he was blanking on the name.

"It's Albert," the small man offered. He had a kind expression, and he nodded to both Stella and to Erik. "We've met before, Mr. Engen. I worked in the Nutcracker Factory, too. I was an accountant, though now I'm retired. Of course, I can't talk Mandy into retiring. She loves that factory too much. But I have convinced her to cut back on her hours."

"We are so fortunate to still have Miss Miranda and all of her institutional knowledge," Erik rejoined "Of course, I do remember meeting you, Albert." He pushed his chair back to stand, but Miranda pressed him down with a gentle hand to his shoulder.

"There's no need to get up, my boy. I don't want to interrupt you young people," she smiled at Stella, waving a bangle-braceleted wrist at the younger couple. "Like the good old days," she murmured. "Who would have thought it? Stella and Erik, the two of you, together again. Stella Larson, how are you doing?"

"Fine, Mrs. Fedie. It's good to see you."

"You give your mother my greeting. We play Mah Jong together once a month on Wednesdays over the summer," Miranda explained to the men. "Well, you have a pleasant evening. Ta ta." Albert in tow, Miranda headed to a larger table where they joined several couples of a similar age.

"How do you know Mrs. Fedie?" Stella whispered, leaning forward on her elbows.

Erik snorted. "Miranda knows everyone and everything that goes on in this town and at the Nutcracker Factory. She also happens to have been my grandfather's last secretary and my father's secretary in Noelle. She stayed on a very part time basis when my father moved the administrative headquarters to Chicago. Miss Miranda is mostly retired and is only at the office maybe ten hours a week. She doesn't trust us enough to fully step away from it. Well, she trusted my grandfather, but I think her jury is still out on my father and me." Erik shared.

"Why doesn't she trust you?"

"Miranda thinks I've lost my way as my father did before me."

"You want to clarify?"

"She thinks that I should be carving nutcrackers, the way my grandfather did. She was upset when my father moved the headquarters, and she wasn't pleased when we diversified our offerings. Miranda believes that we should stick to what we know—nutcrackers."

"Do you carve anymore?" Stella asked, focusing on the first part of his statement.

"No," Erik admitted. "Not since after high school. When my grandfather died, I guess I lost interest. I was busy with hockey and the business. Miranda knew my father had no talent or interest in carving. I was her hope to follow in my grandfather's footsteps, but it didn't turn out that way."

Stella hid a grin and took a sip of her beer. "She's in her seventies but not retired?"

"As I explained, she doesn't trust us enough to retire," Erik offered dryly. "She was a teenager right out of secretarial school when my grandfather hired her. She only worked for him for a couple of years, but she's convinced that she's the only current employee who has an idea of what Grandpa would have wanted for his legacy."

"You mean she's afraid that you and your father will run the Nutcracker Factory into the ground?"

"No, I think it's more that she's concerned that we will lose sight of Grandpa's vision for it. Miranda is sort of the self-designated keeper of the flame. She makes up all sorts of reasons to come in the conference room when Darius and I are speaking with the managers." Erik picked up another deep-fried pickle. "That woman is a force of nature."

Stella was silent, her expression contemplative. "Is she right?"

"About what? The company? Engen Ornaments is doing well." Erik deliberately avoided the intent of the question.

"But what about the Nutcracker Factory? I've heard a lot of gossip around town that you may be shutting it down, mechanizing it more, laying folks off, or shifting the factory to a cheaper location."

Erik groaned and rubbed his eyes. "It's because we care about Noelle and the Nutcracker Factory that we are looking at keeping it vital and profitable. We are invested in this community. My sister and her family live here. My parents still see Noelle as home. I'm not some Ebenezer Scrooge come to take away everyone's jobs before the holidays."

"What are you looking at doing?"

"That's the million-dollar question. How do you keep a fifty-year-old nutcracker factory vital? I thought I would be streamlining production and increasing output while reducing costs."

"And now?" Stella inquired.

"I'm not so sure that increasing efficiencies and cutting costs is the best approach."

"Cheaper and faster isn't always better," she pointed out.

Erik exhaled slowly. "I'm not sure I disagree. That's what Darius and I've been working on."

"Craftsmanship is the answer. Artistry," Stella opined. "If you make something truly unique and special, there's always a market for it."

"That's what my grandpa believed. Art has worked out for

you, hasn't it?" Erik inquired. "I mean, you still create art, and you teach. You're doing everything you ever wanted."

Stella considered. "Art is my life. I can't imagine not painting. To be honest, I didn't realize how much I would enjoy teaching. I got the license in college as sort of a failsafe. I was doing reasonably well as an artist when my brother passed, but it was the right thing to do to come back here for Sam and Barb. Everything sort of came together. I got the job at the school. Now I can't imagine living anywhere else. Don't get me wrong, I still love to travel, and during the summer I take commissions all over the world, but Noelle is home. You have to admit, there is no better place to be at Christmas time."

"You're right about that," he replied.

"Do you miss carving?" she asked, resting her chin on her hand.

Unable to meet her gaze, Erik looked away from Stella. "You're one of the few people in the world who know that I carve, or I did at one point. I didn't realize I missed it until recently. You understand what making something is like... how special it is."

She nodded sympathetically.

"I miss that feeling of a carving coming to life in my hands." He held his large hands up and open, staring at them as if seeing them for the first time. "Stella, I've realized that I've missed a lot of things these past few years. Coming back to Noelle has shown me what I've been lacking or, rather, who."

Swallowing hard, it was her turn to look away. She wasn't ready to have this conversation. The feelings were all too new, too volatile.

"Here are your meals." Chue set two enormous platters of

food before Erik and Stella, momentarily halting the conversation again.

"Thanks, Chue," Erik responded. "As always, it looks delicious."

Seemingly in agreement about avoiding hard topics for the rest of the meal, Erik and Stella chatted companionably, sticking to uncomplicated topics. The food proved to be excellent.

An hour or so later, feeling pleasantly warm and full, they emerged from the Wiley Cat and drove over to the snowmobile oval. They parked in the public lot on the far side of the complex, proceeded past the four multi-story buildings that housed the indoor seating, concessions, and bar. On other nights, Stella would have headed into one of the buildings from which she generally watched the races. Instead, Erik led her to a restricted area directly in front of the open-air stands. Here, below a platform on which the officials stood, were the hard-core race fans as well as some race officials and a handful of sponsors. Several layers of fencing separated this area from the track.

Despite the single digit temperature, excited fans decked out in full winter gear packed the bleachers behind them. Erik looped Stella's arm through his own, but the two didn't bother trying to speak over the roar of the snowmobile engines.

Stella had always enjoyed going to the snowmobile races. The atmosphere was electric with excitement and adrenalin. They had arrived at a time when the races were well underway. She found herself bouncing on her toes, trying to see the snowmobiles as they sped around the track.

Erik rested his forearms on the top of a fence, taking it all in, the track, the cold night, the racing snowmobiles, the roar of the crowd. He leaned over to Stella. "I'd forgotten how much fun this is."

She beamed back at him. Her cheeks and the tip of her nose were adorably rosy. "I know. It's so cool."

They watched several races. Noticing that Stella was shivering, Erik got them Styrofoam cups of cocoa. Stella gratefully accepted hers, gripping it with a mittened hand, and sipped at the hot liquid. Her lips encountered the small, hardened marshmallows slowly softening. They reminded her of past occasions of drinking instant cocoa as a child, after coming in from sledding or skiing. The memories and the beverage warmed her despite the chill of the increasing winter wind.

"I have to hand out the trophy after the vintage race," Erik explained. "We can head out after that. Can you make it through one more race?"

She nodded. "I'm fine, really. This is fun. You're giving out a trophy?

"Engen Ornaments is the sponsor of the vintage race. It's coming up. I have to get the trophy. I'll be right back."

About ten minutes later, Erik returned bearing an enormous trophy. The trophy consisted of a large cup mounted on a base on which the engraved names of prior winners were carved. In front of the cup and fixed to its base was a nutcracker plated in bronze to match it.

Erik's fingertips gently moved over the nutcracker.

"Wow, that's quite a trophy," Stella commented.

"My grandpa carved this nutcracker." He looked up from the statue to Stella. "I didn't know they'd mounted it here."

"Really?" Stella studied the small figure. It was of a traditional king nutcracker. The detail remained exquisite despite the bronzing. "How do you know it's one of his?"

"I'd know his work anywhere. I watched him carve from the time I was a little boy. I'm sure my dad designed this trophy or gave them the nutcracker to attach to it. Grandpa would have loved this." Moved, Erik cleared his throat.

The emotion in his voice touched Stella in an unexpected way. Respecting his privacy, she crossed her arms over her chest, hugging herself.

"Now for the signature event of the evening," a voice boomed over the loudspeaker. "It's Noelle's own Vintage Holiday Nutcracker Classic. This is a nonprofessional event sponsored by Engen Ornaments. Folks, let's hear it for our sponsor and for our drivers."

The crowd and the snowmobiles roared as the drivers revved their engines. The old school machines were popular with the spectators. The announcer went through the names of the drivers and their respective snowmobile numbers, and then the start gun fired. Stella squealed with excitement as they took off.

Without looking down, she felt Erik reach for and entangle his warm fingers with hers. Hand in hand, they cheered, hooped and hollered as the snowmobiles swooped around the snow covered, banked oval.

On about the seventh lap, two snowmobiles began to pull ahead, one was a black and red Skidoo and the other a Moto-ski with a white and orange paint job. The jumbotron screen in the middle of the track zoomed in on the drivers as they leaned deep into the corners, trying to steal a few more precious inches. The announcer was doing the play by play of the race, but Stella and Erik couldn't make out his words over the roar of motors because they were so close to the track.

A few more laps, and the black snowmobile squeezed past the white and orange one. By the time the event's marshal waved the checkered flag, the black Skidoo was several lengths ahead. Overwhelmed by roar of the crowd, Stella placed her hands over her ears.

"Folks, we have a winner. Driving the Minnesota Monster," the announcer proclaimed, "we have Kale Stern. He's a local fellow, originally from Noelle, though he now resides in Still Lake, Minnesota. Let's give him a big round of applause."

Once the other snowmobiles had cleared the track, Kale Stern drove the Minnesota Monster over to where the race officials awaited him. Raising his clasped hands over his head in triumph, the driver dismounted from his Skidoo.

"Kale Stern!" Erik repeated in disbelief. He grinned broadly, revealing strong, white teeth. "I haven't seen him since high school."

"The name sounds familiar." Stella replied. "Did he go to school with us?"

"A couple of years older. He played football and hockey. He was a total beast. It's a small world."

Stella snorted. "You're not kidding. It is a small world for everyone who is connected to Noelle."

"True."

"Hurry up," Stella prodded, catching sight of the announcer who was waving for Erik to come up onto the platform with him. "You're needed up there."

Erik turned to head up the stairs, but he paused. "Come with me?" he asked.

"No, you go ahead," Stella waved him up. "I'm good here."

"I'd like you with me."

Stella's heart pounded at his unexpected words, but she was saved from answering as Kale Stern appeared behind her.

"Pardon me." He gently ushered her to one side and ascended to the platform behind Erik.

Gazing up at the two men, Stella sought to calm herself. *Once burned, twice shy,* she reflected. *Erik's only passing through Noelle. He has no intention of staying. He didn't last time, and he doesn't now.* She repeated this mantra, but her tender heart wouldn't accept it. Her heart rebelliously pounded as she watched Erik and Kale Stern grin and greet each other. They shook hands, and then Erik handed Kale the trophy. Still beaming, Kale grabbed him and the trophy in a hug. Erik clapped Kale on the back, laughing out loud.

That's the thing about Erik Engen, Stella reflected, *he's too appealing.* Too handsome, too charming, too unforgettable, too ready to move onto the next thing, whatever it was. She believed Erik liked her. Cared about her, in fact. His feelings for her were apparent in the warmth of his brown-eyed gaze, in the thoughtful things he did for her and said to her. But he would only hurt her in the end. That was the way it was and always had been. She intended to stay in Noelle, while he was only here for the duration of the Nutcracker Festival.

Feeling like she was going to cry and not wanting to face him, Stella abruptly turned and headed toward one of the viewing buildings, intending to get lost in the crowds there for as long as it took her to regain her composure.

Up on the platform, unaware of Stella's turmoil, Erik chatted with Kale, the champion snowmobiler, but his eyes and his heart followed Stella as she walked away. *Why is she leaving? Where is she going?*

About an hour later, Erik located Stella. Kale and the track officials had detained him after the race. As the sponsor and as the representative of Engen Ornaments at the event, he had to do some meeting and greeting which didn't usually bother him. But this time, all he could think of was Stella and wonder where she'd gone. Once his duties were completed, he wandered around looking for her.

After about fifteen minutes of aimless searching, hoping to catch a glimpse of her, he texted her, "Where r u?"

To which, she responded, "In the food court."

She hadn't gone home. Relieved, but aware that something was amiss between them, he made his way there, slowed by greetings from old acquaintances on all sides. It was with relief that he finally caught sight of her white, shaggy, faux fur vest and matching hat in the dining area.

He headed over to her. To his dismay, he realized she wasn't alone. Darius and his family sat with Stella at a round table. Erik waved a greeting to Darius, who had his precious, little daughter asleep in his arms. Stella sat beside Darius's wife, Jayda. He knew Jayda from high school. He noted that Jayda didn't smile at his approach.

What's gone wrong? What did I do to anger Stella? Everything seemed to be going fine before I went to hand off the trophy. But how could that have upset her? It doesn't make any sense. Why would Stella walk away without saying anything to me?

"Jayda, Darius, hi," Erik greeted them both before taking an empty seat by Stella. *Did she just shift her chair away from me?* Despite the heat in the building, he was aware of a distinct chill in the atmosphere around his date.

Oblivious to the undercurrents, Darius waved back at Erik, gestured at his daughter, and then held a finger to his lips.

Erik nodded in understanding

"Evening, Erik," Jayda leaned forward and held out her hand to him. "I don't know if you remember me, but I'm Jayda Watkins, formerly Evans."

He shook her hand. "Of course, I remember you. Darius talks about you all the time. It's a pleasure to see you and Lyrique."

At the mention of her daughter's name, Jayda's expression softened. She glanced over at the sleeping toddler.

Jayda was exactly as Erik remembered…fit, assertive, and loyal. In other words, a formidable woman who wouldn't tolerate any perceived abuse of her friends. Erik knew he had to win Jayda over if he had any hope of seeing where things went with Stella. "Thank you for being so understanding about the long hours your husband has been putting in with me. I believe we're in the homestretch now."

"That's good to hear. Did you enjoy the races tonight?" Jayda's eyes were measuring and critical. Obviously, Stella had communicated whatever she was upset about to the other woman. Again Erik wondered what had gone wrong. It was a genuine mystery to him. They'd been having such a pleasant evening. They hadn't fought about anything. They hadn't even disagreed.

"It's been a blast," Erik answered Jayda's question.

"How are you liking Noelle?" Jayda inquired. Apparently, she, too, felt the tension between them.

"I'm enjoying my trip." Erik clasped his hands in front of his waist and leaned back in his chair. "There's no place better than Noelle during the Christmas season."

"So you're just here through the holidays?" Jayda continued.

"Originally I was supposed to stay until the night of the

Nutcracker Ball," he explained, acutely aware of Stella listening intently to each word he said. "My plans have changed."

"How have they changed?" Stella challenged. "Are you leaving sooner?"

"No, just the opposite actually. I've asked Freya and Benji if I can stay on until after the holidays."

As if she was observing a tennis match, Jayda's gaze flicked between her best friend and Erik.

Lyrique whimpered and began to fuss. Darius adjusted his daughter's knitted hat on her head and then secured her blanket about her little body. "We need to get going," he whispered to his wife.

Jayda nodded, getting to her feet.

"We should get going, too," Stella agreed. "It's getting late."

"Good to see you, Erik," Jayda said. "See you tomorrow, Stella." She winked at her friend.

"See you in the morning," Stella replied.

The Watkins family headed for the exit across the dining area.

Stella and Erik sat in silence. Abruptly, Stella stood up. "I'm tired, and I have a mural to finish tomorrow. Are you done here?"

Erik nodded. They made their way down to the parking lot and the car in silence. He had remotely started the car while they were still in the building, so it was already warm inside when he opened the car door and she got in. "Thanks."

Erik shut the car door, but as he moved around to his side, he decided he'd had enough. He opened his car door, sat down, shut off the radio, then turned to face her. "What happened? What did I do? We were having a good time. What went wrong? You're angry because I left you to give out that award? I'm sorry about that if that's the problem. I didn't mean to be gone that long."

She hung her head. "No, of course not. That wasn't the problem at all. It's just you, Erik. You sweep into town, and everyone gets carried away by your charm. It's the way it's always been. People like you."

"Do you like me?" he teased.

Her stricken expression faced him. "That's the problem. I do like you, just as I did once before. And then you broke my heart. You said just now that you're leaving after Christmas. There's no future here," she gestured with her hand between them. "This time, I'm calling it. We aren't going to see each other like this anymore. This thing between us is just memories and Christmas magic. That's all it can be. We're friends, and that's it. You understand? That's the way it has to be."

His hands clenching in his lap, Erik listened.

"That being said, I'd still like it if you'd continue helping me with the hockey team. If that's okay with you?"

"Of course, it's okay with me," he replied with some exasperation. "I'm not a bad guy. I enjoy working with those kids, and Hayden is having a ball getting the hang of playing goalie."

"But that's it. That's all there is between us," she repeated, raising her hand for emphasis. "Erik Engen, we can't go back in time. Our lives are in different places. Please take me home now."

"Why are you doing this, Stella? Why can't we see where this goes?"

"We shouldn't see each other," she repeated.

"Why not? Friends can see each other."

"People may get the wrong idea."

"When did you start caring what people think?" he challenged. "Where is my free-spirited artist? What people are you worried about? From what I've seen, people are happy to see us out and about together."

"I'm an artist, but I'm not free-spirited, not anymore. I can't be. My life is here in Noelle. My work, my friends, and my family are here," she hesitated a moment. "We both have responsibilities. You have Engen Ornaments and your family. My family has needed me since Elias's death. Barb, his wife, does the best she can, and Sam's a great kid, but being a single mom is challenging. I don't have the time, energy, or inclination to get caught up in a whirlwind holiday romance that has no future."

Erik gripped his steering wheel, unsure of how to respond, of what to say to convince her that his intentions were good. To be honest, possibilities and emotions had overwhelmed him since coming back to Noelle. He wasn't yet ready to tell her how he felt or what he wanted. He intended to show her.

"Please take me home now, Erik," Stella pleaded.

"Okay." Reluctantly, he backed out of the parking slot. Neither said a word the entire way to her house. Once he stopped in her driveway, she dashed out of the car and into the house before he had a chance to do more than wish her a good night.

After dropping Stella off at home, Erik wasn't ready to return to his room at the Lingonberry Lodge. Feeling restless and out of sorts, he drove around the familiar streets of Noelle. Heavy snowflakes began to fall as he headed down Hans Christian Anderson Street. Despite the hour, and it was almost eleven, Noelle was well lit with holiday lights. Every lamppost was adorned with either an LED snowflake, wreath, or candy cane. Garland and bows festooned every shop front. Silver and gold adorned the evergreen trees around the Town Square. When he cracked the car window for some fresh air, Erik heard Christmas carols playing from unseen speakers. He rubbed his forehead. Tonight he didn't have the Christmas spirit. He hadn't since things went south with Stella.

Christmas Eve was now only four days away, he realized. He'd experienced Christmas in many cities in the world, but none had moved him in the way that a Noelle Christmas did. With Stella and the fate of the factory and the town weighing on his mind, he pulled into the parking lot of the Engen Nutcracker Factory. Still pondering his course of action, he wandered around to the factory's enormous display window that faced into the square. As was tradition, on this night and every night until the evening of the Nutcracker Ball, the interior curtains remained drawn. On that night, the culminating event of the festival was the great reveal of the Engen Nutcracker Factory holiday window display which always incorporated the current season's winning nutcracker. The background of the display varied with the year, but each one paid homage to the history of the Nutcracker Factory and the town of Noelle.

Erik knew that Miranda and Darius had been working hard with the creatives on this year's vision. However, as he stood there, contemplating the blank canvas of that empty space, inspiration struck him. His plan would address both his personal and his professional concerns. It would take his best effort, but all good things did. *This just might work.* Not wanting to lose the idea, he hurried to the factory door, swiped his ID badge, disarmed the alarm, and headed straight to his grandfather's workshop. There he flipped on the lights and pulled a sheet of paper out from one of the shelves beneath the worktable. He shook it out to get the dust off, selected a pencil, and began to draw. At first, his pencil moved haltingly across the paper. He was out of practice. He hadn't drawn anything other than doodles in forever. But with time, his pencil began to move across the paper with greater purpose and more confidence. His long unused muscles and mental faculties remembered this passion from his childhood.

The image became clearer his mind's eye. When he finished and sat back to study the sketch, he frowned. He was dissatisfied with it. He wadded up his sketch and threw it at the wastepaper basket. It wasn't until several hours later that he completed a sketch with which he was reasonably pleased. He exhaled, nodding slowly. It wasn't the first nutcracker that he had drawn since high school. It wasn't anything like the slick, mass produced nutcrackers that the Engen Nutcracker Factory had put out in recent years. This sort of design hadn't been released since his grandfather's days at the helm of the company. However, as he studied his drawing, another idea began to take shape in his mind.

After setting the sketch aside on the worktable, he got his laptop from his father's office. This idea for bringing the Noelle Nutcracker Factory into the twenty-first century required a great deal of fleshing out, but it could work if the numbers supported it. *It can work.* Erik turned on the work light over the desk. With his sketch right beside him, he got to work.

Hours later, the door to the workroom swung open, and the bright overhead lights flashed on, blinding him. Darius stood in the doorway with Miranda right behind him. Erik looked over at the window. The blinds remained drawn, but he could see from the light shining through them that it was in fact already morning. He realized he'd stayed up the entire night in his grandfather's workshop. He couldn't ever remember being so excited about an idea.

"Yes, Freya. He's in here. He's fine, just working. I'll tell him. Bye." Darius spoke into his phone. "Erik, that was your sister wondering where you were. She pointed out you could have texted her so that she didn't worry." Darius put his hands on his hips, his gray button-down cardigan coming open. "You look rough. Did you spend the night here?"

Erik grinned, attempting to pat down his dark hair which was messy from running his fingers through it. "I guess I did. I haven't pulled an all-nighter in years. Crazy, isn't it?"

Miranda sniffed, shaking her head. "He's just like his grandfather. He gets an idea in his head and then doesn't stop to eat or sleep."

Darius moved closer to him, Miranda in his wake. "Are you okay, Erik?"

"I'm fine. Great, in fact." Seeing that Darius had zeroed in on his drawing, Erik flipped the paper over. "I have an idea. It's a big one, and I need you both to help me. Miranda, what is this year's theme for our display window?"

Miranda clasped her fingers in front of her chest. "My vision for this year is a Christmas Masquerade. It's top secret, of course, but I'm confident it will be completely adorable."

"Scratch that idea," Erik waved one hand at Miranda, cutting her off.

"Well, I've already ordered all of the materials," the secretary harrumphed. "I've always planned the window display."

"And you are fabulous at it. Your Christmas Masquerade idea is great, and we can hold onto those materials for next year. But this year, we have to do something a little special. The window display is going to help communicate our vision for the future of the Engen Nutcracker Factory and for the town. My idea is to involve some of the historical nutcrackers, some my grandfather carved as well as others. I need you two to help me do this. Are you with me?"

Darius rested his palms on the worktable. "We don't even know what you're planning. Fill us in."

"What do you have in mind, Erik?" Miranda inquired, pushing her gold framed glasses up the bridge of her nose with her forefinger.

"It came to me last night," Erik rose to his feet and began to pace excitedly around the room. "It's been in the back of my mind this whole time. I don't know why I didn't think of it before," he smacked his head demonstratively.

"Slow down, Erik. What are you talking about?" Darius demanded.

"The window display, the nutcracker lines, the entire Nutcracker Factory. My grandpa knew all along. I sat right here at his knee watching him carve, and he told me."

Miranda pulled out a stool and sat down. "Erik, you're miles ahead of us."

"Here, I'll show you." Hesitantly, perhaps a little self-consciously, Erik flipped over his nutcracker drawing from the previous night.

Leaning closer, Miranda inhaled sharply.

"Man, oh man," Darius commented, peering down at the drawing. "I had no idea you could do this. But what does this have to do with the factory?"

Grinning, Erik pointed him to a stool and drew his laptop over so that Darius and Miranda could see the screen. "Let me explain."

CHAPTER 7

That night, the Rockets were scheduled for a pond hockey scrimmage against the Bruins, one of the other in-house hockey teams. Because it wasn't a formal league game and because Erik believed that his nephew had progressed to the point where he was ready to play, Hayden was suited up as goalie. Freya, Benji and the twins planned on coming. Erik's sister and brother-in-law planned to surprise Hayden with the news that he could continue to play hockey, if he so chose, after the game.

After Erik consumed more than his usual evening coffee quota at dinner, he and Hayden left for the rink. The others would follow later. Erik was exhausted but also euphoric. There was no way he was going to miss this scrimmage and a chance to see Stella again. Upon arrival, he noted that the outdoor skating complex was lit up and unusually packed for a weeknight.

"What's going on over there?" Erik asked, gesturing over at the skating rink where an increased amount of Christmas lights illuminated people moving about both on the rink and around it. The Madrigal singers from the high school, adorned in Victorian winter wear, including top hats and dark suits for the boys and long red or green dresses accessorized with warm muffs for the girls, were assembled in the band shell, singing Christmas carols. Now, they were performing a rousing rendition of *Jolly Old Saint Nicholas*.

"I dunno," Hayden announced, practically bouncing in his seat with excitement and anticipation of the upcoming game. "Do you think Mom and Dad will come?

"I'm sure they will," Erik soothed. "They said they would."

"I gotta go get geared up. Connor and Justin said they'd help me. Do you think I'm gonna see a lot of shots? Brady says the Bruins are good. Do you think Mom and Dad will make it on time? What if they miss the game? Should we text them again to make sure they know the time?"

"I texted them when we left the house. They'll be here. Don't worry about how many shots you're going to take or if they're going to be good ones. Just play hard, stop one puck at a time, and have fun. That's all that matters. When I played, I focused on the next shot, that's all. There's no point in thinking about the rest of it. If you over think it, you'll probably play worse. One at a time."

"I know, but I wanna do good, too," Hayden slumped back in his seat, "so that Mom and Dad will let me play hockey. If I'm bad, maybe they won't let me play, and that would stink."

Hayden's words warmed Erik's heart. He gently pushed at his nephew's shoulder. "You like it, don't you? As far as your parents not letting you play if you're not good, why that's ridiculous. They love you and are proud of you no matter what. You know that," he pointed out.

"Yeah, I like it a lot. I've been watching YouTube videos to see how goalies move. Dubnyk's my favorite."

"He's good," Erik agreed. "But try and watch some Dominik Hasek videos, too. He was my hero growing up. Watch videos from the Nagano Olympics if you can find them. Maybe talk to Samantha. Apparently, she's quite good at finding old hockey videos on YouTube. Hasek was incredible throughout his career and pretty much won the gold medal for his team. His goaltending style is unorthodox. He was a flopper, and he relied on his own innate athleticism to stop pucks. He's amazing to watch."

"Was Hasek a big guy like you, Uncle Erik?" Hayden asked. "I don't know if I'm going to be as big as you and Dubnyk."

"No, but he was an incredibly athletic goalie. You'll develop your own style, too. Have fun tonight, okay?"

"It's been fun coming to practice with you and Miss Larson. She's nice and pretty, too. Don't you think?" Hayden observed his uncle with keen and eager eyes. "All the kids at school think she is."

Erik nodded. *Out of the mouths of babes.* Apparently, his interest in the pretty art teacher hadn't escaped his nephew's notice. "I like her," he finally admitted.

"Do you think you might really like her?" Hayden asked. "Because that would be cool with me. I think she likes you because she's always giggling and smiling when you two talk." Hayden batted his eyelashes and tittered, mimicking a flirtatious woman.

Erik chuckled. "Kid, you're too much." He opened his car door. "Come on, we've got to get you suited up."

Carrying their gear, the two headed into the warming house. Most of the Rockets were already there. Erik's gaze immediately went to Stella. She sat on one of the benches, tying her own skates. Her pretty eyes went wide upon seeing him, and then, deliberately, she looked down, turning her attention back to her skates.

Sam came dashing up. "Hayden, you ready to play tonight?" she demanded. "Don't be nervous or anything. I'm going to score lots of goals," she beamed.

Erik looked around the space. There was plenty of room, but he chose to sit on a bench opposite Stella. "Your niece doesn't lack confidence," he observed wryly.

"You're right about that," Stella replied.

"That's good. Goal scorers need confidence and a short memory."

"Come on, Aunt Stella. Hurry up. We play in like half an hour. We have to be on the ice for warm-ups soon," Sam prompted.

Connor and Justin joined Sam, and the kids swept Hayden to the corner of the warming house where the goalie gear awaited him.

Stella continued to tie her skates, and then, feeling Erik's gaze on her, looked up. "What?" she challenged.

"Nothing." Erik yawned broadly, covering his mouth with the back of his hand.

"If you're tired, I've got this," Stella offered.

"I'm good. Pulled a late one last night, but I wouldn't miss this scrimmage for anything. Thank you for letting Hayden participate. This means the world to him."

"He's a good kid," Stella nodded, her stern expression, softening. "I hope he does well tonight. He's really been working hard."

Erik snorted. "I want him to have fun. That's what all of this is about. Hockey should be fun, the way it was for me when my grandpa brought me out here to mess around on the ice. Those are some of my best memories of childhood."

Stella finished tying her laces and, placing her hands on her hips, studied him. "You've changed, Erik. You used to be all business when it came to hockey."

"I was wrong," he shrugged. "It took me all of college and a very brief pro career to figure it out. Somewhere along the line, I lost the joy of it. Seeing these kids out here has brought that back to me. Kids get into hockey because it's fun. Guys and gals stick with hockey for the same reason. That's what I want Hayden to get out of it. During my career, I got too caught up in making the next tryout, making the next team, earning the next contract. All of that comes to an end eventually. Then you're left considering *was it worth all of the effort?* And yeah, for me it was. It took me to so many interesting places, and I still love the game. It's part of who I am."

Stella's eyes were suspiciously bright. "I totally understand. I was chasing the art dream for all those years, too. I loved doing the public installations, but I was living out of a suitcase. Bigger exhibits in bigger cities. I was running from place to place, there long enough to fulfill a commission and then moving on to the next one. I had art, but no life outside of it. After Elias died, I came back here. Benji approached me about working at the elementary school. The old art teacher had health issues and had to retire midyear. I got an emergency license renewal, and here I am."

"You still do your art," Erik pointed out. "I saw your mural today. You finished. It's amazing."

"Thanks," she beamed, the full force of her smile, melting something inside Erik that he didn't know was frozen. "I think it turned out rather well, too. I'm also glad it's done. It's a challenge working in such a tight time frame with so many contributors. I'm pleased with it."

"I'd like to discuss you doing a mural at the factory, telling the story of my grandpa Ole founding it, and how it and the town has grown. Would that interest you?"

"Yes, it sounds fascinating. I take commissions over the summer, so if that would work with your timetable, we can definitely talk about it."

"You like living here in Noelle, don't you?" Erik probed.

"I'm content, happy to be here now," she raised her chin. "Don't get me wrong. I wouldn't change the traveling artist time in my life. I saw so many beautiful places, and it makes me proud to think I left a little bit of myself at many of them."

"I saw another one of your murals in Stockholm. That season, I was playing in the Swedish Hockey League. The guys and I were walking around the city. There was a festival going on."

Stella nodded, smiling slightly. "Stockholm, that was the ABBA mural, right? The whole experience was outrageous. There was a citywide ABBA festival in honor of the band's anniversary, and there were groupies everywhere. There were so many people working on that mural, and I didn't speak Swedish. It was a blast."

"Well, I saw you working on that mural," he admitted. "You were in the middle of it anyway. You and the rest of your crew were dressed up in disco clothes, and there was music playing. You were all painting and dancing. It was crazy."

"You were there? Why didn't you come up to me or say anything?" Stella was dumbfounded.

"What could I say?" There was pain and embarrassment in his brown eyes as well as sadness clouding his features. "Remember me, I'm the guy..." he hesitated before finishing his thought.

"Who broke up with me at a high school graduation party,"

Stella finished for him with a self-deprecating laugh. "Yeah," she wrinkled her pert nose at him. "I haven't let you live that down. I probably wouldn't have been friendly had you come up to me in Stockholm."

"I did go back a few days later," he admitted. "But you were done with the mural and gone by then."

"You know, maybe it's time for me to quit holding that against you. You were right. We were too young, and we both had big dreams. Maybe I held onto the anger for so long because it made it easier for me to dislike you."

"And now?" Erik's voice was deep and soft and wrapped around her body like smoke from a bonfire.

"Come on, Aunt Stella," Sam interrupted. "What's taking you so long to get your skates on? Coach Erik, everyone is waiting for you guys. There are a ton of people here to watch the game," she announced excitedly.

Erik clapped his hands onto his thighs. "Let's play some hockey."

The scrimmage went well and ended in a tie. About an hour later, Erik stood at the side of the rink chatting with Freya and Benji as the Rockets and the Bruins, their opponents, lined up for the traditional post game handshake.

Benji was pleased. "Hayden did okay, didn't he?"

Freya lightly smacked her husband on the arm. "He did better than okay, Benj. He stopped six shots. Hayden was good, wasn't he, Erik?"

Beaming with pride, Erik agreed. "He played well, and he has the fever."

Benji nodded. "I can see that. I was wrong to keep him from it." Exhaling forcefully, he announced. "We'll find some way of making hockey work with cross country skiing."

Pleased, Freya beamed. "Wave him over here. Let's tell him."

Catching sight of his parents gesturing to him, Hayden skated over.

Other parents moved about on the ice, taking pictures with their kids. Erik stayed where he was, leaning up against the boards, taking it all in. Coaching felt good, he decided.

Stella moved away from the group of parents she was chatting with and glided over to him. She looked so lovely she took his breath away.

"We tied!" she shouted euphorically.

"Next time, the Rockets win," Erik replied laconically.

"No, you don't understand," she gripped his forearm in her excitement. "We've lost every other scrimmage by at least five goals. This is the first time we haven't lost. That's why the kids are so excited! I know winning isn't everything, but not losing sure feels good."

"Winning feels even better. And Sam had a hat trick. She has some serious wheels. She's genuinely talented. In a couple of years, you and your sister-in-law will have to make a point of getting her seen by people who can advance her career."

"Oh, isn't it a little early for that?" Stella frowned.

"Yes, but time flies. Right now, she's doing exactly what she should be doing, having fun."

"Look how happy she is," Stella grinned, eyeing her niece who continued to buzz around the ice shooting pucks, beating imaginary opponents.

"Our work is done here tonight," Erik announced.

Stella glanced about. "I think all of the kids have connected with their parents. I don't see any Rockets left alone. I agree. I think we're done."

"Now what?" Erik asked.

"Well, I think most people are heading over to the winter carnival. There's cocoa and cookies, Christmas carolers, and a skating party."

"You game?" he winked at her.

"For what?" she replied.

"Would you go skating with me?" He grinned boyishly at her. "I remember going skating with you a few times back in high school. I mean unless you have to get Sam home?"

"No, Sam's with her mom." Stella gestured to where a dark-haired lady with a sweet face stood watching Sam and the other hockey players. Noticing Stella and Erik looking at her, Barb waved. "Actually, I think I'd like to go skating with you, Erik," Stella declared. "Let me put the pucks in my car."

"Great," Erik clapped his hands together. "I'll wait here for you. There's an ice trail over to the figure skating rink, so we should be able to skate right over to it."

Stella nodded and skated away, toward the warming house.

Leaning up against the boards, Erik waited for her, watching the interactions between the players and their families. A big man who was nearly eye to eye with Erik in height, significantly wider at the girth, with an impressive mustache, about ten to fifteen years older, and whose arm was held fixed in an arm brace approached him. "Hey there," he greeted Erik, walking carefully on the iced path.

"Hello," Erik answered. The man looked vaguely familiar, but he couldn't come up with a name.

"You Engen?" the other man prodded.

"I am."

"You did good with these kids. Doubt you remember me, but I'm Jim Severson," he stated.

"Hi, Jim. It's good to see you again." Erik spoke with

genuine warmth and held out his hand. Jim shook it with his good hand.

"You may not have recognized me right off because I've put on twenty or thirty." Jim patted his belly good naturedly. "My boy's Brady. Number ten on the Rockets. A bigger D-man. I was supposed to be the head coach, but I got hurt trying not to fall on a kid back during tryouts. I've felt terrible that I haven't been able to help Stella much. She's trying hard, and she's good with the kids, but..." he paused.

"...she doesn't know anything about hockey," Erik finished for him.

Jim nodded. "Which is why I'm grateful that the kids have had you for these past few practices. Brady has been super excited to come to practice lately, whereas he was kind of reluctant before. A couple of nights he even told me he'd rather be playing a video game with his buddies than come skating. Can you believe it! That's not like him at all. It's changed these two weeks because of you. I'm not putting down Miss Larson at all. She's done her best, but we all have our talents, and hockey has never been hers. I want to say thank you for taking the time for these kids. It's meant a lot to them."

"I've thoroughly enjoyed my time coaching the Rockets," Erik responded with sincerity. "They're good kids, and they're improving. They tied a game tonight. Hopefully, they'll win one soon. No big deal," Erik said.

"It is a big deal," Jim's eyes were suspiciously bright, "to Brady and those kids out here tonight." He cleared his throat. "Which is why I feel obligated to talk to you about another matter."

"Okay," Erik was curious where the conversation was going.

"I have to say my piece. You're a local hero, and your family employs a lot of people in this town. But that lady there, Miss Larson, she's a special girl, and she means a lot to our kids. I don't know what your intentions are, but if you plan to sweep her off her feet and out of Noelle, well, people won't take kindly to that. I sure won't."

Erik hesitated before answering. *What do I intend?* "I haven't asked Stella to leave town. We haven't even talked about the future."

Jim frowned, his handlebar mustache emphasizing the motion. "If you're just having fun with her while you're here, that's no good either."

"I know, and I agree, but we are both adults." Beginning to take some exception to the direction this discussion was going, Erik straightened to his full height and puffed out his substantial and impressive chest. "No offense, Jim, but why do you feel the need to tell me this?"

Jim shrugged and then flinched from the pain at his shoulder's motion. "Miss Larson has taught two of my children, and then she took on this hockey team when no one else would. She's a good person, and I don't think I'm the only one in town who wouldn't want you hurting her. Her folks aren't around, and her brother Bam Bam was a popular guy. We all kind of look out for her, Barb, and Sam."

For a moment, Erik bristled. He debated telling off the other man. Then he sighed. Jim was intruding, but his intentions were admirable. "I don't disagree with you, Jim. Stella is a special lady."

"Well, good." With his good hand, Jim clapped Erik's shoulder. "I'm glad we got that over with. I'm not one to interfere, but my wife, Anika, she has a nose for these things. She said you two have been making eyes at each other at every hockey practice. Anika's been driving Brady, you see. During practice, she sits in the car with the motor running and reads her romance novels. She wanted me to talk with you, man to man. Now because I've done it, I'll be in the good books with the wife. I was a little nervous coming over here. I've seen those YouTube videos of you fighting during hockey games, but I didn't think you'd hit a man in an arm brace," Jim remarked with jocularity.

"Excellent point," Erik agreed. "I wouldn't."

"You ready, Erik?" Stella asked, coming around the building. She had switched her hockey helmet for a black stocking cap with a furry pom pom. "Oh, hi Jim," she skated with her usual stiff kneed style over to Erik and Jim. Her eyes bright, she declared, "It was a good night for the Rockets, don't you think?"

"I'll say," Jim approved. "Nice chatting with you, Erik. I'll see you both around." He turned and shuffled back toward the warming house.

"What was that about?" Stella questioned, her eyes following Jim.

"He asked me my intentions."

Stella huffed. "You're kidding, right? About the factory?" she inquired, her forehead furrowing.

"No, about you." Erik linked his arm through hers as they made their way down the narrow path to the skating rink.

"What?" Stella froze, a blush rising in her cheeks. "You're joking, right?"

"No, actually it was kind of refreshing. Since I've been in Noelle, everyone I see asks me about the factory. Will we be cutting jobs or laying people off? I totally understand their concerns. Jim, on the other hand, addressed me about my intentions with respect to you. Apparently, most people in town are suspicious of me."

"Should we be?" Stella fidgeted with her scarf.

"Should you be what?"

"Suspicious of you?"

Erik lifted his chin. Evasively, he answered, "I want what's best for the company, for the factory, and for this town. But right now, I just want to skate with you." He grinned boyishly, taking her hand in his and weaving their fingers together. The two glided slowly along the light lined path to where it widened out into the skating rink.

For Stella, it was hard to concentrate on the mechanics of skating with his hand in hers. It was like every nerve cell in her being migrated to that connection between their hands, the awareness, the contact and the heat between them.

"Wow," she murmured breathlessly. "I haven't been out here lately. Most nights, I'm in such a hurry coming from school that I rush over to the hockey rink. I never take the time to look over here. I didn't know that they'd decorated this rink so much. I didn't expect it to be so beautiful."

"All of these decorations are new this week. You're seeing the finishing touches tonight. I've been checking the progress."

"I'd heard the Christmas Village is almost finished. Sam, Barb, and I went last year. It's pretty amazing, but so is this." She extended her arm wide to include the holiday scene spread out before them.

They paused in their progress to take it all in. The circular skating rink had white Christmas lights hung over it to resemble a circus tent. Red and white poles where the lights were suspended resembled peppermint sticks. Around the outside of the rink, beyond the banks of snow surrounding it, were assorted illuminated Christmas decorations, trees, gingerbread figures, Santa and his elves, and a colorful Christmas train. People were already skating around the oval accompanied by the Christmas carols sung by the Madrigal singers. An enormous bonfire around which more people were gathered crackled and sizzled off to the left of the band shell.

A young man dressed in Victorian apparel, including a top hat, a dark frock coat, and a plaid scarf, stepped to the front of the stage. In deep, dulcet tones that would have made Bing Crosby proud, he began to croon *White Christmas*. People who weren't skating hastened over to the front of the band shell to hear the performance. Some of the skaters moved into couples and began to glide over the ice together.

Erik squeezed Stella's hand. "Let's dance."

She leaned back away from him. "No, I can't keep up with you. I'm not a good skater. You know that."

"I'm not going to be speed skating out here."

"I don't know. All these people are good skaters. You should find a better partner. I'll watch."

"But you're the only person I want to skate with," he replied. He cast his eyes around the rink. He spied a small grouping of metal bottomed chairs set in the snow over by the Christmas train. "I have an idea." Leaving Stella, he skated over to the chairs, picked one up and then headed back across the rink to her. "Remember?" he asked, with a wide, easy grin.

"Oh yes, I remember."

"Sit down. Let me push you. The way we did when we were kids."

Not thinking, caught up in the magic of music, moonlight, Christmas, and Erik, Stella gave him her hand. Chivalrously, he led her to the chair. She sat down. He took up the position behind her with his hands on the back of the chair. Then, using his long, powerful stride, he began to push her around the rink. Her skates slid across the ice. Lights turned into streaks. Stella felt as if they were flying. After a few moments, she closed her eyes, savoring the feel of the wind in her face, the speed. It was exactly as she remembered it when as teenagers Stella and Erik had come to this same rink. Those were special memories and ones that she'd never expected to repeat so many years later. For Stella, this was one of those perfect life moments that come upon you unexpectedly and linger in your mind's eye, evoking a joyful feeling whenever they are recalled.

Finally, as the singer finished wishing everyone a white Christmas, Erik slowed down. He allowed the ice and his motion to carry the two of them over to the far end of the rink. Here he stopped, as did the movement of Stella's chair across the ice. Breathing heavily and resting his hands on his thighs, he leaned forward, toward her. His cheeks were ruddy from his exertion.

"My grandpa used to push me when I was learning to skate. I was a little nipper, like four or five, and he took me out on the pond behind the Lingonberry Lodge. That's how I got into skating. Grandpa was the first person who took me out on the ice. He was the one who got me into hockey. Wow, I'd forgotten that or never really thought about it. My dad's a great guy, but sports were never really his thing. Grandpa loved winter sports. It was what we did together, that and carve."

"I remember him," Stella commented. "I mean, I remember seeing him around town. He was from Norway, wasn't he? I think I always saw him wearing that big furry hat, the one that went down over his ears."

"Yes, he loved that hat. Grandpa came over from Norway as a teenager. He came here to work on the railroad," Erik explained. "Grandma was from Sweden. She'd come to the United States as a baby. Back then, in Noelle, the Swedes and the Norwegians didn't mix. Remember, the Norwegian Methodist and the Swedish Lutheran churches are across the street from each other. Grandma caught Grandpa's eye one day on the way out of church. He never did explain to me why he was checking out the Swedish girls coming out of church," Erik commented dryly. "But from that day forward, Grandma was the only one for him. I can remember him in his seventies looking up the staircase at the lodge at her. Grandma was irritated with him for some reason. But he just stood there gazing up at her, and he commented that he still couldn't believe how lucky he was to get her."

"Wow, that's incredibly romantic."

"That's how Engen men are. Once they meet the girl of their dreams, that's it. My dad was the same. He and my mother met in middle school, and they've been together ever since."

Stella didn't trust herself to reply.

He reached out and cupped her face in his hands. Then, ever so gently, ever so softly, he kissed her. Her eyes were still closed when he spoke again. "Stella, I want to be someone you can trust and believe in."

Stella considered his words and, listening to her heart, nodded slowly.

"Will you come with me to the Nutcracker Contest?" he asked with a serious mien.

She cocked her head, still befuddled by the power of that butterfly delicate kiss, surprised by this sudden turn in the conversation. "What?"

"I'd like it if you'd come with me to the Nutcracker Contest."

"What? Oh, that's right. You're the Grand Marshal this year. Are you judging the contest, or do you want me to judge?"

"No, a panel selects the winner, and I can't be on it. The nutcracker selected that night is the one featured by the Engen Ornaments for the holiday season. Haven't you ever been?"

"Years ago."

"There is a special reason I want you there," he gazed at her pensively. "Please tell me you'll come."

Slowly, because she was under his spell, she nodded again. "I had already planned on going. Every year, Barb, Sam and I usually go to the parade and then to the tree lighting in the square. The Nutcracker Contest is right after that. I'll be there. We could meet up."

"Good. There's something I want—"

"Aunty Stella! Coach!" A familiar youthful voice shattered the moment. Sam appeared, skating toward them. "That looks so awesome. Can you push me, too, Coach Erik?"

Seeing her niece's intrusion as a good time to get her unruly emotions in order, Stella stood up and moved away from the chair. "Do you mind, Erik?" she asked apologetically.

"Of course not," he replied gamely. "Hop on, Sam."

Erik zoomed Sam around the rink and then some of the other Rocket players as well. Finally, knowing that he was going to be sore the next day, he straightened up and skated over to where Stella remained chatting with some friends. A posse of hockey players trailed after him.

"Aw, come on, Coach," Connor of the chipmunk cheeks

and dirty blond bangs protested. "Can you push me one more time? No one goes as fast as you do."

"Yeah, you're awesome," Brady, Jim Severson's son, agreed.

"No, I'm done," Erik leaned back, stretching his back out. "I'm probably not going to be able to walk tomorrow. You kids take turns pushing each other."

Stella beamed watching Erik interact with her players.

Erik felt the sunny warmth of her smile all through him. The future and life in general seemed brighter and clearer to him. He stroked his bearded chin.

"You okay?" Stella asked, noting how he was favoring one side.

"I'm not used to skating this much. I haven't in years, and it's the old injury. Nothing an ice pack and some ibuprofen won't help."

Stella gestured to her companion, a coiffed, well-turned out, petite blond. "You remember Lauren Olson?"

Lauren beamed at him. "You probably don't. I was a few years ahead of you two in high school."

"Nice to see you," Erik replied, having no idea of who she was.

"My son Luke is on the Rockets. He's been over the moon about having you as a coach."

"Thanks. He's a great kid," Erik agreed automatically, his eyes on Stella.

Aware of the electricity in the air, Lauren glanced between Stella and Erik. "Well, thanks again. Stella, I'll see you soon, and Erik, I hope to see you at future practices."

"I plan on helping out with the team as much as I can," he responded.

Stella glanced at him in surprise. "I'll see you, Lauren," she replied hastily. "Really, Erik? You plan on helping out with the team more?"

"Of course, it's fun. I'm enjoying it. The kids are a blast. I'll help out for as long as I'm in town."

"Oh," Stella echoed. "For as long as you're in town," she echoed. *How long are you planning on staying in town?*

Placing his fists on the small of his back, Erik straightened up in a gingerly fashion. "Wow, am I out of skating shape." He grinned even as he grimaced at the ache.

"You look super fit," Stella pointed out. "And the beard is nice. Impressive even."

In bemusement, Erik stroked it again. "I'm growing it out for Sam. She wants me to look like Paul Bunyan, but it's definitely starting to grow on me, too."

"It's a good look for you."

"I'm glad you think so." He winked at her. "I've always enjoyed hitting the gym. It's good for the mind and the body. But skating fit is different. Different muscles than benching or squatting or even running. Do you still run?"

"A couple days a week," Stella answered, blowing some hair out of her eyes. "I love that quiet time in the morning, but it's tough to get up and get going the morning after an evening hockey practice with the kids. My bed will feel divine at six tomorrow morning."

Glancing down at his watch, Erik groaned. "Wow, it's almost nine. Stella, I have to get going," he informed her regretfully.

"Why? Are you that sore?" she questioned.

"No, it's not that. It's just I have a project I have to finish back at the factory."

"Now? Tonight?" she challenged incredulously.

"I do have to go," he explained. "There's not much time left."

"For what?"

Erik exhaled. "I can't tell you yet. There are a couple of projects I'm working on at the factory. You'll see soon, I promise. But I have to go now."

Stella considered. "Okay. Well, I guess I'll see you later."

"At the Nutcracker Contest?" Erik asserted. "We have a date?"

She nodded.

He took her hand once more. "I had fun tonight," he told her, squeezing her hand.

"Me too."

"Good night."

"To you, too." Nonplussed, Stella watched as Erik skated the trail that led back to the warming house.

"He was in a hurry," Lauren commented, arriving back at Stella's side as Erik vanished behind the closed door of the warming house. "What was that all about?" she queried, her pretty features bright with curiosity.

Feeling somewhat bereft, Stella shook her head. "I have no idea. I guess he has a lot of work to do before he leaves town." The thought made her sad. With sudden clarity, she realized she was falling for Erik Engen. Again. *Fool me once,* she censured herself. Even though she'd sworn countless times that it wouldn't, it had happened again. For the second time in her life, she was faced with Erik Engen heading out of town with her heart in his back pocket.

CHAPTER 8

Erik used his company badge to get into the factory and disarm the alarm. Walking briskly down the darkened hallways, he headed immediately to his grandfather's workshop where he unlocked the door and flicked on the lights. He had told Darius, Miranda, and all the other employees that the workshop was completely off limits for the time being. He headed over to the worktable where a throw cloth covered his creation, the reason he'd reluctantly left Stella's side this evening.

He gently lifted the cloth off and studied his nutcracker, running his hands gently over her carved features. The figurine he'd dubbed *Princess Inga* was still rough, nowhere near finished. Tonight, he planned to complete the carving. Tomorrow, he'd work on the textures and fine details. He'd paint her on the actual day of the Nutcracker Contest, the twenty-second of December, now only two days away. He fully intended to have his Inga decorated and ready for that contest.

Erik wanted to shout his feelings for Stella from the

rooftops. This nutcracker was his love reveal or proclamation to her. He nervously anticipated her reaction when Princess Inga was projected up onto the big screens during the contest. *Stella will understand my message. Artist to artist, she will get it. When you recreate your beloved's face in any medium, you're telling the world what that person means to you.* Erik had always been a go big or go home person. Stella was a part of the fabric of Noelle. He understood that loving her meant returning and rejoining the life he'd once left behind in this town. *For Stella, I'm more than ready to come back to Noelle*, he realized. He hoped and prayed her feelings were the same.

He examined the face of the figurine. In her features, he'd sought to capture Stella's, as well as he could express her delicate and lovely facial characteristics in wood. True, he was rusty as a carver, and he'd had to relearn skills he'd learned a lifetime ago, but what he'd lacked in proficiency he'd made up for in effort and commitment. To his eyes, Princess Inga was a beautiful nutcracker, inspired by one of the images in Stella's mural. He had carved Inga in her winter gear, wearing a cloak with an embroidered red dress beneath it. One long, blond braid hung in front of her shoulder, and the other, behind it, as she carried Prince Haakon strapped to her back. Her face was unmistakably Stella's. Her expression was strong, stern, and resolute as she fled her son's enemies, seeking to carry him to safety. Erik was well pleased with the nutcracker. She was pretty much how he had envisioned her. Now he wondered *how will Stella see her. How will she interpret his gesture?* Erik ran his thumb along the smooth wood of the nutcracker's skis. He wasn't entirely sure of how things would work, but somehow, he seemed to have chosen a new life path these past few days, one which led him back to Noelle, back to

Stella. The next few days would prove whether she felt the same.

Finally, a few hours later, having finished the night's work, knowing that he was exhausted, and that the next two days promised to be action packed, Erik turned off the workroom lights and headed home.

The next morning, on six hours of sleep but with a steady and resolved heart, Erik showered, dressed, had some coffee, and then headed straight to another marathon planning session with Darius. To this point, they hadn't yet shared their plan for the Nutcracker Factory with the rest of the staff, and most of the employees continued to regard him with suspicion and skepticism.

"What's with the long faces?" he questioned Darius on returning from the break room where he again encountered cool stares. In addition, all conversations ground to a halt as soon as he'd entered the room to get a cup of coffee.

Darius chuckled grimly, rubbing his hands together. "What do you expect? Everyone is sure you're going to shut us down or fire people right before the holidays. You swore me to secrecy, and I'm a man of my word. But as I told you before, you must tell them something, or they're going to assume the worst. Everyone's been all over me, asking me what I know. I've been a vault. I know you're planning a happy surprise for the employees and for the town, but you have to have some mercy. I've warned you, everyone is imagining the worst possible scenarios, and you don't want people to be worrying about job security right before Christmas."

Erik nodded slowly while pressing his fingertips to his forehead. "Maybe keeping all of this secret wasn't the best plan."

"The problem is we are now right before Christmas, and everyone is amped up. All the employees know it is the most important time of the year for the factory. Rumors are flying around. I walked in on a discussion over by the pop machine that there won't be any jobs listed anywhere until after the New Year's holiday. People are genuinely concerned about finding work if they get laid off. They're also worrying about whether they are going to have to sell their houses if they lose their jobs. You should put their minds at ease. This is a small town. The Nutcracker Factory is a big employer and a source of pride."

Erik ran his fingers through his hair. "You're right. I should have been more transparent, but I wasn't sure about our strategy until now. Then I wanted to make this a good surprise." He snapped his fingers. "Here's what we'll do. We'll make the announcement and provide an explanation for employees on the twenty-third. We'll also craft a press release sharing the same information to go out at exactly nine o'clock on the twenty-third before the holiday break."

Darius pointed his pen at Erik. "You mean you're making the announcement at the ball, after the Nutcracker Contest and the parade?"

"Exactly," Erik rose to his feet in his excitement. He began to pace around the room. "You know the annual board meeting is right before the ball. I've kept in close contact with the board members through this process. I'm confident our plan will be approved. After the vote, we'll make the announcement of the new vision for the Nutcracker Factory in front of the employees and the board. Then the message will go out to everyone else, the shareholders, any employees not there, and to the press. The press release will explain our plan to everyone. Employees will get an extra email that will include information about their Christmas bonuses which we're going to increase to ten percent of salary for this year."

Darius whistled in appreciation. "Ten percent. That's very generous."

"We've done well this year, and this plan will demand even more of our employees and this town. We have our work cut out for us."

The remaining endless days of work finally passed. The day Erik had longed for, December twenty-second, the day of the Noelle Nutcracker Contest had arrived. He could feel the excitement and Christmas spirit building in Noelle all day long wherever he went. His plan was in place. His nutcracker was ready. There wasn't anything left for him to do, so he restlessly roamed about town. Christmas carols played from every shop. The holiday spirit was contagious, and, despite his rising stress levels concerning Stella and how the Engen Ornaments board and the town would react to the changes he was proposing, Erik found himself humming along with *Jingle Bells* while waiting for his coffee at the Roasted Bean Coffee House. Tonight, his Inga would be revealed as well as his feelings for Stella.

Later that afternoon, after waiting until everyone else had left the factory, Erik crept into his grandfather's workshop. He wrapped his nutcracker in a soft cloth and spirited her out of the building and down into the square. Outside, the night sky was already dark. In contrast, the square was well-lit with countless Christmas decorations and lights. Erik could hear the winter parade forming a few streets over, but the square remained essentially empty. It wouldn't fill until after the parade. Occasionally, he glimpsed the flashing lights of a decorated city work vehicle passing by, but he figured he had time to accomplish his task. The parade would end here, so police had cordoned off all parking areas. He saw ice sculpting teams working to bring their visions to fruition on the opposite, flood-lit side of the square. He figured they were too focused on what they were doing to pay attention to him.

Sticking to the shadows, he hastened down the street. Feeling like he was going to be *caught* at any moment by someone who recognized him, he paused just beyond the soft glow of a LED streetlight. Peering through the occasional snowflakes which were beginning to fall, he gazed at the Nutcracker Factory's still curtained display window. He considered the spectacle which was to be revealed as the culminating event of tomorrow evening's festivities, the Nutcracker Ball. He, Miranda, and Darius and a crew of creatives, all of whom were sworn to secrecy, had worked on the display in marathon sessions. It was complete now except for this year's winning nutcracker, which would be selected in an hour or so.

Erik hastened to the small parking lot across from the factory. The road between the lot and the factory was fully cordoned off here to save space for the soon-to-arrive winter revelers. Workers had spent the day assembling a raised stage with three enormous screens mounted behind it, so that everyone in the square could see what was happening. In front of the stage, in an enclosure surrounded by red velour ropes and stanchions, were waist high stands decorated like candy canes upon which the nutcrackers entered in the contest sat. A sparkly red cloth covered each nutcracker. Locating an empty stand was Erik's current objective.

Entries into the Engen Nutcracker Contest were meant to be anonymous. Artists and carvers had the day to put their creations on the stands and cover them up until the evening's reveal. It was part of the magic of Noelle and of the Christmas season. The contest had never been marred by someone trying to steal or deface one of the creations. Still, for the past five years or so, the factory had discretely posted a guard in the general vicinity of the contest entrants. Erik glanced around but didn't see the security guard in sight.

Most of the stands were already taken. Each nutcracker remained covered with a cloth trimmed with silver words that read, *Engen Nutcrackers-Celebrating the Most Wonderful Time of the Year.* Erik noticed an empty stand at the back of the grouping, in a darker corner and to the left of the stage. Setting his nutcracker carefully on the ground, he bent down under the rope and was making a beeline for the stand when he felt a gentle tap on his shoulder.

Darn, he thought, though he didn't say a word.

"Can I help you?" A blond, beefy security guard in his early twenties whom Erik couldn't recall having met stood facing him.

How come I didn't see him? "I want to set up my nutcracker up for the contest," he explained, gesturing at his little statue.

"You have to actually enter those in the contest. It's new this year."

Why didn't Darius or Miranda think to tell me that? Erik wondered.

"The lady taking the entries should be back any minute. But I can't let you back here. Please take your nutcracker and leave this area. It's off limits right now. The contest is starting in a half hour. You're too late to enter one. Maybe next year."

Erik was too close to an important moment to have it foiled by him not knowing some rule minutia and a well-intentioned security guard. "It shouldn't be a problem." He pivoted and picked up the empty stand to move it to where the other nutcrackers were already set up. He had so wanted Inga's creator, himself, to be an anonymous participant in the contest. The last thing he needed was an overzealous security guard.

"Sir, please take your hand off the nutcracker stand. I don't want a problem," the security officer declared, "but I have my orders. Some of these nutcrackers are real valuable. I can't let anyone mess around with them. Miss Fedie laid down the law before she left me in charge and headed off to watch the parade," the young man stated.

Erik nodded. "I understand, and I appreciate your devotion to your job. I simply want to add my nutcracker to the entrants. I won't touch any of the others that are here. You can watch me. Then I'll be on my way."

"I'm sorry, man, but I can't let anyone touch anything here. Orders are orders."

"Officer," Erik peered at the security officer's name tag. "Johnson, I have no sinister intent. I simply want to add a nutcracker to the contest, without anyone knowing it's mine."

"Everyone has to register with Ms. Fedie. Those are the rules," Officer Johnson shook his buzz cut head. "Can't have any monkey business on my watch."

Time was passing. For his plan to work, Erik needed to get his nutcracker on a stand now. "I promise there won't be any issues with me or with this nutcracker." He held up his opened hands. "I merely want to leave it here."

"No can do," Officer Johnson replied self-righteously. He looked Erik up and down and apparently decided the bigger man was more than he wanted to take on alone. "You need to get out of this off-limits area, or I'm going to call for assistance."

Erik smothered a groan as Officer Johnson reached for his walkie-talkie. "Stu, you want to come join me down by the nutcrackers? I may have a situation. We may need additional back up. He's a big one."

"Sure," a voice squawked back. "I'll be right there."

"What's going on here?" trilled a familiar, soprano voice from across the street. Miranda Fedie, a Mother Christmas vision in a long red and white Christmas coat with the hood pulled up over her red hair, bustled across the road to where Erik and the young guard stood at an impasse.

"This guy wanted to put something out on a stand," Officer Johnson gestured at Erik. He held up his walkie talkie. "I told him he had to submit an entry and that he was too late. He wouldn't listen, so I called Stu for back up."

Taking in the situation, Miranda clapped her hands together. Her elaborate, gold cat's eye glass frames reflected the light. "Oh Erik," she laughed. "We forgot to tell you about the entry process. I'm so sorry. We had it posted in the lobby at the factory."

"You know him?" Officer Johnson asked.

A heavy-set older man, also wearing a security guard's uniform and running heavily on stiff knees, burst into the scene. Panting heavily, he put his hands on his hips and leaned over. "What's the problem here? Ms. Fedie, Mr. Engen," he straightened immediately. "What's going on, Adam?" he questioned. "Where's our problem?"

"Evening, Stu," Erik replied.

The young officer's eyes flicked between Erik, Miranda, and Stu.

"Oh Erik," Miranda laughed. "You are the problem?"

Erik nodded his head.

"Adam, this is your boss, Erik Engen," Stu explained, gesturing at each person as he introduced them. "Mr. Engen, this is Adam Johnson, our newest and overly eager member of the security staff. Adam joined us this week. He just finished training. I guess you two haven't met yet."

"You're Mr. Engen?" Adam, the young security officer lamented. "Oh man, I'm sorry. My orders were to watch the nutcrackers and not let anyone mess with them. I was doing what Ms. Fedie told me to do. I'm so sorry."

"I appreciate your commitment. No harm done." Erik held out his hand and shook the young security officer's hand. "You were doing your job. It's my own fault I was trying to be all mysterious. I wanted to add this nutcracker before anyone came over here." Sheepishly, he reached down to pick up his Inga.

"Sweet boy," Miranda exclaimed, clasping her hands. "Ole would be so proud. I suspected as much when I heard that the lights had been on late in Mr. Engen's workshop." She waggled her finger at him. "Can I see it?"

Erik shook his head and adjusted the cloth covering the nutcracker. He grinned boyishly. "I mean, not yet. Not while I'm standing here. You're welcome to peak at her when I walk away, but please don't share with any of the judges that she's mine."

"*Mums* the word," Miranda raised one, long, silver sparkle tipped fingernail to her lips. "You know, as an Engen family member, I don't think you can win. It may be against the rules. I'll have to check and let you know."

"It doesn't really matter if I win or not. I merely want my nutcracker revealed to everyone tonight. I want her shown on those big screens up there for everyone to see." *For Stella to see.* "If I recall correctly, the rules state anyone can enter the contest, but only non-family members can win the prize money." Fearing the impending arrival of more people, Erik glanced around the square. *The coast is still clear.* But he could hear the parade with its accompanying music getting closer. "Would you please enter this nutcracker in the contest for me?" He gently extended his nutcracker toward Miranda.

She took the figure carefully in her hands. "What's it called?"

"Her name is Princess Inga," Erik replied. "As I said, I don't want anyone to know she's mine. I want her to be judged on her own merit."

"We have the option to leave the artist's name blank on the entry form, Erik. We assign your nutcracker a number for identification. That's what we used to do with all the nutcrackers. Now some of the artists appreciate having their names recognized with their works, for promotional purposes. That's why we changed things up this year."

"Assign her a number. That's a good plan. I have to go," Erik murmured, his eyes, scanning the square. "Thank you all. Stu, good to see you again. Adam, nice to meet you, and welcome aboard. I'll be going now. I have some plans for the parade. I can't miss the start."

"Oh, you have a good half hour until the parade, Mr. Engen," Stu said. "They pushed the whole thing back so that it's completely dark. They want folks to be able to see the Christmas lights on the floats."

"Good to know," Erik replied. "That's helpful." Relieved, he turned, nearly jogging in his eagerness to leave the vicinity of the Nutcracker Contest before anyone else observed or recognized him

"What's gotten into him?" Stu asked, gesturing at Erik with his thumb. "The boss is awfully jumpy tonight."

"A woman," Miranda nodded wisely, clasping her hands before her. "His woman. The one that got away. Although I think he may be trying to make things right this time around. Tonight's contest should be very interesting."

With the rest of the gathered masses, Stella and Jayda stood on a rise alongside the road which passed from Walker Park to Sibelius Square in downtown Noelle. Stella had gotten there early to hold the spot so they could get a good view of the parade scheduled to pass directly by them. In addition, they were strategically positioned opposite the line of trees that were to be illuminated right before the start of the parade in honor of the holiday season. It was a spot that never failed to capture the essence of Noelle's holiday festivities.

Jayda had a well-bundled Lyrique strapped to her back in a baby backpack. The toddler's eyes were huge and bright with excitement because of the people milling about, the music, and the lights.

"I don't know what to make of him," Stella lamented to her friend. "Erik's saying and doing the right things. He's diligent about helping at hockey practice with Sam and Hayden and the other Rockets, and he's an excellent coach. He's super fun to be with, but then he always has been. The thing is," Stella worried her lower lip with her teeth, "he's been preoccupied. I've noticed it. The factory is on his mind, but I'm afraid to ask what's bothering him. I don't want him to be the villain in this story."

"I know he's been working long hours," Jayda acknowledged. "Darius has been, too. There are big plans in the works for the Nutcracker Factory. Indeed, for the whole town. Darius won't tell me a thing, but I think things are going to be okay. Positive signs are there." Jayda gestured with her hands. "Darius seems anxious and overworked, but also excited and happy. If they were thinking about shutting down the factory or laying people off, Darius would be miserable and unable to hide it from me. I truly believe the factory and the town will be fine. But what about you? I know Erik is good with kids, pleasant and charming with everyone, but how has he been with you?" she probed pointedly.

Stella blushed, looking down and away from her friend.

"Oh, girl, you have it bad," Jayda pronounced. "He's been in town for what? A few weeks and he already has you wrapped around his little finger? You never got over him, did you?" Lyrique began to move about restlessly, so her mother swayed from side to side to settle the child. "You deserve happiness, Stella," Jayda stated. "You're always doing for other people. It's time to think about yourself. What do you want?"

Magically and without warning, the white lights came on, illuminating the maple and elm trees opposite them. As one, the gathered crowd oohed and aahed.

Jayda gripped Lyrique's mittened hand. "Will you look at that, honey? How pretty." The little girl kicked and squealed as *A Holly Jolly Christmas* rang out from mounted speakers lining the street.

This was the signal for the Winter Parade to begin. A fire truck aglow with Christmas lights was the lead-off vehicle. Illuminated floats of all sizes and shapes followed that truck.

Other city vehicles were interspersed between the various club and team floats.

Stella cheered especially loud when she saw Noelle's city Zamboni accompanied by hordes of jersey-wearing hockey players of all shapes and sizes as well as their beaming moms and dads pass by. Many of the kids were wearing light up necklaces or waving glow sticks.

"Look! Look! There are the Rockets. There she is! There's Sam! Hi Barb! Hey Sam!" Stella waved her hand frantically.

Barb grinned and waved back. Sam did, too, with both hands. The girl was beaming.

Stella found herself a little choked up and teary eyed. It was wonderful to see Barb and Sam happy and having fun. They would never recover from losing Elias, but it seemed they were beginning to heal a little. She watched Sam and Barb until they disappeared. Following the hockey players came the Shriners, zooming about in their miniature cars. After them came the city curling league members. They wore ugly Christmas sweaters with Santa hats and carried buckets from which they tossed fistfuls of candy into the crowd.

The parade went on and on. It was brilliantly lit, magical, and seasonal. Truly enjoying sharing this experience with her daughter and her friend, Jayda clasped her hands. Beaming, she turned to Stella. "Could it be any nicer out here? The weather is perfect. What a wonderful night." Stella didn't respond, so Jayda turned to check on her friend.

Stella remained somewhat withdrawn and distracted, likely preoccupied with thoughts of Erik. Jayda wanted Stella to share her enthusiasm for the evening. She squeezed her friend's arm. "Stella, come on. You need to get into it. Usually, you're the one counting down until Christmas. What's the problem?"

Stella didn't reply right away. She wanted to be as happy and joyful as Jayda and seemingly everyone else around her. After all, she loved Christmas, the anticipation, the music, the cookies, the giving. She loved the buildup at school and in town with the festival. It was without a doubt her favorite time of the year.

"Stella, you're my best friend, and you know I call things as I see them. You've fallen for Erik Engen again, haven't you?"

Stella rubbed at the back of her neck. "I don't know. It's all so complicated. What happens when the holidays are over, and he heads out of town again? Do you have any idea how awful it is being the one left behind?"

No longer watching the parade that continued to roll by, Jayda put a hand on her hip. "Stella, have you asked him that question?

"To be honest, no," she finished lamely.

"It seems to me that's where you need to start. You've never been afraid of *courageous conversations*. We have them all of the time at school, and you are one of the first people to speak up."

"I know," Stella admitted, lowering her chin. "This feels different."

"Because it involves your heart, right?"

"You got it."

"Will you take a look at that," Jayda exhaled through pursed lips.

"What? What are you talking about?" Stella demanded, her eyes on her friend's face.

Following Jayda's gaze, she turned.

A horse drawn carriage was advancing down the road toward them. An enormous pair of Belgian horses with antlers attached to their bridles pulled it. Evergreen boughs, red ribbons, and colorful lights adorned the white carriage. The sign on the carriage doors displayed the Engen Ornaments logo of a traditional nutcracker prince against a red and blue background. Sitting behind the driver in the back seat of the carriage, dressed in black with a Noelle Nutcracker Factory ski cap, was Erik Engen.

The carriage pulled up directly in front of Stella and Jayda, and there the driver stopped, halting the progress of the entire parade. No one protested or hurried the carriage along. Clearly, the moment was planned. Erik opened the carriage door and stepped down. He was smiling, his gaze fixed on Stella. He headed straight for her.

"Will you look at that," Jayda breathed. "How romantic. Like in a fairy tale."

Erik held out his hand to Stella. "Will you ride with me?"

Stella was too dumbfounded to reply. Jayda pushed her a little in Erik's direction. Stella stumbled forward.

"Oh my gosh, is he going to propose?" someone called out.

Another person started chanting, "Pro-pose. Pro-pose." The crowd joined in and accompanied the chant with clapping.

"Come on, lady," the Cub Scout leader called from the float behind Erik's carriage. "Get on the carriage so we can get moving. You're holding things up."

Erik didn't falter or waiver. He simply waited for Stella's hand. When she took his, the crowd applauded.

"Where are we going?" she asked him.

"To the square. Will you ride with me?

"I'd planned on going there after the parade for the Nutcracker Contest," she finished lamely. *What is wrong with me? Why can't I think straight?* "You're not going to, are you?" she whispered to him.

"What?"

"Propose. Right here and right now?" Her voice had an edge of panic to it.

He laughed out loud. "No, I just wanted to impress you, sweep you off your feet, and ask you to go for a carriage ride with me. Isn't it every girl's dream to be swept away in a horse drawn carriage or to be in a parade in a horse drawn carriage? I figured one of those options would appeal to you. I am trying to be romantic." He winked at her.

"You're one hundred percent right. I mean, yes, I would love to ride in the parade with you." She turned back to her friend. "Jayda, are you and Lyrique all right if I go with Erik?"

"Girl, we're fine! You have fun!" Jayda whooped as Stella took Erik's arm, and he led her back to the carriage. Once there, he handed her up into the seat as the crowd around them continued to go wild.

Once both Stella and Erik were safely ensconced on the plush, red cushions, the driver clucked his horses on. The seat was snug, and Stella was aware of every inch of Erik's warm, long frame pressed against her own. He gently laid a blanket over her knees. Then he leaned back, and their shoulders bumped. She giggled nervously. There wasn't quite enough room for their shoulders with both of them sitting upright and straight, but then Erik linked his arm with Stella's, and she sort of curved into him. Nestled together, they both settled comfortably back into the cushions.

Stella waved at Jayda as the carriage started to move off. "I'm impressed, Erik Engen. This is quite the grand gesture," she observed.

Erik chuckled, and Stella felt the sound vibrate through his body. "I remember you telling me I didn't have romantic bone in my body back in high school."

Stella waved at some students who were shouting her name. "You didn't. I gave you your Valentine a day early so that you would have a heads up to get one for me."

"There's a bucket of candy by your feet. You can throw some to your students," Erik directed. He reached down and got his own bucket which was overflowing with Double Bubble bubblegum. "I'd like to believe that I've improved with age, like a good brandy. I have some plans for us tonight. I hope it's all right that I sort of swept you away?"

"No, it's better than all right," Stella beamed. "I feel like royalty, and I'm all yours for this evening." She continued to throw candy and wave at the crowd assembled along the road. "Like everyone else in town, I want to see where you're going with this."

"Well, as you agreed to at practice the other night, we're going to the Nutcracker Contest first."

"Oh, great," Stella replied. "I love seeing all the new nutcracker designs. I thought you'd forgotten about asking me to go to the contest. I didn't hear anything from you after that practice. You didn't even text me."

"I was pretty confident you'd be here, and I wanted to surprise you."

"You succeeded."

The float ahead of them began to play *We Wish You a Merry Christmas*, and the crowd joined in, drowning out Erik's and Stella's voices. Mutually content it seemed with not speaking, the two of them leaned even closer together, both enjoying the shared intimacy of this moment on a carriage in front of the entire town of Noelle.

The parade followed along Hans Christian Anderson Street and then turned a sharp left into the Sibelius Square. The area of the Nutcracker Contest, where forty minutes before Erik had spoken with Miranda and the two guards, was now brilliantly lit and filled with parade goers.

The parade route continued around the square, past the store fronts as well as the ice sculptures, cheerfully illuminated in rainbows of bright colors. Finally, Erik's and Stella's carriage pulled off the parade route and stopped on a side road next to the Nutcracker Factory. The two of them disembarked from the carriage, and Erik thanked the driver. Arm-in-arm, they headed along a side road to join the throngs of people going to the Nutcracker Contest. It was clear that the event had remained and even grown in popularity since Erik had last attended. The seating was already filling up in front of the stage. They followed the now milling crowd to the back row of chairs where they found seats.

More than five hundred chairs were set up in front of the stage, and more people were standing or wandering between the contest and the ice sculptures. Feeling a little nervous now, Erik adjusted his knitted, ivory turtleneck around his neck. *Everyone in town will know how I feel about Stella after seeing my Inga. Maybe I should have chosen a slightly less public venue for sharing my feelings with her. What if she doesn't reciprocate them?* He darted a gaze at Stella, and she raised an eyebrow at him curiously.

She leaned over to Erik. On the fresh winter breeze, she caught a whiff of his cologne, a smoky, spicy fragrance. It was something she'd always remembered about him, even back in high school. He'd always smelled so good. Very few of the other guys she'd dated had successfully competed with him in the cologne department. The guy had good taste, and he enjoyed nice scents, as evidenced by the Jicky that he'd brought her and his own cologne selections.

She studied his rugged profile, the pronounced brow, the slightly hooked nose, and his sensually full lips. She remembered doing the exact same thing while reading *Macbeth* in eleventh grade English class. He'd sat a row ahead of her and a seat over. Even now, she remembered trying to catch a whiff of his cologne. Like most teenage boys, he hadn't known to wear it subtly. Stella recalled spending most of that semester of English class mooning over his profile and his cologne. She certainly didn't remember anything they'd studied in that class.

Over the years and through countless hockey games and probably a few fights, the nose was no longer straight. There was distinct hump to it. There were also some scars and lines around his eyes, but something else almost indefinable had changed. Erik had always been intense, and now, to Stella's eyes, it appeared that he had eased up a little. He was more relaxed, more comfortable in his skin, perhaps a little less driven. She sought a word to describe the change she saw in him. What came to mind was content. Erik looked content with his life, no longer rushing toward some distant ambition.

"I thought you were supposed to be announcing the winner," Stella whispered to him. "Shouldn't you be up there? I'm fine here by myself. Don't worry."

"I thought it might be a conflict of interest, so I recused myself." Erik replied, smacking his leather gloves lightly in the palm of his hand.

"Well, hello Erik, Ms. Larson," Freya accompanied by Benji, Hayden, and the twins had appeared at the end of their line of chairs. Erik's sister's eyes were bright with curiosity. "It looks like there are enough seats in your row for all of us. Can we join you?"

"Freya, wouldn't you rather sit closer to the front, so that the kids can see better?" Erik prompted, not wanting his sister's overly shrewd eyes on him for what was about to happen.

"No, this is perfect," Freya replied, smiling sweetly at her brother. "Would you mind, Stella?"

"Of course not," she answered. "Hello Hayden, Hazel, and Felix."

"Hi, Miss Larson," Hayden replied. Stella waved, and a more disgruntled looking Felix, who was sucking his thumb, nodded a greeting to her.

Erik scowled at his sister which Freya ignored. He stood up so his sister's family could pass in front of them in the row. To her amusement, Stella thought Erik's mulish expression resembled Felix's.

Freya made sure to elbow her brother lightly as she passed him.

"I kind of wanted to have a moment alone with Stella," he muttered to Freya.

"I know," Freya replied with a chuckle. "You're out of luck. By the way, we need to save room for two more."

Feeling a sense of foreboding, a frowning Erik demanded, "Who else is coming?"

"We're here!" A distinguished looking, well dressed older couple appeared at the end of the row. The man was about six feet tall with a lean and craggy face that strongly resembled Erik's. He wore a long, black, winter overcoat with a gray, wool Herringbone hat with ear flaps. The woman was almost as tall as her husband, elegant and thin in a buff, full length cashmere coat with a faux fur collar. She sported a sleek blond bob and carefully made-up features. She was beaming with delight and waving frantically at the children.

Erik nearly groaned in dismay. *Not tonight.*

Felix and Hazel squealed on seeing the new arrivals. The two pushed aside the chairs and leaped into their grandparents' arms.

The heavily pregnant Freya followed a bit more slowly. "Mom! Dad! You made it! You should have called when you got to the airport."

"We didn't want to bother you. We weren't sure we would make it in time," Oliver Engen explained. "The whole thing was very last minute."

"We left the cruise early and caught a flight to Miami," Meg Engen exclaimed, hugging Felix tightly to her.

Oliver Engen had both Hazel and Hayden wrapped up in his arms. He looked equally pleased with the situation.

Erik stepped forward. "Dad... Mom. I ah—"

"Now, son," Erik interrupted with a raised hand. "We know you have everything with the festival and the factory well in hand. We didn't come because we doubted your ability or your plan."

"The truth is your father couldn't handle missing Christmas in Noelle," Meg finished. "Nor could I," she admitted. "The cruise was lovely. The islands of the Caribbean are magnificent, but you need snow and family for Christmas."

"That's exactly right," Oliver agreed, nodding. "I know we said we'd stay away, but we couldn't do it. We won't step on your toes, Erik. That's quite a beard you have there, son," he observed.

"I think you look handsome," Meg approved. "It's so thick and dark. You look like a pirate. Perhaps you should get it shaped a little, then it would look especially nice."

"Dad, Mom, I'm glad you're here." Erik hugged first his

mother and then his father. Benji stepped forward to greet his in-laws.

"We couldn't miss this," Oliver murmured, raising his eyebrows to his wife. She nodded in tacit agreement. "It makes me feel like a kid to see all of the new nutcracker designs," he explained.

Meg nodded. "Though I'm not a big fan of the modern looking ones. I prefer the ones done in the traditional style."

Freya cleared her throat. "Oliver and Meg, I think you may remember Stella Larson." She gently pressed Stella forward.

"She's our art teacher," Felix explained.

"And my hockey coach," Hayden offered excitedly. "I'm a goalie now, just like Uncle Erik."

"Really?" Meg asked, raising one artfully crafted eyebrow and darting a glance at her son. "She's all that?"

Erik cleared his throat.

"You're playing hockey?" Oliver asked Hayden. "Isn't that something?"

Hayden radiated joy.

"I'm going to play hockey, too," Hazel inserted, eager to get back her share of grand parental attention.

"It sounds like there has been quite a lot happening up here," Oliver declared.

"It's good to see you both," Stella shook hands with Freya's and Erik's parents. "I don't know if you remember me."

Oliver and Meg exchanged another expressive glance.

"Of course, we remember you, Stella," Meg said, giving her a kiss on both cheeks in the European style. "Freya has been filling us in on all of the news from town, so of course your name came up."

"I'm sure it did," Erik muttered to his sister.

Looking like the cat that ate the canary, Freya grinned back at him.

"Aunt Stella... Aunt Stella, can we sit with you, please?" Sam appeared, having darted through the crowd upon catching sight of her aunt.

Barb, Sam's mom, followed her daughter. She had curly dark hair, a rounded figure, bright, sparkly eyes, and an amused expression. Having caught sight of the one remaining chair at the end of their row, she cupped her mouth and called out to Stella. "Do you mind if we join you?" she asked, referring to herself and her daughter. "Sam wanted to sit with you and Hayden."

"I'm not sure there's room," Stella began as she looked down the row of seats.

Hayden immediately replied. "We can share a seat. I'll scoot over," he offered Sam, moving over.

"Of course, Barb," Stella drew her to the chair beside her as the Webers and the Engens accommodatingly moved down an additional seat. "You know everyone here, right?"

Barb nodded and waved a greeting to Erik, Freya, Benji, their children as well as to Oliver and Meg Engen.

"We are about to begin our annual Nutcracker Reveal and Contest, so if everyone could please take their seats. We want everyone to be able to see this season's creations." From the stage, Miranda Fedie's clarion tones rang out over the assembled crowd. The large screens behind her flickered to life, offering a blown-up, larger-than-life view of the proceedings. As Miranda turned to her attendants on the stage, the audience could hear her directing them to *Please turn down the Christmas music.*

She waited until the entire crowd, including Erik, Stella, Freya, and everyone else had settled. At that point, Miranda raised the microphone to her bright red lips. "The town of Noelle and the Engen Nutcracker Factory would like to welcome all of you to our thirty-third annual Nutcracker Reveal and Contest."

The crowd exploded with applause and cheers.

Miranda smiled and waited. "We would like to thank all of you for sharing this unique Noelle tradition with us tonight.

"We would also like to thank our sponsors, Engen Ornaments, the Engen Nutcracker Factory, and the Engen Family." She raised a hand to shield her eyes against the spotlights trained on her. "I believe the entire Engen family is here at tonight's festivities. Engens, if you would please stand and be recognized. Let's give them a round of applause."

Oliver, Meg, Freya, and the kids all stood. Erik and Benji remained in their seats but waved.

"Now, the moment you have all been waiting for. It's time to select our judges. Darius, if you please."

Darius, who was sporting an eye catching red, candy cane covered Christmas suit, stepped forward holding an elaborately decorated silver and gold box. With a showman's flair, he removed an elaborate gold key from the chain around his neck and inserted it into the box. He opened the lid.

"For those of you who are new to our town or unfamiliar with our traditions," Miranda explained, "this locked box has been set out in the entrance vestibule at the Engen Nutcracker Factory since Black Friday back in November. Next to it was a stack of entries. Folks could sign up for the opportunity to be a judge for this year's Nutcracker Contest. The only rule is that entrants must be over the age of eighteen, and they must be here this evening. Sorry, kids. Once we have selected our judges' panel, then the entries in the contest are presented one at a time. After viewing all the nutcrackers, the judges select this year's winning nutcracker. That's all there is to it."

The crowd rustled in anticipation as Miranda continued, "First prize for the artist creating the winning nutcracker is ten thousand dollars. Second prize is five thousand dollars, and third is two thousand. The winning nutcracker is the inspiration and showpiece for next season's entire line of Christmas nutcrackers and is featured in the Engen Nutcracker Factory's window display, which will be revealed tomorrow night during the Nutcracker Ball."

Again, the gathering whooped.

"Our judges will each receive an honorarium of one hundred dollars and tickets to the Nutcracker Ball. So, Noelle, Wisconsin, are you ready to select your judges?"

A swelling roar rose from those assembled. Gripping the elaborately decorated box with both hands, Darius shook it dramatically over his head, then set it on the stand. "Who would like to draw the first name?" he asked.

Hands shot up in the crowd.

Darius selected a stout boy who dashed up the stairs to the stage. Darius carefully tied a blindfold over the boy's eyes and then unlocked and opened the box. He guided the boy's right hand down. The boy reached in, stirred around the ballots, and then raised one high. Darius took the paper and handed it to Miranda.

"Anders Olson, you have been selected as a judge," she read aloud. "Are you here, Anders? Ah, there you are." Anders, a bowlegged octogenarian, made his way to the stage.

"Who would like to choose our second judge?"

This time, a gap-toothed girl with a huge bow in her long, brown hair headed up the steps. She drew another entry, gave it to Darius, who then passed it to Miranda.

"Sue Mathison," Miranda stated.

Sue, a young mother, handed her baby off to her husband and ascended to the stage.

On it went, until all six judges were selected. Eagerly and nervously, each one took a seat on the row of chairs behind Miranda.

"Judges," she turned to address the panel now assembled on the stage. "One at a time, each nutcracker will be placed on that podium there," she pointed. "Cameras will zoom in on each creation and project it onto the screens behind you, so that everyone here can see the detailed workmanship of these nutcrackers. In order to assure a fair competition, the artists who created these nutcrackers will not be named until after the judging. We have fourteen nutcrackers entered tonight. Each nutcracker will be on display for a total of three minutes. Judges, you have a numbered list. After viewing all the nutcrackers, you rank your top five. The nutcracker receiving the most votes is this season winning nutcracker, and that's all there is to it. Does anyone have any questions?" The judges shook their heads. "Noelle," Miranda called out, "are you ready to see this year's nutcrackers?"

The crowd erupted with shouts and cheers.

"Ms. Fedie's a natural show person," Stella observed, gripping Erik's arm and leaning into him.

Too nervous to respond, Erik smiled tightly. He looked over at his parents who were eagerly watching the events. He observed the excitement on the faces of his nephews and niece, indeed, on the faces of all the children in attendance.

He wondered, *why did I miss out on this for so many years? Why didn't I remain longer in Noelle during Christmas time these past few years?* Reflecting, he realized he'd been running away from his own disappointment at the end of his hockey career. He'd been trying to prove himself as a businessman because, like many other professional athletes at the end of their careers, he'd sort of lost his identity when he couldn't play anymore. First, hockey had been the most important thing to him, then work. Now, he realized, he'd been missing out on what mattered most, the people he cared about, his family and Stella. *Things are going to be different now,* he resolved. That's what this evening was all about.

A covered nutcracker was set on the stand. Darius theatrically lifted off the cloth covering it, revealing a broad-shouldered Green Bay Packer nutcracker. Predictably, the audience went wild as the cameras zoomed in on every detail of the carved figure, from the beard to the thick eyebrows, to the number twelve on the jersey, to the football gripped under the nutcracker's arm. However, the craftsmanship of the entry was merely adequate.

Next up was a blue organza covered fairy creation, complete with wand, sparkly blue eye shadow, and abundant glitter.

"I'm not sure the Sugar Plum Fairy up there could crack a nut with that jaw," Erik remarked snidely.

Stella tittered. "I agree. I'm not sure she'd be up to the job, but she is pretty."

One after another, the nutcrackers were presented. Each one was unique. There were trolls, superheroes, social media stars, and politicians, all depicted in wood and carved and painted with varying degrees of skill. In addition, there were several traditional looking kings and warriors. Some of them had clearly been made by amateurs, some even by children. But the crowd celebrated each one. Finally, a slightly larger nutcracker was set on the podium. Under its concealing cloth, this one looked somewhat wider than the ones that had come before it.

As Darius drew back the cloth, there was an audible gasp from the spectators. For this nutcracker was a depiction of Lady Godiva on a rocking horse. Long, blond hair exquisitely carved cascaded over the rocking horse-style rounded base as well as Lady Godiva's upper torso. Her pale legs, draped off one side, were mostly covered with more of her hair. The figurine's expression was bold and confident.

Stella whistled low. "She's magnificent."

Erik's heart sank. He, too, was awed by the Lady Godiva nutcracker. She would be virtually impossible to beat. She was beautifully carved and painted, a true work of art.

It was then, right after that incomparable Lady Godiva nutcracker, that Erik's Princess Inga nutcracker was placed onto the stand. He recognized her because of the skis sticking out from under the covering cloth. Holding his breath, he closed his eyes as his nutcracker was revealed. Seconds later, he heard murmurs and appreciative comments, so he carefully opened one eye and peered at Stella. Like everyone else, she was staring at the screen where his nutcracker stood for all to see.

With a critical eye, Erik examined his creation. For the most part, the wooden figurine resembled Stella's mural character. She wore the same long, red cape that was up swept at the bottom, as if caught by the wind. Her blue dress was delicately trimmed and detailed with gold thread. Even to Erik's critical eyes, the detail was exquisite, the carving and the painting were first rate. The camera panned around the wooden figurine until it rested on the nutcracker's face.

Erik was aware of the moment Stella recognized the face on the wooden statue. He felt her stiffen beside him. She inhaled sharply, drawing away from him. Erik's nutcracker version of Inga had gamine features that were like Stella's own, including the slightly upturned nose and cheeks that were lightly dusted with freckles.

Stella didn't look away from the screen, but Erik was uncomfortably aware of his mother's, father's and sister's eyes upon him. *The cat's out of the bag.* It was obvious to everyone that knew her that Stella's face was on the nutcracker. True, the nutcracker was wooden, which was a rigid medium and not particularly adroit at expressing facial details. But Stella was there, to his eyes at least, from the arch of the cheekbones to the slight slant at the corner of the eyes.

At this moment, the real Stella's face appeared equally wooden.

A child finally stated what everyone else in the row was thinking. "Hey, Aunt Stella, she looks like you. That nutcracker looks like you," Sam observed, her voice, ringing out over the crowd.

"She does, doesn't she?" Hayden agreed.

Fortunately, at that moment the Princess Inga nutcracker was removed from the display stand. Her three minutes were up. A troll nutcracker was put up in her place, and the audience oohed and aahed, and seemingly forgot about Erik's nutcracker.

Erik had always considered himself a brave man, one who was unafraid to take chances in life, but now he found himself more than a little terrified to make eye contact with Stella. He stared at the screen, not really seeing the remaining few nutcrackers.

After all the nutcrackers were revealed, there was a brief lull while the judges' votes were tallied. Finally, the winners were projected onto the screen and simultaneously announced by Miranda. Predictably, the Lady Godiva nutcracker was the winner, and his Inga came in second. After the announcement, people got to their feet and began to mill about, some to leave, and others to head over to check out the ice sculptures. The Engens, Webers, and Larsons also stood.

Finally, Erik snuck a peak at Stella. He saw that she was chatting with her sister-in-law, Barb. His father, Oliver, gripped his shoulder. "I didn't know you were carving again, son. Your nutcracker was fine."

"She didn't win," Erik observed wryly.

"The Godiva was unique, but yours was beautiful as well. I know my father's factory is in good hands when I see that kind of craftsmanship. Your grandpa would be very proud of you."

"Thanks, Dad."

"I want you to know that I'm in full support of the plans that you're presenting to the board tomorrow night. I think your idea is inspired and exactly right for Engen Ornaments, the Nutcracker Factory, and this town. I'm proud of the work you've done here."

Erik exhaled slowly, watching his breath plume up in the cold air. "Tomorrow's the night. We have the Board Meeting and then the Nutcracker Ball. It's all coming together."

"As it should," Meg concurred, linking arms with her husband. "You plan to attend the ball, don't you Erik? And are you bringing a date?" she gazed pointedly at Stella.

Her son didn't reply.

"Erik," his mother shook her head. "It appears to me that there is someone special you'd like to have with you at the ball," Meg reflected.

"It's obvious to everyone else who saw that nutcracker," his father pretended to cough into his fisted hand.

"What are you going to do about it?" Meg prompted.

It was at that moment that Erik's eyes met Stella's. To his dismay, hers were as cold, remote, and as wooden as that of his Princess Inga nutcracker. There was no warmth or softness for him in her expression. He recognized how well he'd carved his nutcracker. It wasn't surprising given that every line of Stella's features was etched into his mind.

"I'll see you later, Mom and Dad. We can catch up tonight at the lodge."

They waved their understanding and joined up with Freya and her family.

Erik headed over to Stella and Barb. Their discussion ended on his approach.

"Stella, I ah—" he began.

"Erik," she cut him off, holding a hand up. "I think I'm going home with Barb and Sam. Thanks for the carriage ride." With that, she turned and walked away from him. Barb cast him an apologetic glance over her shoulder, leaving Erik standing with his heart trampled under the heel of Stella's Mukluk boots.

CHAPTER 9

Stella met Jayda and Addy for spin class at five-thirty the next morning at The Wheelhouse Spin Studio. All three women were barely awake and didn't say much of anything to each other, except to grunt an early morning greeting.

Sally, the class's instructor, was perky and full of energy, clearly a morning person who sought to share her enthusiasm with her class. "Today, ladies and gentlemen," Sally announced after dimming the lights and turning on the oscillating fans, "we will be spinning to a generational battle. We'll be flipping between tunes from the sixties, seventies, and today. We'll start with some Santana and then go to Pit Bull. We'll spin to some Doobie Brothers and finish off with the Killers. This should be quite a ride. Mount up."

Usually, Stella could lose herself in the music and the biking motion. Most mornings, she was barely awake when she got to her bike, and she made it through the first ten minutes of class in the same state. Inevitably, as her blood started pumping, she got into it as the class progressed. Forty minutes later, she felt recharged and ready to face a new school day. She believed few things were better than having the day's workout behind you before breakfast.

But today was different. She hadn't even wanted to go to spin class when the alarm went off. It was only because she knew that the other women expected her that she got dressed and drove to the studio. This morning, Stella had little to no enthusiasm for strapping her feet into the stirrups. Her right foot slipped out more than once and then the pedal smacked her painfully in the back of the calf. Her mind was elsewhere. On Erik. On the nutcracker he'd carved...of her!

The resemblance had been obvious to everyone. Barb had elbowed her in the side on seeing Erik's nutcracker on the big screens. But now what? What would happen to them, if there even was a *them*, when this Christmas season came to an end? Erik lived in Chicago, and she lived in Noelle. Would they simply return to their lives after the holidays? The thought depressed her.

As was their custom, when the class ended and they'd wiped off their bikes, the three friends headed over to the dry sauna to unwind. Stella paused to fill her bottle at the water filling station, then joined the two other women.

"Wow, it's so hot in there this morning," Addy remarked, laying a towel down on the wooden bench before sitting down.

"It makes me feel alive," Jayda commented from where she already sat across the little room from Addy on a bench a tier up. She tilted her head back and closed her eyes.

Taking a seat, Stella leaned her elbows on her knees and stared down at the sweat dripping off her forehead and onto the wooden floor.

"Are you ladies going to the Nutcracker Ball tonight?" Addie asked. "Jak got us tickets weeks ago as a perk from work. I wasn't sure I wanted to go at first. It seemed like a lot of hassle. But now I must admit I'm excited about dressing up and doing the whole makeup thing. I feel like I'm going to a big girl prom."

"I'm going," Jayda replied. "My mother promised to babysit Lyrique, so tonight is date night for Darius and me. He has to be there for work anyway, but we thought we'd make an evening of it. We're going to dinner at the Local Lounge before heading over to the ball. Darius will have to do some meeting and greeting, but then we plan on dancing the night away. How about you, Stella?" Jayda opened her eyes and leveled them on Stella. "Are you planning on going with Prince Charming? And what happened after he swept you away in that carriage?"

"What?" Addie asked, her eyes, wide. "Stella, why are you keeping us in the dark? What happened last night?"

"It was something else," Jayda shared. "Erik Engen pulled up in a horse drawn carriage in the middle of the parade and carried Stella here away. I texted her a couple of times, but all she said was that she went to the Nutcracker Contest and then went home with Barb and Sam. I know you're holding out on us."

"That's what I did." Stella shrugged and raised a towel to dab at the sweat dripping down her neck.

"It was totally romantic. Tall, dark, and handsome swept you away in a carriage, and you aren't telling us anything," Jayda snorted. "Come on, Stella. What happened after that?"

Stella took a deep breath and then a sip from her water bottle. She studied two of her closest friends who were leaning forward, eager to hear something romantic and charming. "Well, I kind of blew him off."

"What?" Jayda challenged.

"Why did you do that?" Addie demanded. "I thought you liked this guy."

"I do, or I did. I'm confused." Stella threw her hands up into the air.

"You do like him," Jayda observed shrewdly. "That's why you're such a mess."

"You're right. You're right," Stella groaned, covering her face with her hands. "I've had other boyfriends, but Erik's always been the one who makes my heart go pitter patter. What a disaster."

"That's so dreamy," Addie gushed. "Have you let him know how you feel about him?"

"No. In fact, I had Barb drive me home last night so I could avoid him. The thing is, he carved a nutcracker to look like me. He took a character from my mural, Inga, and he put my face on her. During the Nutcracker Contest, everyone saw his nutcracker. It was up on those big screens, and he carved me! I didn't know what to say."

"Oh, my gosh," Addie enthused, clasping her towel to her heart.

"I think it's a little weird myself," Jayda observed. "But the man owns a nutcracker factory, so I guess that's his way of telling you he loves you."

"I took off with Barb and Sam right after that," Stella explained dourly.

"What?" Addie questioned. "Why did you do that?"

"I'm not getting this," Jayda inserted. "After Erik picks you up in a horse drawn carriage and shows nearly the entire town a nutcracker that he carved of you, you left him there alone? You didn't even talk or anything?" She rubbed the back of her neck. "That doesn't make any sense. What is wrong with you, girl? You have to let him know how you feel."

"He broke up with me the last time I did," Stella muttered.

"You were in high school," Jayda protested. "You were kids. It was like ten years ago. What would you have done if he hadn't broken up with you then? You would *not* have gone to art school and stayed here in Noelle? Would he have quit hockey and remained in town, too? No, both of you were ambitious and wanted to see the world."

"The time wasn't right for you then, and timing is everything in love," Addy remarked sagely. "You were both too young. Things are different now. You have to take a chance on love."

"A leap of faith," Jayda advised.

Stella scuffed her sneaker against the dark floorboards of the sauna. "Maybe you're right, but I'm afraid. I don't want him to break my heart twice in one lifetime." She gazed up at them wryly. "That would not be good."

"You admit you are in love with him," Jayda observed, a broad grin popping up on her face.

"I may be," Stella conceded miserably. "But tonight is the twenty-third, the day before the night before Christmas. That means that even if Erik plans on staying through Christmas, that's only a few more days that he's guaranteed to be in town. There aren't any hockey games or practices until after the holidays when I know I'd see him. He may just leave Noelle, and we'll never know…" her voice trailed off.

"What? You'll never know what?" Addy demanded.

"That the two of them are meant to be together," Jayda observed dryly, "even though it's painfully obvious to everyone else."

"I was going to say *what might have been*," Stella agreed. "I blew it last night," she muttered. "I was scared. I didn't trust him or myself."

"Yup, you did," Jayda agreed. "You blew it, but it's not over yet."

"This is your chance to fix things. Have a comeback from that disaster years ago. You could see him tonight," Addy encouraged, "at the Nutcracker Ball. You know he'll be there. His family hosts the event."

"He'll be there," Jayda agreed. "Darius told me there's supposed to be some big announcement at the ball. This is your chance, Stella. Don't let love slip away."

"I don't have a ticket. I'm sure it's sold out by now," Stella said. "I think he was going to ask me, but I left right after the Nutcracker Contest," her voice trailed off.

"Erik really carved a nutcracker of you himself?" Addy questioned disbelievingly. "He didn't just have one of his employees carve one of you?"

Jayda nodded. "Darius told me all about it when he got home from the contest. Also, WQSW did a segment on the news last night and this morning. They featured the three top nutcrackers, and one looks an awful lot like Stella here."

Addy pondered. "Erik's an artist, too?"

Stella nodded. "I don't think he's carved in years. The Inga nutcracker was beautiful," she admitted.

"You're both creative and driven," Addy enthused. "Don't you see? He's your soulmate."

Stella groaned.

"We can fix this," Addie offered. "You have to go to the Nutcracker Ball and see Erik. It may be your last chance because tomorrow is Christmas Eve. There's room at our table, I think. I'll text Jak. I'm sure he can get you a ticket," Addie persisted. "If you want to come, that is," she finished, unsure of how to take Stella's silence.

Stella shrugged. "I guess I'm afraid of getting burned a second time."

"You have to decide if he's worth it." Jayda pointed out while getting to her feet. "Ladies, I'm getting well done here. Are we ready to go?"

"I am," Addie stood up. "I feel like a wet noodle, totally relaxed. Stella, if you decide to go to the Nutcracker Ball tonight, do you have anything to wear?"

Stella considered for a moment. "I have a couple dresses from art exhibits that could work. There's one that comes to mind. I think I have a picture of it in my gallery on my phone. I'll show you."

"She's going after her man," Jayda crowed triumphantly, holding up her hand for a high five.

Stella slapped it.

"That's the spirit," Addie approved.

It was still dark outside when Erik found himself wide awake and staring at his alarm clock which read five-fifteen. *It's too early to head to the office, and there's no way I'm going to fall back asleep.* He was too keyed up by the events of the night before, by the uncertainty of what was to come for himself, Stella, the Engen Nutcracker Factory, and the town of Noelle. *Today is the big day when it either all comes together or all falls apart.* Erik tossed and turned for maybe five more minutes, but then he sat up in bed, yawned and stretched, hit the light and set out to find his running gear. *Nothing better than an early morning cold-weather run to clear the mind, settle the thoughts, and get ready for the day.* Once he was fully dressed in his winter weather running gear, his all-terrain running shoes, balaclava, and black ski hat, he tiptoed through the lobby of the lodge and out the door.

Once outside, he realized that he'd forgotten his high visibility runner's safety vest inside. Not wanting to awaken any of the lodge's other guests, he decided to adjust his plans. *I won't run on the road. It wouldn't be smart without the vest, and drivers would have a hard time seeing me with the snow drifts. I'll run on the ski trails instead.* He knew from a conversation with Freya that the ski trails were recently groomed to make the most of the weather conditions. He also understood that running on a recently groomed ski trail was completely unacceptable. *I'll run on the side of the trail,* he concluded. *That should be fine so long as I don't damage the trail.* Erik had run in snow before, and the idea of jogging through a still and peaceful winter forest appealed to him.

He set off slowly, the several inch-thick snow, crunching under his footfalls. His warm breath plumed out in the cold air through the balaclava material covering his mouth. There was no breeze for which he was grateful. Still, it was bitterly cold. It almost hurt to breathe. He could feel the bite of the frigid air around his eyes, his only exposed skin. Frost was beginning to form on his eyelashes. *It must be below zero,* he reflected.

In the beginning, he was aware of his usual early morning stiffness, and he ran with a short, choppy stride. With time, as he grew warmer and looser, his stride lengthened, and his running grew more fluid. His deliberations reflected the motions of his body. For the first part of the run, his thoughts flipped about from idea to worry in a completely undisciplined fashion. Foremost in his mind was Stella. *Why did she leave so abruptly last night? Is there any hope for us?* But after he reached mile three and his turn-around point, he began to relax. At a half mile from the Lingonberry Lodge, he felt calm and even peaceful.

Erik always walked the last half mile or so of a run as a cool down. Mentally, he was rehearsing the speech he planned to give the Engen Ornaments Board that night. Coming to an abrupt bend that permitted no view of the trail beyond it, he was so lost in his thoughts that he didn't notice he'd stepped onto the actual ski trail. At that exact moment, a cross country skier swept around the bend from the opposite direction, nearly colliding with him. Fortunately, he caught sight of the skier in the last possible moment and, using his athlete's reflexes, threw himself off the trail and into the snowbank on the side of it. Once clear of him, the very pregnant skier stopped and turned ponderously on her skis to face him.

"Erik, what are you doing out here? You about scared me to death," Freya berated him. "You look like some kind of criminal, running around out here all in black. And what's with the balaclava? You look terrifying."

Erik leaned back in the snowdrift and pulled off the balaclava. Under it, his face was bright red from his exertion, and his beard and eyebrows were tipped in frost.

Freya laughed. "I'm not sure that's a better look. I'm surprised you're up so early. You have a big night tonight. I would have thought you'd have slept in."

"I couldn't really sleep," Erik admitted, getting to his feet.

"Walk back with me?" Freya encouraged.

"Don't you want to ski some more?" Erik asked.

"I already did a two-mile loop, and this youngster is feisty this morning," Freya cradled her belly. "I'm ready to head in. Will you walk with me?"

"Sounds good."

Side by side, the siblings returned to the path, both headed, this time, in the direction of Lingonberry Lodge.

"What happened last night?" Freya prompted, one thin eyebrow arched.

"Nothing," he replied, kicking at the snow. "You saw. Everyone saw. Stella left after she glimpsed my nutcracker. I don't want to accept it, but maybe she doesn't share my feelings."

Gliding beside Erik on her skis, Freya shook her head. "No, I observed Stella throughout the contest. She wasn't even really watching the contest. Not to give you a bigger head, but she couldn't keep her eyes off you."

"But she left," Erik pointed out as he kicked his sneaker into the snow.

"Stella thinks you're going to leave town after the holidays. That is what you told us. What you told everyone. Has that changed?"

Erik didn't answer right way.

"Well?" Freya demanded.

"I think maybe it has," he admitted. "Yeah, I know it has. You know, for a little sister, you're pretty smart." He reached down into the snow, grabbed a handful, shaped it into a soft snowball, and promptly lobbed at his sister's arm.

"Hey, that's not fair," Freya protested, brushing snow off her arm. "I can't bend down over this belly, and I have these ski poles in my hands."

"I know," Erik winked at her. Suddenly, he froze. "Will you look at that?"

"What?" Freya turned to face the same the direction as her brother. The pair stood gazing into the clearing where the lodge stood. At this moment, the morning sun over the lodge painted the sky in brilliant pinks and purples against the gradually lightening horizon.

"Wow," Freya breathed. "Now that's a sign."

"A sign of what?" Erik questioned, glancing from the amazing sky to his sister.

"Of magic. Pure magic," Freya replied. "You have to be open to the magic around you, Erik. That's the great thing about having kids. They're so aware of the beauty in the world. When you see beauty like that, you have to hold onto it."

"I agree," Erik affirmed, but it was clear to both that he wasn't ruminating on the sky. "You know," he reflected, "it almost makes it worth getting up in the morning to see that kind of sunrise. The sky never looks like that in Chicago. There are too many lights."

"Another reason to come back to Noelle," Freya whispered. "You have to follow your heart, Erik. You won't be happy until you do. Now I have to get breakfast made for the kids, and I promised the twins we would make sugar cookies. I'll see you at breakfast?" She stole a glance at him.

"Yes, and thanks, Freya. You have a way of putting things in perspective. I'll be there in a minute. I want to watch the dawn a little longer."

Erik remained where he was while his sister skied away. He stood at the edge of the clearing, watching the sky lighten, contemplating what the future might hold for him and Stella.

CHAPTER 10

That evening, Stella stood in her bedroom in front of her floor length mirror, studying her reflection. She wore her hair smooth and down, evoking a darker haired Veronica Lake, with elaborate silver chandelier earrings. Her dress was a vintage, draped, burgundy velvet cocktail dress that she'd found in a consignment store on the Rue Saint Honoré in Paris. She had a pair of heels to wear that were dyed to match it. The dress had a smart, sexy, nineteen forties aesthetic to it. It was dramatic and eye-catching. She had good memories of wearing it to a very successful exhibition of her work and that of several other artists. It was a little much for a holiday party in Noelle, Wisconsin, but for tonight, Stella was determined to look her best. She had decided to take the leap of faith and follow her heart. She was going after Erik.

The doorbell rang. Stella took one last look, spritzed herself with Jicky, and grabbed her cape and purse from the chair. She opened the door.

Addie and her fiancé were standing there. They had offered to bring Stella with them to the ball. Her friend, who looked radiant in a black chiffon, high necked cocktail dress, clapped her hands together. "Oh Stella, you look stunning."

"You both do," Jak, Addie's significant other, observed. Jak, a local attorney with shoulder length auburn hair, looked dapper in his tuxedo. "How lucky am I," he observed, "to get to escort you two bells of the ball tonight."

"Thanks," Stella was pleased. "You look sharp tonight, Jak, and Addie, you are breathtaking."

"Ladies, your chariot awaits," Jak held the door wide and stepped aside to allow Stella and Addie to pass by.

Jak's SUV was well-warmed, and he had Christmas carols playing, which Stella was relieved to note, made it nearly impossible to carry on a conversation, though Addie and Jak did try. Nevertheless, Stella was pleased that the music absolved her of having to contribute to the exchange.

She was on pins and needles. *What do I say to Erik? Where could this thing between us go?* He'd carved his nutcracker of her. What did that mean? *It has to mean something. Right? What does Erik intend to do regarding the Nutcracker Factory? What is the big announcement Jayda mentioned?*

That was an important question as well, for the town and for her friends. There was supposed to be a Board Meeting of Engen Ornaments tonight before the Nutcracker Ball. Jayda had told her that was one of the lesser known festival traditions. Stella didn't think she could forgive Erik if he harmed the town or the factory. Once she couldn't get out of town fast enough. Now, she loved and appreciated Noelle. She wanted it to stay a going concern for Barb, Sam, Jayda, Lyrique, Darius and everyone else who lived here. The Nutcracker Factory was an integral part of the spirit of Noelle.

She intended to fight for Noelle and for the people she

loved here. She intended to talk to Erik, find out his plans, and try and convince him to do the right thing by the town. Then, she intended to lay her heart at his feet.

From his position on the third floor, Erik gazed down into the central atrium of the Engen Nutcracker Factory. He adjusted his bow tie which matched his satin lapels. Dinner had been delicious and was over. For the most part, the servers had removed the plates, silverware, and glasses. Erik had dined with the board members. The rib roast, winter squash, double stuffed baked potatoes, and creamed peas proved delicious. The spicy mulled wine with its hint of anise had been a delightful companion to the meal, and the desert had been an elegant ganache-topped chocolate cake. That part of the evening had gone well. He nodded with satisfaction, taking in the entire scene, the elaborate Christmas decorations, and the festively attired citizens of Noelle.

The theme for this year's Nutcracker Ball was *The Enchanted Forest*, and Miranda and Darius had gone all out to capture the spirit of the season. White trees dripping silver and gold ornaments formed a perimeter around the large room. Tree branches hung from the ceiling, festooned in delicate fairy lights. Tables and chairs were scattered among the trees. The tables were draped in silver trimmed cloths with white roses, cranberry bunches, and pinecone centerpieces of modest height, permitting people to see over them. In the cleared center of the atrium, a wooden dance floor had been laid out. At the back, a local band played Christmas tunes. Over the dance floor hung a chandelier of illuminated glass globes in a variety of sizes and hung at varying heights. Erik inhaled and caught a whiff of bayberry and pine over the omnipresent scent of wood. The transformed factory even smelled like Christmas.

The Nutcracker Ball was Engen Ornaments gift to the employees and the people of Noelle as well as the social event of the holiday season. It was always well-attended. He wondered if Stella would be there. He'd intended to invite her as his guest after the Nutcracker Contest, but she'd left, or more like, fled right after with her sister-in-law. She hadn't returned his texts or calls since. Still, his gaze scanned the crowd, searching for the woman who'd captured his attention and his heart for the second time in his life. Closing his eyes, he pictured the morning's sunrise. *As Freya said, sometimes you need to have faith and hope, and count on a little bit of Christmas magic. Stella will be here tonight,* he assured himself.

A hand clapped down on his shoulder. He turned to face Darius who was resplendent in a double-breasted, green velvet jacket.

"The board meeting," Darius grinned, "couldn't have gone any better."

"Thanks to the data you shared with the board. They're seeing dollar signs."

"All of the credit goes to you, Erik," Darius continued in all seriousness. "You came up with the vision and the strategy. I merely gathered the data to support it. It feels good. I can't wait to see people's reactions when you tell them your plan tonight."

"Our plans, Factory Manager," he corrected.

"Our plans," Darius agreed. "I'm also looking forward to telling Jayda about the promotion. It means a lot to my family. That's another secret that's been tough to keep."

"You did a great job of keeping it secret. I know it wasn't easy," Erik continued.

Darius rolled his eyes demonstratively. "Jayda has been all over me. She almost refused to come tonight because she is so enraged that I wouldn't give her any details. She only agreed to come because my wife can't resist an opportunity to get dressed up."

"Everything is out in the open tonight. I think it's time," Erik exhaled forcefully. "Wish me luck."

Darius stopped him before he turned to go down the stairs. "Good luck with all you have going on tonight."

Erik didn't answer right away. He stared down at the crowd below him. "Have I been that obvious?" he finally asked.

Darius laughed out loud. "If the whole carriage thing didn't make it crystal clear, the nutcracker carving of Stella Larson did. I think everyone recognized her face on that. By the way, you are a very talented carver. I think it could have gone either way, the Lady Godiva or the Princess Inga. Turns out, one of our newest creatives carved Lady Godiva. None of us had any idea of his talent until last night. It was quite a discovery. In my opinion, a lot of good things came out of this year's contest."

"I'm not disappointed about not winning." Erik lightly patted his white silk pocket square.

"No, you're worried you're going to lose the girl."

"You're right, my friend. With how things ended last night, I'm not sure that she has any interest in giving me another chance. I pretty much handed her my heart, and she walked away. I don't even know if she's here tonight," he sighed heavily. "But I need to get myself together. It's show time.

Let's do this." The two men fist bumped, then Erik headed down the staircase.

He was halfway to the first floor when he glimpsed her. He paused mid-step, taking her in. Stella had always had a flare for the dramatic, even as a teenager, and she didn't disappoint tonight. This evening, she took his breath away. She was wearing a burgundy dress that clung to her mouth-watering curves. Her long hair hung in a slick curtain over one elegant, white shoulder. She was, in a word, stunning. He took her in as she chatted with some friends by the bar. *How was I such a fool to let her get away the first time? Can I convince her to give me another chance?* But now was not the time to address her.

First, he had to deliver the news that the whole town of Noelle anxiously awaited. He glimpsed his parents seated at a table with Freya and Benji. He gave them a thumbs up, which they reciprocated, and then he walked briskly to the stage where the band was still performing. He gave the singer their prearranged signal. She nodded, wound down her song, then handed him the microphone. From somewhere, a spotlight flashed down on him. Darius was responsible, he guessed. Erik waved to the crowd.

"Ladies and gentlemen, if I could have your attention please for a few moments. As you may be aware, each year on this night, in fact, right before this ball, the board of Engen Ornaments meets for the final Board Meeting of the year."

After some preliminary whispering and jostling about, the crowd stilled, and conversations ceased as everyone focused their attention on Erik, whose size and handsome, tuxedoed presence would have dominated the room even without the spotlight.

"Most years, I'll be honest, little is accomplished at this

end of year meeting." There were some chuckles from board members dispersed through the crush. "It's generally a matter of reviewing sales information for the year coming to an end, some discussion of future plans, and then everyone wishes each other *Happy Holidays*, and that's it. We all head on our merry way. But this year, things are different." Erik paused. He felt more than heard a murmur sweep through his audience. He was aware of the intense focus from the crowd on what he would say next. He was particularly conscious of a beloved pair of green eyes.

"I know that rumors have been flying around Noelle about why I'm here. As you know the ornament business has become progressively more competitive, in part due to discount online retailers. But Engen Ornaments is now a global concern, and we have been successful and even grown because we have been creative with our business model."

He gave the audience time enough to absorb that before continuing. "I came to Noelle this winter in order to assess the future health of this nutcracker factory. The factory has been doing fine, but the question in my mind and in the mind of the board members is what does the future hold? What are our expectations for the Engren Nutcracker Factory?"

Erik could have heard a pin drop. Then dissenting voices swept through the crowd. He raised his hand, signaling for the audience to wait and hear him out. "In a world where people can order a nutcracker off Amazon for twenty dollars and have it delivered within forty-eight hours, how can a nutcracker factory like this one survive and be competitive? This is our fundamental question."

Again, people in the audience began to mutter and react. "Well, there's something to be said for craftsmanship," Albert Fedie called out. Other people chimed in, in agreement.

"Excellent point, Albert," Erik acknowledged. "Hear me out. Working closely with Darius Watkins, I came to understand that the future of the Engen Nutcracker Factory doesn't lie in cheap, mass produced items but, instead, in true craftsmanship."

He had their attention now. The factory workers, board members, Engen family members, town folk, and tourists simply listened to Erik.

"Please allow me to explain. I came to Noelle this holiday season expecting to address issues like further mechanizing our assembly line. Upon reflection and with a great deal of consideration, and armed with real numbers, both current data and projections, the Engen Nutcracker Factory will be de-mechanizing to a certain degree."

Again, there was a rising swell of reaction. Erik waited until it subsided.

"We will be returning to my grandfather Ole Engen's vision for this factory, a workshop producing true works of art inspired by the holiday seasons. Will these nutcrackers cost our customers more? Yes, undoubtedly. Will we be able to sell enough of these works of art to ensure that this factory remains profitable? I certainly hope so, for that is our long-term plan. Darius and I have run the numbers multiple times. We believe that this new approach of creating unique works of art that also happen to be nutcrackers will ensure that this factory continues to exist into the future and beyond."

Spontaneously the crowd burst into applause. Erik felt a little choked up. He took a deep breath and blew it out through pursed lips.

"How are you going to get enough skilled woodworkers to make this feasible?" a woman called from somewhere at the back of the large room.

Erik held his hand up, trying to see the speaker, but he answered to everyone in the crowd. "That is an excellent question, and one that has caused us considerable concern. We do have fine craftsmen here working at the factory. I know that some of our most established artists have been frustrated with the direction that the factory has taken in recent years. Admittedly, we have lost some of our most talented creatives due to burgeoning frustration with our emphasis on increased production and lower costs. All of that is now out the door."

"Hear! Hear!" someone shouted.

"Our plan is to create an apprenticeship program, working with the local tech college to first identify and then train those with the talent and inclination to become expert woodworkers. We will also recruit and seek to identify new talent. For example, Kellen Samuels who designed and carved the Lady Godiva that won this year's Nutcracker Contest has now been promoted to a Master Carver. Let's give Kellen a round of applause."

An extremely tall young man with a bashful smile standing near the front of the crowd waved.

"People of Noelle, this is your nutcracker tactory," Erik continued. "We will continue to seek to train, hire, and promote the sort of craftspeople who will ensure that Engen Nutcrackers remain a special and integral part of the holiday season for families for many years to come."

He paused so the applause and noise could die down. "I'm not going to lie to you all. There will be some time and money spent in transition. We will continue to produce the lines that we have currently in production, and no one will lose his or her job. That I promise you."

Cheers rang out.

Erik again waited until people settled before going on. "We will need to be flexible and willing to learn. Our vision is not going to come to fruition right away. We will slowly transition away from the mass-produced nutcrackers, and we may be adding some non-nutcracker products to this factory as well. But it is my firm belief, and one that is shared by the Board of Directors of Engen Ornaments, that the Nutcracker Factory can and will continue to remain a vital part of the Noelle community.

"When I agreed to take my father's place as Grand Marshal of the Nutcracker Festival, he informed me that each year on the twenty-third, he personally gave out Christmas bonuses to all of the employees."

"I put them in red envelopes," Miranda exclaimed.

"That is correct," Oliver Engen agreed. "I personally handed out the bonus checks at the factory on the twenty-third."

"There was nothing but a Christmas card in the envelopes handed out at work today," a tall woman wearing a black velvet sheath dress which revealed the sleeves of tattoos on her arms remarked.

"I warned you, Erik," Darius shook his finger at his friend and employer. "I told you people would get the wrong idea from being handed merely a holiday card."

"Thought you'd skipped on the bonus this year," a jovial, male voice called from the thick of the crowd.

"All right," Erik admitted. "Maybe I should have provided an explanation, but we wanted to share the good news with all of you tonight. This year, we went with the electronic transfer of your Christmas bonuses to your preferred account. You will find this year's bonus to be a bit healthier than usual. It should have gone out," he glanced down at his

Apple watch, "approximately five minutes ago. We hope you will be pleased. We wanted to be able to share our message with you, our employees, their families, and the people of Noelle, together.

"Now, without further ado, I would like to reveal this year's Engen Nutcracker Factory display window." Again he glanced down at his watch. "Yes, it's almost eight o'clock. If you would please get your coats and head outside. It's time for the unveiling. Merry Christmas to you all and a very happy New Year."

The atrium thundered with applause.

I've done my job. Now time to follow my heart. Erik handed off the microphone to Darius and headed straight to Stella. The crowd seemed to part in front of him. Then he was standing before her. Wordlessly, he offered her his arm. She took it. Tears shimmered in her eyes.

"That was amazing," she began. "You are incredible."

Tenderly he touched her cheek, gently wiping away a tear. "Stella, why are you crying?"

"Because I'm so happy."

"You look amazing tonight."

"So do you," she replied.

"Come on," he urged with a wink. "It's time. Let's go see the window display."

Oliver stopped them as they passed through the room. "Good work, Erik," he uttered, patting his son on the shoulder. "Your grandfather would have wholeheartedly approved of your plans for the factory. This is the right direction. I only wish I'd seen it sooner. This factory needs a craftsman at the helm, and you are that man. I couldn't be prouder."

"Artist," Stella corrected.

"Excuse me? I couldn't quite hear you," Oliver said.

"Erik is an artist," Stella clarified.

Erik couldn't find the words to respond. Instead, he gazed at her lovely face. *Love. It's love. I love Stella,* he realized.

Oliver cleared his throat. "I agree, Stella. I'm so pleased that this boy has started to figure out what really matters." He winked at her. "Erik, you have a window display to reveal. Everyone is waiting."

"Of course," Erik smiled, but he and Stella remained standing there, staring into each other's eyes.

"Get going, Erik," his father prompted.

Arm in arm, Stella and Erik joined the mass of guests moving toward the cloak room. There, guests picked up their coats and then headed back out through the front door of the factory. Erik took Stella's coat from the attendant and held it open for her, so that she could slide her arms in.

"I'm so happy that you aren't closing the factory," she whispered to him as she drew her coat closed.

"Is that all you're happy about?" he teased, breathing in the warm, perfumed scent of her neck.

She turned and gazed up at him through her lashes. "Maybe not quite all."

They joined the flood of people as they headed outside and around to the storefront of the Nutcracker Factory. They made their way to the back of what was already quite a large assembly. In addition to the attendees at the Nutcracker Ball, the mass of people had swelled with parents and children who had come for only this part of the evening's festivities. Some people had set up lawn chairs directly in front of the window. Catching sight of Hayden, Sam, Brady, Connor, and the rest of the Rocket hockey team in the thick of it, Erik waved. Hayden and several others waved back. It was at that moment that the streetlights directly by the factory shut off. A murmur of excitement swept through the crowd. The glow of Christmas lights and streetlights from the other two sides of the square and from the moon ensured that it was plenty bright enough to see.

"What else are you happy about?" Erik whispered so that only Stella could hear.

Grinning and enjoying the feel of his arm about her waist, Stella giggled. "Does this mean you plan to come home to Noelle more often?"

"That's what I wanted to talk to you about," Erik began, but then Christmas music, a hand bell version of Jingle Bells, drowned him out.

Squeals of anticipation and oohs and ahhs rang out. Children with cheeks rosy from the cold leaned forward eagerly. Spotlights flashed onto the enormous storefront window, drawing everyone's attention there. Suddenly, dancing and capering snowmen, Christmas trees, ornaments, presents, and candy canes were projected onto the curtains. The images romped across the space in time with the music. The light show lasted for several minutes, then the projected lights went solid and bright, and the curtains dramatically and slowly drew back to the tune of *Deck the Halls*.

A snow-covered, miniature landscape filled the display. One hill was at the forefront, and two hills were recessed back and on either side of it. The tallest hill resembled Mount Martin over on the east side of Noelle and was complete with a ski jump. There were some buildings and trees scattered about in the winter scene. Sparkling lights began to flash on and off. The shadow of a skier swooped down the hill and launched into the air, seeming to take off over the audience's heads. Suddenly, little trapdoors opened at points all along the hill. The nutcrackers from this year's contest emerged through the trapdoors. Each, in turn, was spot lit. The crowd cheered at each one. Stella squeezed Erik's hand when his Princess Inga nutcracker came up. Finally, the tip top of the hill sank down, and the Lady Godiva nutcracker rose out of it, eliciting a resounding round of applause.

"I liked yours better," Stella breathed right by Erik's. "The details of the face are amazing. I can't believe you carved me."

He turned to face her. "Your face is what I dream about when I close my eyes at night," he admitted.

"My face?" she echoed.

He simply nodded.

A train whistle rang out, once and then twice. A Christmas train appeared on a track that ran along the base of the display window. The steam locomotive was fully decorated for the holiday season and pulled several flat railway wagons displaying progressively older nutcrackers.

"That train wraps around the entire atrium of the factory," Erik told Stella, leaning closer and catching another whiff of her perfume. Jicky, he was pleased to note. A very good sign.

"You laid a train track around the factory?" Stella inquired. "I can't believe it. I mean, I'm all about the Christmas spirit, but laying a model train track through your factory? That's amazing."

"You see that nutcracker there," he pointed to a mountain troll with a fierce expression painted in natural, woodsy colors. "My grandfather carved him. He was my favorite when I was a little guy. We plan on displaying all of our factory designs on this train. We'll add new cars each Christmas season to display that season's nutcrackers. It will be a new tradition. My grandpa always said you need a train at Christmas time."

"Oh, Erik, it's wonderful," Stella sighed. "You're wonderful."

"Come with me," he prompted, taking her hand. His expression was serious and intent.

"Is the show over?" Stella asked.

"Not quite, but we have to talk."

"Where are we going?" she allowed him to squire her away from the factory window and through the mass of people into the relative darkness further out in the square. He escorted her around two sides of the square. Here they could still see the festivities at the factory but with the only direct illumination provided by an LED streetlight a few yards away. The spot was relatively dark and offered the two of them some privacy.

"Would you look at the moon," Stella remarked, turning her beautiful features up to the sky. "It's a full one tonight. It looks like you could reach out and touch it. It reminds me of that Eric Carle book, *Papa, Please Get the Moon for Me.* She reached demonstratively up, as if trying to grasp the glowing orb. "The father waits until the moon is small enough, then he climbs into the sky, takes it, and gives it to his daughter. It continues to shrink until it totally vanishes one day and then reappears back up in the sky."

"It's a children's book?" he inquired.

"Yes, by one of my favorite artists and authors," she explained.

"Right now, I wish I could give you the moon."

She reached out and rested a hand on his bearded cheek. "You don't have to. All I want is you."

He closed his eyes and pressed a kiss into the palm of her hand while savoring her words and the feelings that they evoked in him.

"How did I get so lucky," he tucked a loose strand of hair behind her ear, "to get another chance with you?"

"I never got over you," she admitted.

"I'm glad you didn't. Back then, we both had a lot to learn," Erik began. "I know we can't go back and change what happened."

"Nor would we want to," Stella finished, her face, bright with feeling.

"Right," Erik responded nervously, "but is there a possibility we could go forward together?"

Stella tilted her head, studying him, not yet willing to let him entirely off the hook. "What are you saying, Erik? The last time I saw you this serious, you broke up with me at a high school graduation party," she teased him.

"You won't ever let me live that down, will you?"

"No, probably not."

"I have something I want to show you." He reached into his overcoat pocket and grasped his black leather wallet. Opening it, he pulled out what appeared to be a small, square, laminated card. He scrutinized it and then slowly, hesitantly, extended it to Stella.

"What is it?" She took it. It was a picture from those strips of four taken in booths at high school dances and weddings. It was of the two of them together at what she guessed was the Winter Carnival of their senior year. Stella was wearing a red, strapless dress and Erik, a black suit, and they were beaming at the camera. Their arms linked, both leaned in close to each other. Their faces were flushed with joy.

Stella swallowed the lump which had risen in her throat. "We look so young."

"We look so happy," he countered.

"You held onto this picture all these years?" She handed it

back to him. "Why didn't you message me or call me or try to get back into contact with me?"

He shrugged. "I've carried that picture with me for more than a decade. Somehow, I always thought that we were meant to be together. It was like me buying that perfume not knowing when I would see you or if ever. Some things happen in their own time. I guess I had faith in us. Well," he prompted, "will you let me come back to you?"

Stella hesitated. "What does that mean, Erik, in terms of you and me and Noelle?"

He gripped her hands in his. "Noelle's home. I know that now. It's home for me if you're here. I want to be with you wherever you are. I want to carve nutcrackers and coach squirt hockey players and watch snowmobile races with you."

Stella nibbled her lower lip. "Don't you have to live in Chicago for your work?"

His forehead furrowed. "I'd have to travel sometimes, and I do like my work, but Noelle with you is my home. I'll ask you again, can I come back?"

"You know what they say?" The two were moving closer still, drawn together by Christmas magic and moonlight.

"What do they say?" he prompted, his lips curving in a slight smile.

"Well, someone said *You can't go home again.*"

Erik shook his head. "I don't care for that one. Charles Dickens said something like *you appreciate home more for traveling.*"

"Did he now?" Stella asked, tipping her chin up, those long lashes dusting down on her cheeks. "Aren't you literary?"

"It impressed the girls at Princeton," he taunted.

"Did it now? I'm not sure it will work on a Noelle woman."

"I'm just hoping it will work on this Noelle woman." Ever

so slowly, he leaned down and their lips touched, and then the kiss deepened. It was one of those epic, perfect kisses that both would forever remember, a kiss flavored with the memories of first love and the promises of a future together.

At that exact moment, the sky exploded with Christmas fireworks.

THE END

For news on upcoming releases,
please sign up for Caroline's mailing list at:
http://eepurl.com/djcntz

Don't miss out on your next favorite book!
Join the Satin Romance mailing list
www.satinromance.com/mail.html

THANK YOU FOR READING

Did you enjoy this book?

We invite you to leave a review at your favorite book site, such as Goodreads, Amazon, Barnes & Noble, etc.

DID YOU KNOW THAT LEAVING A REVIEW...

- Helps other readers find books they may enjoy.
- Gives you a chance to let your voice be heard.
- Gives authors recognition for their hard work.
- Doesn't have to be long. A sentence or two about why you liked the book will do.

ABOUT THE AUTHOR

Caroline Akervik has always been a voracious reader of most any genre, with the exception of horror, because it's scary. Blessed with a wonderful husband and three amazing grown children, Caroline has worked as a horse trainer and as a school librarian. She remains an animal lover and believes that libraries are among the most magical of places. Her writings reflect the eclectic nature of her life and reading taste, and her books include sweet romances, horse stories and even science fiction. Caroline seeks to write from the heart, to transport her readers and to give wings to their imaginations.

More information on Caroline's books can be found on her website:
http://carolineakervik.blogspot.com

**For news on upcoming releases,
please sign up for her mailing list at:**
http://eepurl.com/djcntz

 twitter.com/CAkervik